Lea Croft
By: Angela Rigley
ISBN: 978-0-908325-10-8

C000320090

Bluewood Publishing Ltd
Christchurch, 8441, New Zealand
www.bluewoodpublishing.com

Also available by Angela Rigley

Looking for Jamie

A Dilemma for Jamie

School for Jamie

Coming Soon:

Choices for Jamie

For news of, or to purchase this or other books, please visit:

www.bluewoodpublishing.com

Lea Croft

by

Angela Rigley

Dedication

I would like to dedicate this book to the members of Eastwood Writers' Group who have supported me so much.

Chapter 1

Six-year old Tommy Holloway ran into the kitchen where his mother, Martha, stood kneading bread. "Mam, Mam, they've found a body!"

"Really, dear? How nice." She wasn't really listening, as her thoughts were elsewhere.

"But, Mam…it's a real one."

"A real what, darling?" She looked up, brushing her floury hands over her heart-shaped face.

"A…real…body." Hands on hips, defying her to mistake his meaning, he glared, his little upturned nose twitching.

"A person?"

"Yes, Mam, in the gully. They say it looks like it's been there ages."

"A man or a woman?" He finally had her full attention.

"Um." Screwing up his face, he scratched his nose. "I don't know. It's just a body. I'm going to see if Jimmy's playing. He always knows everything." He pulled his cap over his long fair hair. Martha had been intending to cut it for the last week or so, but had not found the time.

She took off her apron. "I'll come with you. This is something I don't want to miss."

Grabbing her hand, he dragged her out the door. "Come on, then. Quick, before they take it away."

A throng of people had gathered by the time they arrived at the gully on the outskirts of Lea Croft. A tree-covered rock-face sloped steeply upwards as far as the eye could see, and down below the plateau where they stood, the trees thinned out towards the river.

Martha pushed her way to the front of the crowd

where her seven year old daughter, Amy, stood peering over the edge.

"Don't go too near," Martha warned, pulling her sleeve.

"Isn't this exciting, Mam? An actual dead body." Her daughter's pretty blue eyes shone with animation. "I've never seen one before."

"Do they know who it is?"

A neighbour brushed her arm. "They think it might be Herbert Grant. He disappeared a few months back, if you remember."

"You mean Farmer Ed's son?"

"Yes, that's him. A right rum 'un he was. Always gambling and running riot. Serves him right, if you ask me, if someone's bumped him off. There's plenty that would want to."

Including my Charlie, thought Martha, but kept her mouth shut. If Herbert had been murdered, her husband could well be a suspect.

"But he might have just fallen and not been able to climb back out," she volunteered.

"Um, happen. We'll see. The police will..." Her words were cut off as everybody stood back to allow the body to be hauled over the top.

Martha tried to catch a closer look to convince herself the man really was dead, and wouldn't be pestering her any longer.

A hush descended on the crowd for a brief moment, then those at the front stepped back, covering their faces, moaning at the horrible stench. The people behind them grumbled at having their toes stepped on as pandemonium broke out.

Martha peeped over a man's shoulder as they laid the badly decomposed man, dressed in brown trousers and jacket, on the ground.

Lily Grant, the farmer's wife, elbowed her way through and sank down on her knees beside him.

"Do you think this could be your son, Mrs Grant?" asked a policeman.

Grimacing, gingerly picking up a bony finger, she nodded as a gold ring fell off and rolled to the ground.

"And when did you last see him?"

"Five or six weeks ago," Lily whispered, picking up the ring and twisting it. "He went out to fetch some firewood and never returned."

"Didn't you or your husband go out to look for him?"

She shrugged. "Ed did, but dusk was approaching so he gave up. The...my son often went off, staying out, night upon night. We weren't that worried."

"But what about when he didn't return after a few days?"

She shrugged again.

"Good riddance, I expect she thought," said a voice in Martha's ear. She turned to see her youngest sister, Jessica.

"Why do you say that?" Martha asked. "What did you have against him?"

Jessica rubbed her rounded belly. "Only saying what other folks are thinking, our Martha. You too, I expect, only you would never admit it."

"Why...?" No, she didn't want to start an argument in front of the neighbours.

The policeman put away his notebook as a cart pulled up. "Let the undertaker through, please, folks. Let him about his business."

The people cleared a path as the men in black loaded Herbert Grant's body onto the cart and drove away. The crowd dispersed, everybody muttering, each with their own thoughts about the corpse.

"Who found him?" Martha asked nobody in particular.

The neighbour who had spoken earlier turned back. "Some kids playing, so I heard, chasing a sheep that fell down the gully. They panicked, climbed down to rescue it, and saw a boot sticking out from behind a rock."

Martha turned to Jessica, linking arms with her as they walked back. "I'll bet diamonds one of them was our Tommy. He can find mischief at the drop of a hat."

Jessica smiled. She didn't often, and it was a delight to see. "Ah, but he's lovely with it—my favourite nephew, in fact."

"Seeing as he's your only nephew, that's not hard to understand." Martha grinned, knowing her sister had a soft spot for young Tommy. He had been born on Jessica's ninth birthday so they had an affinity, a special bond. "Anyway, how are you keeping? Is Aunt Elizabeth treating you well?"

"She says, just because I'm expecting, I should still pull my weight with the chores, but…" She grimaced, her lips pursed.

"She's right. You can't expect her to keep you for nothing, my lass. You put yourself in this predicament. You should tell us who the father is, and make him pay."

Jessica pulled away. "I keep telling you…" She smacked her cheek. "Ouch, I think I've been bitten."

"Here, let me see." Martha pulled Jessica's hand down. A red mark had already appeared. "Yes, did you see what it was?"

"I think it was a horsefly. Damned insects!"

"Hey, young lady, watch your language."

"'Damned' isn't bad. You should hear some of the words that come out of Aunt Elizabeth's mouth."

"Well, that's no excuse for you to use them. Come, let's put some ointment on that bite. You had one before, didn't you, when you were little? It swelled right up. Ma was really concerned for a day or two. And didn't our Charlotte have one as well?" She pulled her sister towards the lane leading to her cottage.

"She only had a wasp sting, not nearly as bad as mine. Anyway, I'll be fine, so stop fussing." Jessica looked up through the trees. "Is that our Tommy up there?"

A flutter of bird's wings attracted Martha's attention "It is," she sighed, then shouted to her son, "Tommy, come down from there. You'll fall. And you needn't come running to me when you break a leg."

"Aw, Mam, there's a bird's nest up there at the top," he called down. "Me and Jimmy want to see if there's any chicks in it."

"Come down, please. The poor bird doesn't want you hassling her. She'll abandon them. Come on, it's nearly time for your dinner." She pulled a face, remembering she hadn't finished kneading the dough, so the bread wasn't even in the oven, but no need to tell him that.

Jessica had already walked off to her aunt's, so Martha hastened back to the cottage.

A delicious smell of casserole assailed her as she hurried through the open door. The dough sat on the wooden table, flat and lifeless. *Oh well, a quick knead will perk it up*, she thought, knocking a tortoiseshell kitten off a chair.

"You can go," she exclaimed. "I don't know who you belong to, but you needn't come bothering me. I can't afford to feed you. I have enough with our Charlotte, my two children and my greedy husband. He'll be home from work soon." She glanced up at the clock. "Oh, no, I'd better make a move, or his dinner won't be on the table when he comes in, like he expects." Grabbing her pinafore, she wrapped it around her and set to.

With the dough placed on top of the range to rise, she put four plates in the bottom of the oven to warm. Her husband wasn't really greedy, he just liked his food. And he deserved it, slaving away down the pit all those hours.

Amy came in and picked up the kitten, stroking its multi-coloured fur, causing it to purr. "Ah, isn't it sweet?"

"Hasn't that mangy animal gone? I thought I'd shooed it out." Martha nudged her daughter out of her way. "Put it down and set the table, please."

"Aw, Mam, can't we keep it? It's so soft." She put it up to her face, rubbing it.

"No, we can't."

The kitten reached out and scratched Amy's nose. With a yelp, she dropped it and it ran out.

"I bet you're not so keen on it, now, are you?"

Shaking her head, her daughter went across to the mirror hanging on the end wall. "It's bleeding. Mam, it's bleeding. That little tike has made me—"

"All right, all right, it's only a scratch. Now, do as you're told. The table won't lay itself. Your pa will be in soon, and you know what he'll be like if it isn't ready."

With one more look in the mirror, Amy slumped to the drawer, muttering, "If I die, I'll blame you." She took out the cutlery and arranged it carefully at each person's place. "Will Auntie Charlotte be home for dinner?"

"No, I'll have to keep hers warm for later." Martha picked up the bowl, gave the dough a quick knead, then moulded it into a round shape and put it in the oven, slamming the door shut. Wiping her hands down her apron, she turned her daughter to face her. "Let me look." She spat on a corner of her apron and wiped off the tiny spot of blood. "You'll live." Patting Amy's bottom, she nudged her out the door. "Go and find Tommy for me, there's a good girl," she called after her. "You wouldn't see him crying over a little scratch. He's always covered in cuts and bruises."

Watching Amy ambling over towards the trees where they had seen Tommy playing earlier, Martha smiled. Complete opposites, her children—Amy, quiet and withdrawn—Tommy, younger by a year, robust and outgoing, always on the move.

But I don't have time to be pondering, she thought, movement catching her eye as she turned to go back indoors. Charlie, on his way back from the alehouse he frequented each afternoon after his shift, looking at his pocket watch. *Oh, heck, he's early.* She breathed a sigh as Tommy waylaid him, probably telling him about the corpse. Hopefully, it would give her an extra minute or so.

She rushed in, opened the oven door, took out the casserole dish, slammed the door closed, for the bread had not quite baked, and placed the dish on the table. At least, with that there, the table would look prepared.

The plates! Pulling the door open again, she grabbed them, forgetting to use a cloth, and squealed as they fell to the floor with a clatter. With her eyes squeezed shut, she held her breath as her husband's voice asked, "Is it true?"

Her eyes jerked open and, trying to ignore the broken pieces on the floor, she turned, forcing a smile to her lips. "About Herbert Grant?"

"Yes, what else would I mean?"

She nodded. "Yes, so it seems."

He washed his hands at the sink. Maybe he hadn't noticed she had dropped the plates.

"You'll have to eat your dinner off the floor," he said with his back to her. He had noticed. Of course he had, he noticed every little misdemeanour, even if she had not made one.

Luckily, only one of the plates had broken. Tommy ran to help as she picked them up.

"Leave it, boy. You'll only cut yourself," his father ordered as he took the lid off the casserole. "Sit down." He looked around. "Where's Amy? Why isn't she here?"

"I sent her to find our Tommy." She dropped the shards into the sink as he thumped the table.

"You know I like the whole family ready to eat at the same time."

"Yes, but…"

Fortunately, Amy came in at that moment. "I can't

find… Oh, you're here."

"Sit down, lass." Martha breathed a sigh of relief as she placed the three unbroken plates in front of her family and spooned out their food.

"No bread?" asked Charlie.

"Yes, of course. It's keeping warm."

She grabbed a cloth and took out the bread, thankfully now sufficiently brown.

Charlie's gave her an odd look with his brown eyes as she placed it on the table. "It'll be too hot to eat," he complained.

"Well, you would only complain if it wasn't…hot…" she began, but stopped at the sneer on his face.

"This is lovely, Mam." At least Amy appreciated her efforts.

"Yes, it is." Tommy, too.

In the cupboard she found a small plate for herself. They only had the five large ones, and Charlotte would need the other one. Then she sat down and put a spoonful of food onto it. Amy looked up at her with a questioning look, but she gave a slight shake of her head. Charlie didn't like them talking while he ate. They ate in silence until he had finished.

He wiped his mouth. "Not much meat in that, was there?"

"Well, you know it's near the end of the week, and Amy needed a new pair of shoes. The ones she's been wearing have big holes in the bottom. Whenever it rains, she—"

"Don't give me that old excuse. Surely you could've cadged a pair from one of your many friends."

"I did try, but nobody had any the right size. They were all too big or too small, so—"

He stood up, his tall, muscular frame seeming to fill the tiny kitchen. "I'm going back down to the alehouse. I might find some intelligent conversation there." Pulling his coat from the hook on the back of the door, he went out, without waiting to hear what else she had been about to say.

Breathing a sigh of relief at his departing back, she ladled another spoonful of the rabbit casserole onto her plate. Her children sat still at the table. "Would either of you like any more?" she asked.

Amy shook her head, but Tommy handed her his plate. "Yes, please, Mam. It's delicious."

"Good boy. I never need to ask you twice, do I? I sometimes wonder where you put it all. You must have hollow legs."

He laughed, a tinkling sound that always cheered her up. "Amy, are you sure you wouldn't like some more. You didn't have very much."

Her daughter put her plate beside the sink. "No thanks, Mam. Would you like me to make you a cup of tea?"

Her meal finished, Martha stood up. "That would be lovely, thank you, darling. We'll all have one, shall we? Then I'll wash up and we can play a game. Which one would you like tonight?"

"Snap," yelled Tommy. "I want to play snap."

"Aw, must we? We played that last night, and the night before," retorted Amy, opening the door of the cupboard where they kept their games. "Let's play Ludo for a change."

Tommy stuck out his bottom lip. "But I'm not very good at that. I never win."

"Well, maybe you choose the wrong colour counters." She took out the battered box and opened the board. "Try green today."

"But I like red."

"But you never win with red, so try green." Amy turned to face them. "What colour do you want, our Mam?"

Martha put the last plate away in the rack and joined her children. "I think I'll be blue."

"And I'll be yellow, so, Tommy, green or red?" She raised her eyebrows at her little brother.

"Oh, I can't make my mind up. What do you think, Mam?"

"Don't bring me into your squabbles. You have to make the decision yourself."

He tutted and turned away. "But I don't like making *drecisions*, or whatever they're called. I never know what to pick."

"Ugh, tell him, Mam," screamed Amy. "Tell him not to do that."

"What's the matter now?"

"He's pulled out a big bogey." She screamed even louder when he put it in his mouth.

Martha tried to pull his hand away but it was too late.

He swallowed with deliberation, grinning. "Um, delicious. I love the green ones."

"Go and find a handkerchief. You're revolting," moaned Amy. The look on her face would have melted a weaker boy, but not Tommy.

"I don't need it now, unless there's another one…" He made as if to poke his finger up his other nostril but Martha slapped his hand.

"Please, no more of your disgusting habits. It's a good job your father isn't here to witness it."

"He wouldn't do it if he was." His sister poked him in the ribs, making him yelp. "He only dares when Pa isn't here."

"Are we playing this game, or not?" asked Martha. "There won't be time to finish it before your bed time if you don't make a move."

Amy looked up at the clock. "I still have half an hour. You…" she poked him again. "You only have fifteen minutes. That's not nearly long enough to win a game."

"Mam, tell her…" he began.

Martha stood up. "If you are going to bicker at each other all evening, I may as well do some embroidery." She began to walk away, but Amy pulled at her skirt. "Please, Mam. We won't. Please play."

With a warning glare at them both, she sat back down. "Very well, who's going first?"

"Me!" Tommy put up his hand.

"It's whoever throws the first six." Amy picked up the dice and threw a three. Tommy pounced on it, and threw it so hard it fell off the end of the table. Scrambling underneath to find it, he banged his head, and, rubbing it with a grimace on his face, he threw again, resulting in a four.

Martha took her turn. A six!

"You start, our Mam," moaned Tommy, looking downcast, still rubbing his head. "I bet you'll win."

"Not necessarily." She moved her first counter out of its home. "There's plenty of time yet."

Amy threw another three.

"Me next." The dice spun, landing as Tommy had hoped. With his tongue stuck out at Amy, he made his move.

She soon caught up to be neck and neck, until the last throw. "Four, four," she prayed. It stopped on a three.

Tommy picked up the dice, eyes wide and mouth open. "Yes," he squealed in delight. "Five. I win, I win. Ha, ha, I win." He danced around the kitchen, waving his arms in the air.

Amy stood up, her face the picture of innocence. "Only because I let you."

"Now, darling, you know that's not true." Martha packed away the game. "Have the good grace to concede defeat for a change. Like he said, he doesn't win very often."

"What does 'conscreed' mean, Mam?" Tommy raised his arms and gave a wide yawn.

"The word's 'concede'. It means sort of…admit."

"Oh. Will someone have to *conscreed* that they killed Herbert?"

"I suppose so. And it's Mr Grant, to you. That's if he was murdered. We don't know that yet." She squeezed the flannel in the bowl of water she had just filled and washed his face. "You'll do. Up to bed with you."

He kissed her. "Night, night, Mam. I hope I don't have nightmares about finding more dead bodies." He looked up hopefully. "Can I have a candle? It might help me sleep better, and my head still tingles."

With a pat she ushered him through the door. "Be off with you. It was only a small bump. You're not a baby any more. Anyway, it isn't even dark, yet."

He climbed the stairs slowly.

"And don't forget to put on your nightshirt," she called after him. "You were still fully dressed when I woke you this morning."

"Yes, Mam."

Amy washed herself in the bowl. "I think I'll go up and read my new book, Mam. It has some lovely pictures of animals—lions and things."

Martha hugged her. "Your reading is coming along leaps and bounds, isn't it?"

"Yes, I love it. I can read better than anyone in the whole class, Miss Ewart said today."

"That's lovely, darling. I'm so proud of you, and so is your dad."

With her head to one side, Amy raised her eyebrows, as if she didn't believe it, but didn't speak. She knew better than to belittle him. She would only receive a scolding. No matter what Martha endured from her husband, she would never say anything disparaging about him to the children. They—or at least Amy—picked up certain things, but were never allowed to voice them.

Chapter 2

Jessica scratched her face as she mixed some meal into the mash. "That damned horsefly," she muttered as she went outside to feed the chickens. "I wish it had bitten off that ugly mole on my chin. Then, I wouldn't mind so much."

As she put down the bowl and opened the coop, the birds flew down, one at a time.

"Hello, my beauties. I hope you've laid lots of lovely big, brown eggs today. Aunt Elizabeth won't have cause to moan at me, then. As if it's my fault when you don't!"

She called the last one out. It seemed reluctant to leave so she looked inside. Nothing untoward in there. No dead bodies. The finding of Herbert Grant's body the previous day had unnerved her.

Flicking her brown, straight hair off her face, she arched her back and stood up straight.

"Keep your flippin' shoulders back, don't slouch," she could hear her aunt snapping, as if beside her, as she rubbed her belly and pulled her grey shawl around her shoulders.

Jessica picked up the empty bowl, and wandered over to let out the pig.

"Good morning, Grace," she called as she opened the door, scratching her face once more. The pig lifted its head and she tickled the patch under its chin, which brought a look of ecstasy to its face. "Not long now, is it? I wonder how many piglets you'll have. Aunt Elizabeth says she hopes you have at least ten, maybe even fifteen."

With a hand on her own belly, she prayed she would only have one baby. That would be more than enough to cope with, especially as it would not have a father. His identity could not be disclosed to anybody.

The cow in the enclosure, due to calf any day, mooed, so Jessica wandered over and threw some hay to her. There would be babies everywhere soon.

Her stomach rumbled. Time for breakfast. She hoped Uncle Will wouldn't be back. She always felt uncomfortable around him. His glass eye seemed to follow her, no matter where she was in the room, and his hands... She tried not to think of him as she herded the group of white, gaggling geese into the meadow.

The smell of bacon assailed her nostrils as she entered the back door of the cottage, where she lived with her aunt and uncle. "Um, lovely."

"All done?" asked Aunt Elizabeth, turning the bacon in the pan. "Your Uncle Will should be back from the farm soon for his breakfast. The fecking top field fence blew down again in last night's gale, and some of the bleddy sheep escaped."

"I didn't hear no gale." Jessica washed her hands and sat down at the table.

"You mean you didn't hear any gale."

"That's what I said. I didn't hear no gale."

"Two negatives make a positive. Didn't they teach you anything in that blinkin' schoolhouse?" Her aunt placed a plate in front of her. "When you have this baby, you'll need to learn it how to talk proper. Like what I do." She gave a peculiar smirk.

That doesn't sound right, though, thought Jessica, but didn't want an argument. She just wanted to finish her breakfast and depart before her uncle returned.

"I have a list of chores for you to complete today, so don't go bleddy rushing off."

That scuppered that idea.

"You needn't look at me like that, young lady. You have to earn your keep. Me and your uncle were good enough to take you in when you found yourself..." She pointed to Jessica's belly "...in the blinkin' pudding club, so you've made your bed, as they say, now you'll have to lie in it." Her aunt turned towards the stove and began brewing a pot of tea.

I wish I could lie in bed, thought Jessica. *I'm not allowed to have a lie-in, even on a Sunday.*

"Fetch me the milk, would you?"

Jessica stood up and went into the pantry, where the milk kept cool in a jug on the cold slab.

"I'll have to ask your uncle to teach you how to milk Bessie. That's another job you could help with," her aunt's voice filtered through to her.

That, and the ten thousand others you want me to learn.

"Can't *you* show me?" she asked as she came out. "I'd much rather you did. Or maybe I could go up to Home Farm and watch our Charlotte."

"I don't have time to be doing such things, more's the pity." Her aunt reached out for the jug. "And I don't think Farmer Grant would like you wandering around his cows while our Charlotte's trying to milk them, unless you wanted to ask him for a bloomin' job as well."

"No, thanks. Not while that Mary's there. Charlotte tells me she's a bully. My sister's too coy and won't stand up to her. I would. I wouldn't let her scoff at me and escape unscathed." She sat down. "But, anyway, you have softer hands."

"What does that have to do with the price of fish?"

"Eh?"

Her aunt grinned, her round face lighting up. "It's an expression I heard the butcher use once. He's not from these parts. He's from London, you know. They use all sorts of peculiar sayings down there. Although, he reckons us Derbyshire folk use lots of odd words he's never heard."

"Like what?"

"Well, like being 'mardy' and calling food 'snap'."

"They're not odd, they're how you should talk. It's him that's odd."

"Anyway, here's your uncle."

Her Uncle Will came in, sweat running down his temples onto his ruddy face. "By heck, it's warming up out there."

"Well, it was cold earlier," volunteered Jessica, making for the door.

"I wouldn't know," said her aunt. "I haven't had time to even poke my bleddy nose outside, let alone feel any blinking temperature. And don't go sloping off, our Jessica. You can go and strip the beds. If the weather's that fine, you can wash the sheets. Hopefully, there'll be enough of that gale left to give them a good blow."

"Yes, Aunt Elizabeth." Trudging up the stairs, Jessica thought back to that eventful day when she had lost her innocence. If only she had said no. She had wanted to, but he had been so insistent, saying he loved her. She had thought her youth would have stopped him. She had only been fifteen, after all. But it hadn't, and there she found herself, seven months gone, with no husband. Thank goodness her mother hadn't lived long enough to share her disgrace.

"Oh, Ma, I miss you so much." She slumped onto her aunt's bed and wrapped her arms around her midriff. Reason told her not to harp on the harrowing scenes of her mother growing weaker and weaker until she had died, less than a year since, but sometimes she couldn't stop the images playing through her brain.

Her doting father's death, two years before that, had devastated her. He had been killed in an accident in the quarry where he worked but, at least, he had not wasted away gradually before their very eyes.

"Jessica," her aunt called up the stairs. "What on hell's earth is taking so long up there?"

"Coming, Aunt," she called as she jumped up and pulled off the sheets. They smelled of her uncle's cologne. She screwed up her nose, imagining him and her aunt doing *that*. She could hear them at night, moaning and squealing, the bed banging against the wall, keeping her awake. She usually stuffed her fingers in her ears to try to blot out the noise. Thankfully, it never lasted long.

With as little contact with the sheets as possible, she screwed them up into a bundle and went into her own room. "I needn't have bothered making my bed," she complained to her old, tatty rag doll. She picked her up and placed her on the tallboy, while she dragged off the white sheets. They didn't look dirty, so she felt it to be a waste of time. Folding the brown blanket, she placed it on the bare mattress with the blue counterpane.

A quick look in the mirror told her the bite looked inflamed. No wonder it hurt so much, but she picked up her sheets, and the bundle from her aunt's room, and hurried downstairs. "Look at my face, Auntie." She dropped the washing and stuck out her cheek for her aunt's perusal.

"Oh, my, that does look bad. I've put the copper on to boil for the sheets so, while it's heating up, you'd better smother it with some ointment." She opened a cupboard, brought down a jar and took off the lid. It smelled foul.

"Ugh, I don't know if I want any of that stinking stuff on my face."

"Suit yourself, lass. But don't come blathering to me when it blinking festers."

Her aunt placed the lid back on the jar to put it away, when Jessica changed her mind. "Just a tiny bit, then." She didn't want her face going mouldy, so she scooped some onto the end of her finger and dabbed it onto the sore patch. "It's nice and cool, and it's stopped some of the itching already."

"Thank heavens for that." Her uncle put down his newspaper and took another puff of his pipe. "I thought we were going to have to amputate your nose."

"Will!" His wife shook her head. "The lass has a nasty bite. Have a little sympathy."

"Pah." He folded the newspaper and pushed back his chair. "I'm back off up the fields." With a peck on his wife's cheek, he went out.

"Right, then, let's set about this bleddy washing. The boiler should be hot by now." Aunt Elizabeth rolled up her sleeves. "Find me the washboard while I fetch the wringer. Then you may as well go and change out of that filthy frock. We'll wash that as well. The green one Mrs Williams the baker gave you might fit now. I know it's too flippin' big, but you can't fit into any of your old ones any more."

Jessica looked down at the hem of her old beige dress. Um, rather muddy. And her apron. Better wash that too. She collected the washboard from the outhouse and ran upstairs to change, eager to try on the green dress again. Pink and yellow flowers adorned the low bodice, with birds fluttering around the full skirt.

"My, I must have gained weight," she murmured. "It isn't big at all." Placing a clean pinafore over it, she hastened back downstairs, not wanting to be scolded again for taking too long. Her aunt looked up momentarily and nodded, before punching the sheet against the washboard, her face bright red, her hair plastered to her forehead.

They worked silently and, before long, coloured clothes and lily-white sheets blew merrily in the wind.

"You can't beat a line full of clean washing to raise your spirits." Aunt Elizabeth pegged the last handkerchief on the line and stood back, one hand on her hip, the other wiping her brow.

Jessica shook her head. She never ceased to be amazed at some of the things from which adults drew pleasure.

"It's just a pity there aren't any baby's nappies." Her aunt's face dropped.

Jessica tried to console her. "There will be soon, Aunt." She knew her aunt had already lost two babies in infancy, and had experienced the trauma of three miscarriages.

"Aye, lass, but they won't be mine, and, in a way, that'll be worse."

Jessica put her arm around her. "I'm really grateful to you and Uncle Will for taking me in, even if I don't always show it. I know how difficult it'll be for you, seeing someone else's baby, a baby that shouldn't, by rights, be born."

"Now, then, our Jessica, don't go saying things like that. Every baby has a right to life, no matter how it's conceived. It's God's will. We don't always understand how or why but, as they say, He works in mysterious ways."

"I'll say an extra prayer for you tonight."

"You don't have to wait until bedtime to pray, you know. Just look around you at Nature. You should thank God every minute of the day for her wonders."

"Yes, Aunt." Maybe not every minute of the day. She would never have time to complete any of her chores. She wondered what else her aunt had in store for her, for she wanted to find out if anybody had heard if the police thought Herbert Grant had been murdered.

"Let's have a nice cuppa, and then we can crack on with the rest of the jobs." Elizabeth picked a dolly peg off the ground and tucked it into her apron pocket.

"First, Aunt, please may I go and find out—?"

A raised eyebrow stopped her finishing her sentence. It would have to wait.

Chapter 3

In the byre, Charlotte Bridge picked up the milking stool and carried it to where the black and white cows lined up, waiting to deliver their milk to the three milkmaids. The warm milk spurted into the bucket, pinging as it landed.

She had rejoiced at the news of Herbert Grant's death. At last, the improper advances would never happen again. She had never told anybody about them. He had warned her, if she did, she would go to prison for causing trouble, for nobody would believe her.

Should I tell now? Better not. Would anyone believe a seventeen year old girl? Especially when the son of her employer could no longer refute it?

Ping, ping. The bucket was almost full.

"You're in the clouds, today, Shar," called one of the other milkmaids.

Grrr, I wish she wouldn't call me that, she seethed inwardly. *I like my full name, Charlotte, after the old queen, the one who had been married to King George the third. I bet they never called her 'Shar'.* She shrugged without replying, for she disliked the girl and did not fancy making conversation.

"Probably thinking you've missed your chance, now your beloved Herbert's dead," sneered the girl, a pretty blonde called Mary, who was two years older and thought she could attract any man she wanted, and usually did.

"I...I...I wouldn't want him if...if...if he was the last man alive," retorted Faith, the second girl.

"But he isn't, you nincompoop. He's dead." In her usual intolerant manner, Mary shook her head at the dim-witted milkmaid.

"There's no need to call her names," admonished Charlotte. Even though she could not name Faith as her favourite person, either, she would never stoop so low as to insult her.

"Oh, Miss High-and-Mighty. Who do you think you are, telling me what to do?"

With a sigh, Charlotte picked up her bucket and poured its contents into the churn. "I'm only saying."

"Well, keep your sayings to yourself. We don't want to hear them, do we, Fay?"

"N…n…no," replied the first girl, not looking up, adding in a low voice, "B…b…but my name's 'Faith'."

"Oh, that's too holy. Fay suits you just fine."

Charlotte moved on to the next cow. With a pat to its withers, she crooned in its ear, hoping it would give a higher yield. Probably a dubious theory, but if it helped then why not try? She knew Mary didn't bother with such things, and turned up her nose at the mere idea, but she often heard Faith do so.

She sat on her stool and pulled the udders. "Anyway, Mr Grant must be devastated at his son's death, so don't let him hear you talking about him as if—"

"Who's talking about my son?" Farmer Grant's gruff voice came through the open doorway of the byre.

"Nobody, sir," they all said, as if with one voice.

"Carry on with your work, and no slacking. These milk churns need taking to market. You should have finished by now."

"Yes, sir." They all pulled harder, not daring to look up.

"And you, girl, what's your name?"

Is he talking to me? Charlotte raised her head just enough to see him, but not enough to take her eye off the milk streaming into the bucket.

He walked towards her. "Yes, you, Charlotte, isn't it?"

"Yes, sir."

"Don't stop. Just listen. I've heard rumours that you were seen cavorting with my son a while back. Is that true?"

Her eyes opened wide. "Cavorting, sir? I don't know what you mean." She thought she heard Mary snigger behind her, but ignored it.

"I think you know very well what I mean. Canoodling, or whatever you young people call it."

"Not me, sir. I have a suitor."

"Well, the police will want to hear about it. Whoever told me might very well inform them."

As his footsteps receded she sat back and took a deep breath, wondering who could have snitched.

"You're in the proverbial, now, girlie." Mary gloated, but her attention was diverted when she squeezed the udder in the wrong direction, and the milk spilt on the hay.

"Ha, ha, ha," jeered Faith. "S…s…serves you right. You'll be in trouble now." Her small, almond-shaped brown eyes closed as if she daren't look at the reaction her words caused. But Mary covered the milk with her foot, spreading more hay on top of it.

A large tabby cat jumped down from the hayloft above them and began to lap at it.

"H…h…hope the cat bites you." Faith stood up and flexed her back. "It b…bi…bit me the other day." She pulled up her sleeve, showing a small red mark.

Mary kicked the cat out of the way. It yelped and ran out through the door.

Faith drew a loud breath. "Oo…oo…oo, I'm telling on you."

"Tell all you like. I'll only deny it."

"Y…y…you saw, didn't you, Charlotte? You saw her kick it?" Faith poured her milk into the churn and went to the door, as if to check on the cat.

"Keep me out of it. I have enough problems."

"What are you going to say to the police?" Mary sounded genuinely concerned. "You don't really have a suitor, do you?"

Charlotte shrugged. "Maybe I have, and maybe I haven't."

Mary lowered her voice, looking around as if to check nobody else could hear. "Well, I heard Herbert could be the father of your Jessica's baby."

"Who told you that? It's a damned lie."

"We'll see, when it comes out with bright ginger hair and large ears." Mary poured the remainder of her milk into a second churn and sat down. "What are you doing, Fay? Why aren't you milking? There's still three more cows to do. Come on, lazybones. You can't leave it all to me and Shar—or should I say 'the witness'?"

"Stop it. I have nothing to feel guilty about." After a knowing look from the other milkmaid, she continued with her task.

Later, outside, her heart skipped a beat when she saw Master Ronnie, Mr Grant's illegitimate son, in the distance. The complete opposite to his brother Herbert, she found him to be a gentle man who smiled a lot, and always seemed courteous and warm-hearted. You couldn't miss his lolloping walk. She had been told he had one leg shorter than the other. Or was one longer? Whichever one, it produced the same result, unmistakable even from a distance. She had watched him on and off for a few weeks—since his brother's disappearance she realised. Sometimes she caught him looking at her, but he would look away as soon as she noticed.

Her little white lie about having a suitor had actually been an exaggeration, more a hopeful wish. She knew she would never be allowed to walk out with Ronnie. Despite the unfortunate circumstances of his birth, he had been brought up as one of the family and would now probably be the heir to the farm since Herbert had died, so what chance did she, a mere milkmaid, have? None, she knew, but a little part of her took no notice. It didn't hurt to dream, even if nothing could come of it.

Ronnie Grant unhitched the pony from the trap and set her free into the paddock. Maybe he would catch a glimpse of the titian-haired milkmaid. What a beauty! Her long hair would fall across her face, hiding her eyes, when she took off her bonnet after finishing the milking, but he felt sure she looked at him with a certain…what could he call it? Pique? Could that be the right word? Anyway, whatever the word, she looked at him with it.

Maybe, one day, he would summon up the courage to speak to her. Not with that Mary there, though. That tyrant, the most horrible person on the planet. Why his father employed her, he couldn't understand. She had even propositioned him not long back. He shuddered. He had never walked out with a girl, but desperation would never force him to do so with her. His brother, Herbert, was—or had been—the opposite. He had chased girls all over the county and, word had it, had one or two illegitimate brats hidden away.

"Good riddance," he mused aloud as he dragged the cart into the barn and wiped off the mud. "I, for one, won't miss you, and, apart from our ma, and maybe our pa, I don't think many others will."

The sun blinded him as he stepped outside and he put up his hand to shield his eyes.

That's her! It most definitely is.

Even at that distance, he could identify her slight, slender figure, Mary being much taller, and Faith chubbier. For a second, his heart stopped. His breath caught in his throat.

If only I had the courage.

He quickly looked away from the girl, though, when his father came around the side of the barn, followed by a policeman.

"Ron, Constable Jenkins wants a word with us all. Is your mother in the house?"

"I suppose so, Pa. I've only just come back from the market." Sneaking another glance at the byre, disappointed to see she had vanished, he followed his father into the house.

His mother sat in the kitchen, peeling potatoes onto a newspaper on the table. She stood up when she saw the constable.

"Don't stand, Mrs Grant. I won't keep you long." He took off his helmet and twisted it in his hands.

"I suppose you've come about our Herbert?" she asked, her head high, not at all like a grieving mother.

"Yes, ma'am."

"Have they decided yet? Did he fall or was he pushed?"

"They still aren't sure, ma'am. We need more information."

"You'd better sit down. I'll put the kettle on. Sugar?" She took down four cups and saucers as, with the scraping of chairs, they sat around the table.

Taking his helmet off, the constable took out a notepad and pencil, licked the lead and asked, "Ma'am, exactly when did either of you last see your son?"

His mother turned from filling the teapot and looked at her husband. "Like I said yesterday, about five weeks ago, wasn't it, Ed?"

"That's right." The farmer nodded. "He went out to fetch the eggs—"

"No, to chop some wood," his wife intervened as she placed the teapot on a trivet on the table.

"Oh, yes," muttered his pa, scratching his chin.

His mother poured the tea through the strainer, and spooned two teaspoons of sugar into each cup. "I remember, because the Aga needed fuel."

"Of course, yes. I remember. I went out an hour later, when he hadn't returned, but could find no sign of him." The farmer picked up his cup and sipped his drink, his hand shaking.

"I know this is difficult for you all, but we must unravel the case." The policeman stirred his tea, round and round, his head bowed.

He'll bore a hole in the bottom of the cup, if he doesn't stop, thought Ronnie, the sound jarring in his head.

The constable looked up. "I'm afraid I have to ask you this…is there anyone who might have a grudge against your son?"

The Grants all looked at each other, each clearly with their own ideas, but not wanting to voice them.

"Well…" The farmer was the first to speak. He blew out his cheeks. "Well, that is a leading question. I could think of a few."

The constable put down his spoon, licked his pencil again and began to write. "Yes, go on, sir."

Ronnie thought he saw his mother's eyes widen at his father, as she gave a slight shake of her head, saying, "There'll be all those men he's cheated. Many a one."

"Could you name any of them, ma'am?"

It was her turn to blow out her cheeks. "No, I'm afraid not. He never told us who he was involved with. We only know from hearsay."

The constable turned to Ronnie. "And you, sir, do you know any?"

Ronnie shook his head. "Not me, Constable. My brother…" He had been about to say Herbert had not liked him—had, in fact, hated him—but that might sound incriminating. "We didn't frequent the same establishments."

His parents looked at him in surprise, not being known for his eloquence. He smiled to himself. Just because he appeared quiet and sombre didn't mean he could not use big words. He secretly read in the small amount of spare time he had. He would be the owner of the farm one day since his brother had died, so needed to start showing he could hold his own with the hoi polloi, and come out from under his shadow. "No, I'm sorry. I don't know anyone who might have wanted to harm him."

"Oh." The constable's shoulders drooped visibly.

"You think he might have been murdered, then?" asked the farmer.

"As I said, sir, we won't be sure until we know the results of the autopsy." His notebook and pencil replaced in his pocket, he stood and picked up his helmet. "I'll say good day to you, ma'am, sirs." With a bow, he went out.

"Well, we'll soon know." The farmer put his arm around his wife. "Won't we, dear?" He turned to Ronnie. "But where did all those big words come from? I've never heard you speak like that before."

Ronnie held up his head. "Now I'm the only son, I need to buck up my ideas."

"Good on you, lad. I'm pleased to hear it. Maybe your brother's demise could be the making of you."

His mother cleared away the dirty cups. "Yes, I know it's a truism, but every cloud has a silver lining."

He thought he detected a smirk on her lips. In his heart, he knew he had always been her favourite son, even though she had not borne him. Being the youngest, his older sisters, all seven of them, had spoiled him until they had married and moved away. Despite being his father's illegitimate child, she had taken him in when his natural mother had died in childbirth. Now, at twenty years old, he could prove to her that her actions had not been in vain.

After kissing her cheek, he donned his cap and went out, whistling, hoping to see *her*. Walking past the byre, he glanced casually inside. Drat. Empty. They must have finished the milking. He could have offered to help them roll the churns to the creamery. Maybe next time.

Hands in his pockets, he continued more slowly towards the gully where his brother had been found, his mood decreasing as, leaning over the edge, he peered down the steep sides of the cliff top. The last time he had been there it had not seemed so deep. He needed to find something. Something the police might be interested in, if they came across it.

An overhanging branch helped him ease his lanky body over the edge and, clinging onto tufts of grass and saplings, he inched downwards, until his foot caught on a protruding root, and he lost his balance. Farther and farther towards the fast flowing river below he tumbled, his heart thumping as he tried desperately to find a handhold. Reaching to grab a rock, it cut through the soft skin of the palm of his hand but stopped his descent, just feet from the bottom. Fearful of moving, he took a deep breath.

Eventually, with blood streaming from his hand, he searched around for something to stem the flow, and found some leaves, pressed them hard against it and looked up to the top of the gorge. Such a long way up. No wonder Herbert had died. But how had he fallen, when...?

To give himself a moment to catch his breath, he tried to come up with an explanation of how he had gained the injury. He couldn't admit to being there in the gully. But with no plausible solution forthcoming, he pushed himself to his feet and gingerly began the steep ascent.

Half an hour later he hauled himself, panting and sweating, over the top and lay on the soft grass. The puffy, white clouds above scooted across the sky into a formation that looked exactly like an angel.

"Thank you," he called out. "Thank you very much."

A boy came running over. "Who are you shouting at?" he asked, looking down at Ronnie, still prostrate on the ground.

He managed to sit up, trying to hide his hand.

"What have you done? You're bleeding?"

He hadn't succeeded. "I just...just cut it. It's nothing."

"You're Ronnie Grant, aren't you? The dead man's

brother?" The boy helped him stand, brushing twigs and leaves from his jacket. He gave him a knowing look and pointed down the gulley. "Have you been climbing down there?"

"Don't be silly. Why would I do that?"

"To see where your dead brother was found."

"I have to be going. It's Tommy, isn't it?" At the boy's nod, he bent down, looking him straight in the eye. "Well, Tommy, don't you go telling anybody you saw me here. Is that clear?"

"Why not?"

"Because…" What could he say that would scare the boy enough to keep silent? "Because you'll suffer if you do, understand?" He glowered with the most ferocious glare he could muster, eye to eye, nose to nose, his good hand round the back of the boy's neck.

He didn't like frightening little boys. In fact, he had never threatened anyone before, and he hoped he would never have to do it again.

"Yes, sir, please let go. I won't tell nobody." His eyes full of fear, the boy pulled away and ran off, glancing occasionally behind him as if to assure himself the nasty man was not following.

"He's related to my milkmaid," muttered Ronnie gloomily, as he slouched towards Home Farm. "And I didn't even find it. Drat. But I'm not trying again. I'll just have to hope it's well hidden." He grimaced, gritted his teeth against the pain in his hand, opened it out and removed the leaves. A deep gash, from thumb to little finger, oozed with blood. He would have to ask his mother to dress it. It couldn't be left like that. He pressed hard down on the leaves once more, curling his fingers around them for pressure, before opening the back door, to be greeted by an empty kitchen.

"Ma," he called. She might be in the front room, so he opened the door leading into the hall, but the ticking of the grandfather clock was the only sound to be heard.

He called up the stairs, but still no reply.

The smell of baking bread drifted towards him. "Surely she wouldn't have gone out and left that," he murmured as he returned to the kitchen and opened the oven door. A puff of steam blew out and his injured hand behind his back, he picked up a cloth with the other one and took out the tray of bread. A small patch of black on the top of the loaf saved it from being spoilt. He liked his bread well-done, anyway, the blacker the better. After dropping it onto the table, he kicked the oven door closed and sat down.

One of the farm cats sauntered in through the back door. He leant down to stroke it, but it arched its back and hissed at him. "Suit yourself," he murmured as it sauntered out. "Do you know where my ma is?"

It didn't turn, just lifted its tail as if in insult, and disappeared.

"I suppose I'll have to do it myself." He stood up and opened the cupboard where his mother kept her ointments and potions. Which one should he use out of so many? He took one down, eventually unscrewed the lid, and took a whiff. "Um, nice." He checked the label. 'Comfrey'. No, he didn't have broken bones. He took down another. 'Camomile'. Probably not. After several minutes, an aromatic row of open jars stood on the sideboard, making his nose twitch. But he still didn't know which one to use.

Where's my mother?

Chapter 4

In the dairy, Charlotte tested the temperature of the milk, and then stirred in the rennet. Her arms ached. Even though she performed the task daily, her muscles still protested.

Faith took the paddle from her. "L...l...let me take over."

"Thank you, Faith. I'll fetch the curding knife and start on the other batch." As she walked past the doorway, she saw Master Ronnie hurrying into the farmhouse. It looked as if he had hurt his hand. She didn't have time to go and help, not with so many chores to complete in the dairy.

The third batch ready, she began to chop it into blocks, turning them to dry, to keep them longer—possibly up to six or seven months, if done correctly—as Mary came back from the lavvy in the yard. "I just saw Master Ronnie covered in blood. I wonder what he's been up to."

"Probably caught his hand in the plough or something. Do you remember that time one of the Barnes boys chopped his off?" She continued working on the cheese, picturing Ronnie with only one hand, as well as a short leg. She hoped it wasn't that serious.

"I...I...I heard tell he was seen dallying with one of the girls in the village last week," volunteered Faith.

"Who?" Charlotte looked round at the older milkmaid.

"M...M...Master Ronnie."

Charlotte's heart missed a beat. She had never heard any rumours to that effect. "Are you sure? I mean—"

"Why've you gone all jittery, Shar?" Mary came over and lifted her chin, turning her head from side to side.

"Now Herbert's dead, you're setting your sights on the new heir, are you?"

Charlotte yanked her face from the other girl's fingers. "Don't be so stupid. And I never canoodled, or whatever Farmer Grant called it, with Herbert. I don't know why everyone keeps saying that." Not willingly, anyway. She turned her back on the girl to hide her red face. "Anyway," she retorted, turning back to Mary. "I saw you once, holding hands with him, running into the meadow. So what if I tell the police that?"

It was Mary's turn to blush. Her eyes opened wide and she bit her bottom lip. "I…it…that was months ago. They wouldn't be interested, so there's no need to say anything."

"B…b…but I saw you, an' all," piped up Faith. "More than once."

"Who's going to believe you? You can't even talk right." Mary turned away.

"I…I…I…" Faith stood with her mouth agape, clearly wondering whether to retaliate.

Charlotte knew it hurt the simpleton to be reminded of her situation. "Take no notice, Faith. She's cruel, and will receive her come-uppance one of these days."

"At least I can attract men," retorted Mary. "You will never know the joys of having a lusty man caress your breast." She cupped hers in her hand. "Or running his hand down your leg." She pulled up her dress, revealing soft, white bare skin. "And…" Her hand moved farther up, past her knee.

"S…s…stop! I don't want to hear anymore." Faith put her hands over her ears and ran out of the dairy.

"You've gone too far this time," said Charlotte. "You're so mean, mocking her like that."

"I bet you know what I'm talking about, young Shar, don't you? I bet you're not the innocent little virgin you profess to be."

"That's none of your business."

"I knew it. I knew I was right. Ha, caught you." Mary danced a little jig, her grey dress swinging around her legs.

"You've done nothing of the—"

"What on God's earth is going on in here?" Farmer Grant stood in the doorway, a sobbing Faith at his side.

Charlotte turned the last block of cheese, keeping her back to him. Out of the corner of her eye, she could see Mary sheepishly walk over to the cheese barrel she had been working on.

"What have you been saying to my niece?"

They both spun around to face him. "Your niece?" they asked in surprised voices.

"Yes, Faith is my sister's lass. Didn't she tell you? No, obviously not. She probably didn't want preferential treatment."

"If we'd known…" began Mary.

"You would have what? Treated her with the respect she deserves? It seems to me you two had better collect your coats and leave."

Charlotte was aghast. She hadn't done anything wrong. "But, sir, I…"

Fortunately, Faith came to her rescue. "I…I…it wasn't Charlotte, Uncle Ed, only…" She pointed to a shame-faced Mary.

"Please, sir, I didn't mean no harm," Mary grovelled. "I was only having a bit of fun. Please don't send me away. My mother, she's a widow and she needs my money. Please, I beg you." She ran up to him, her hands held as if in prayer. "Please give me one last chance."

"It's up to Faith." He looked his niece in the eye. "Could you continue to work with this girl, knowing she might assail you again?" When she hesitated, he continued, "No, I think not. And I don't blame you." He turned to go, with the aside, "I want you off the farm in the next ten minutes, Miss Howard. You may collect your wages at the end of the week."

She ran after him, tugging at his sleeve. "Please, sir, please don't do this. My mother will whip me."

"You should have thought about that before you provoked my niece. Good day to you."

Mary turned back into the dairy, tears running down her face. "Now see what you've done." She poked Faith in the ribs, a look of pure hatred distorting her pretty face. "You'll suffer for this. You haven't heard the last of me." Gathering up her coat and her bag, she stalked out, her sobs echoing around the dairy.

Faith wrapped her arms around her body and looked at Charlotte uncertainly. "Sh...sh...should I call her back?" she asked.

Charlotte didn't know what to say. As much as she didn't like the other milkmaid, she felt concern for her and her widowed mother. How would they live without Mary's money? "It isn't up to me. I think you would have a hard time persuading your uncle to take her back now."

Faith slumped onto a stool. "I...I...I wish I hadn't run out. I just..." She also began to cry.

As much as she knew her work was slipping behind, Charlotte went over and patted the girl's bent back. When the farmer's wife came in, she jumped guiltily and hurried across to the cheese vat. "I'm sorry, ma'am. I'll stay late to make up the time."

"What do you mean?" Mrs Grant walked over to Faith, who gazed at her with a face the picture of misery. "Are you poorly, my dear?" she asked, clearly unaware of the fracas that had just ensued.

"N...n...no, Aunt. I've just caused the death of an old lady."

Mrs Grant's head jerked back. "You've what?" She looked over at Charlotte, her eyebrows raised. "Surely this isn't true?"

"Well, what she means is...what she's trying to tell you is she's just caused Mary to be dismissed." Charlotte went on to explain what had happened.

"Well, good riddance. She always was a troublemaker."

"B…b…but…" Faith stood up, wiping her face with her apron.

"Never mind about that now, dearie. Try to forget about it." Mrs Grant rolled up her sleeves. "I'd better help you finish off these cheeses and sort out the milk to take to market. You'll never manage with just the two of you. I suppose we'll have to find another milkmaid to replace her." She turned to Charlotte who, having finished the first one, took out the bung of the next one to drain off the whey. "I don't suppose your sister—what's her name?—Jemima, would be willing?"

"Jessica, ma'am. I'm not sure. I shall ask her."

"Even if it's only on a temporary basis until we find someone. I know she's…" She looked disapprovingly at Charlotte's belly, nodding her head like a puppet.

You don't need to tar me with the same brush as my sister, thought Charlotte, but merely said she would ask her the following day.

* * * *

Martha wiped down the kitchen table. Peace, at last. She had packed the children off to school, armed with their lunch and an apple, and had carried out her chores without hindrance. Would she have time for a cuppa? Charlie would be rising from his bed soon, ready for his first afternoon shift. She had heard him come home late the previous night, and had pretended to be asleep.

First, she had better prepare his dinner.

Shifts were a real bind. He had worked days the previous week, finishing the day before, then a week of afternoons, then the one she loved most of all, nights. A good sleep, on her own. No snoring in her ear, no hardness pressing into her back just as she began to nod off. Not that she didn't enjoy making love. She did—

sometimes. She just didn't want it every night. She always made sure she was up early when he came in from nights, or she would have to endure it then as well.

How happy she had been on her wedding day, so much in love. The thrill of being a wife had not lasted long, though. She had thought Charlie to be in love with her. Maybe he had been, for a while. Already four months gone and enduring a difficult pregnancy, she hadn't had the energy to wait on him hand and foot—and everything else—as he demanded, and they had started arguing. Not over anything important, just little things, like his dinner not being hot enough, or his best shirt not being ironed sufficiently. When she had tried to explain how ill she had felt, he had stormed off, saying, "My mother had ten children, and my father's food was always on the table in time. He never had cause to complain."

That's because he beats her into submission, she had wanted to say, but had kept her mouth closed, not wanting him to start on her. He had done so not long after. Only small cuffs around the shoulders, to start with. She bore them without complaining. That was until the day he had knocked her down the stairs. He had been apologetic, saying he hadn't intended to push her. It had been her fault for goading him, by not answering whatever he had asked her. She couldn't remember what it had been, nothing important. She had worried she might lose the baby. Early labour had been brought on, but, thankfully, no harm had been done. Amy was born, crying the moment she emerged—a healthy, bonny baby.

The beats and knocks, Martha could stomach. They had become a way of life. She hated the mental anguish more. His sullen silences, not speaking for days at a time or, if he did, in single syllables.

At other times, though, he could be gracious and charming, especially around his mates. None of them would ever guess what he was like once he stepped over that threshold. Unless all men were the same, of course.

Maybe they all lived like that. But her own parents had not acted in such a fashion. They would hold hands and look into each others' eyes whenever they were together. Surely her mother wouldn't have been so lovey-dovey if she'd had to tolerate any cruelty. Would she?

As she twiddled her wedding ring, to remind herself of the vows she had taken, Martha heard movements from upstairs, so dropped a dob of lard into the frying pan, and added the last two rashers of bacon from the grilled safe in the pantry. There would be trouble. He liked three. But her housekeeping allowance had run out and she didn't have the money to buy any more until payday on Friday. The old red tin on the dresser should have contained more money than it had the previous day, but she must have misjudged it. Surely Charlie wouldn't have pinched any of her housekeeping?

An extra egg might soften the blow. Her next-door neighbour had given Tommy half a dozen the day before in exchange for running a small errand. Her Aunt Elizabeth usually provided her with plenty, but hadn't done so that week. She would have to ask Jessica the next time she came around.

Carefully knocking the eggs on the side of the pan so as not to break the yolks—he wouldn't eat them if the yolks weren't intact—she splashed the fat over them to cook the whites, just as he liked them. Then she cut three thick slices of the bread she had baked earlier, spreading as little butter over them as she could without inviting criticism.

"Bacon smells good." He came into the kitchen, his braces hanging down his legs, shirt unbuttoned. At one time, she would have been aroused at the sight of him half-dressed, especially when he appeared to be in a good mood, but not that day. The death of Herbert Grant had affected her more than she could have thought possible.

"It's cooked nice and crozzled, just how you like it." She didn't mention the number of rashers, just placed it in front of him.

He picked up his knife, stuck it into the yolk of the first egg and nodded.

Phew!

His mouth full of bread, he mumbled, "Good job about that Grant fellow." At least she thought that was what he said. He swallowed. "Tea?"

She had been watching him eat, and had forgotten to pour it out. Reaching over to the pot, she lifted the red tea cosy and poured hers first, then stirred the tealeaves, before pouring out his, and adding a tiny amount of milk into the blue china cups.

"Have they said whether he fell, or was murdered?" He sipped his tea, wiping his mouth with the back of his hand before tucking in once more.

"No, I haven't heard." Maybe he hadn't noticed the missing rasher.

"Whatever it was, he deserved it. He molested half the neighbourhood females, you included. He never did it again, though, did he, after I gave him that good hiding?" He looked up for her to confirm it.

"Thank God, although you didn't need to attack him so ferociously. You almost killed him." She hadn't dared tell him Herbert had done it all the more.

"If the police find out…"

"Well, I won't tell them. Anyway, perhaps he did fall."

"Mebee. We'll see." The remains of the bacon fat mopped up with his bread, he washed it down with the remains of his tea and sat back, holding out his cup. "Any more?"

She put down her own cup and refilled his.

"Pour some warm water into the bowl, lass, so I can have me wash." He lathered his chin with the soft, round, white-handled brush and scraped his razor over his bristles. "I might go straight round to the Fox and Hounds tonight after I've changed." He peered into the mirror, dragging the razor up his neck, his lips pursed, as a figure walked by the kitchen window. He stood up straight. "Who's that, calling at this time of day? Don't they know I'm about to go to work?" Checking in the mirror once more, he moaned, "Damn and blast. I've cut meself. That's with folk arriving when they're not wanted." He looked pointedly at the constable knocking on the open door.

"Sorry to bother you, sir. I just need to ask a few questions." The constable shifted uncomfortably from one foot to the other.

"Well, they'll have to wait." Charlie splashed water over his face and dried it, then pulled up his braces and buttoned his shirt. "I'm off to work." He turned to Martha. "Is me snap ready?"

"Yes, of course." She reached into the pantry, handed him an old battered tin, and lifted her face for his kiss. Planting a peck on her cheek, he pushed past the policeman.

"Ta-ta, see you later," she called after him, but he had already sprinted halfway up the entry.

"Come in," she told the constable. "And thank you."

He hesitated. "What do you need to thank me for, ma'am?"

"Oh, nothing." She couldn't tell him he had probably saved her from a beating. She wasn't sure if Charlie had noticed the missing bacon, but just because he hadn't mentioned it at the time, didn't mean he hadn't. She hoped he would have forgotten about it by the time he came home.

"Do they know anything yet—about Herbert Grant, I mean?" she asked, indicating to the man to sit down.

He shook his head, but remained standing. "No, ma'am. As I tell everyone, we'll find out for certain when they perform the autopsy. I just need to ask when you or your husband last saw him."

Her eyes wide, she pulled at her lips, to give the

semblance of trying to remember. "Oo, some weeks back. I wouldn't be able to say for sure." Not that she would admit to, at any rate. "And it's about the same for my husband. Have you asked around the village?"

The man wrote something down in his book. She tried to look at it over his arm but he held it too close to his chest "Oh, yes, ma'am, I'm interviewing everybody. Nobody, as yet, knows anything, or saw anything. It's as if…" He squinted at her.

With raised eyebrows she stood to attention, wondering what he could be about to say, but he merely put his notebook in his pocket. "Well, Mrs Holloway, if anything does come to mind, please be sure to inform either myself or one of my colleagues. Keeping information from the police is a serious matter, can even result in imprisonment."

She attempted to keep the look of dread from her face and turned away as if to examine something on the sideboard. "Of course, Officer. Yes, of course."

"I'll be back another time to see Mr Holloway, ma'am. When would be best?"

"Um…let me see. He's on afternoons for the next six days."

"Any morning, then, ma'am?"

"Oh, well, he doesn't like…he…yes, I suppose so, but not while he's having his dinner…or his breakfast."

"Thank you, ma'am, sometime in-between, then?" He sounded irritated, but he should not blame her for her husband's pickiness.

She nodded. What else could she say? She wouldn't be able to put him off for good. He would come anyway.

"I shall bid you good day then, ma'am. And, remember…anything at all." He picked up his helmet and went out.

Blowing out her breath in a long sigh, she watched him walk across the back yard towards the next house.

Chapter 5

A group of geese threatened to trip her up as Jessica checked her aunt wasn't watching through the kitchen window, so she shooed them out of the way and scuttled up the lane. Surely, someone had heard something! Before she had made it to the end, she met the constable on his bicycle.

He stopped, standing astride it. "Mistress Jessica Bridge?"

Her breath caught in her throat. What could he want with her?

Her face still itched, but she tried not to scratch it as she debated if she could pretend to be one of her sisters. They all looked similar. But she would only be found out so she nodded, looking at his bicycle as if it were a two-legged monster.

"I need to ask you a few questions, miss. But we can't do it out here. Shall we go to the house, and then I can interview your aunt and uncle at the same time?" He put his foot on the pedal. "Are they around?"

She glanced back at the house with a grimace. Her aunt would know she had gone out. She could think of no excuse not to do as he ordered, though, so turned and followed him and called through the back door into the kitchen, "Aunt Elizabeth, there's someone here to see you."

"While we wait for her, miss, I can address my questions to you." The constable sat down at the table without being asked, and took out a tatty notebook and a pencil. "How well did you know Herbert Grant, ma'am?"

"Herbert Grant? Um… Oh, you mean the dead body?"

His head jerked up as if in surprise. "Yes, miss, the

deceased person." He enunciated the words precisely, shaking his head.

She stuck out her lips. "I didn't really know him at all. He was just the farmer's son."

"So, miss, you never had a conversation with him?"

"I wouldn't say that… Ah, here's my aunt." She ran and grabbed her aunt's arm and dragged her into the room. "Aunt, this policeman wants a word." She turned back to the constable. "Have you finished with me, sir? May I go? I have so many chores to complete, don't I, Auntie?"

Aunt Elizabeth gave her a disbelieving glare as the constable stood up.

"Yes, Miss Bridge, for now. I may need to see you again later." As she turned to go out, he called, "Just one more thing…when did you last see him?"

"Oh, absolutely ages ago. Months, in fact."

He scribbled in his notebook.

"May I go?"

"Yes, miss."

She scooted out before he could change his mind.

Wilson approached her. People called him the village idiot, and children often threw stones at him to rile him, but she always found him pleasant enough.

"Good day, Wilson," she called.

He shuffled towards her, his wide nostrils flared, a look of anguish in his eyes, until he recognised her. Then a wide beam spread across his face. "Mistress Jessica, have you heard?" he asked in his deep voice, as he kicked at a stone, his arms hanging loosely by his side.

"What about?"

"Herbert the pervert."

"Herbert Grant? Why do you call him that?"

He shrugged.

Had he heard something? "No, Wilson, what about him?"

"He's dead."

"Oh, yes, I knew that. Do you know anything else?"

He looked about him shiftily. "They say he was…"
He pulled his ragged sleeves down over his hands.
"Murdered."

"Who says that?"

"Um…just they."

Most folk thought he couldn't understand what they
were talking about when he listened in on their
conversations, but she knew he understood a lot more
than they realised.

"What do *you* think, Wilson? Do you think he was—
" She opened her eyes wide and put her hands up in front
of her face just as a lion might "—mur…dered."

He shied away, his arms over his head. She felt guilty
then, but she found him so easy to scare. She eased her
hands down. "I'm sorry, Wilson. Tell me what else *they*
say."

His old brown cap came off and he scratched his
bald head. Without his cap, he looked completely
different, his face looking rounder and his eyes bluer,
somehow. She wondered about his age. He seemed quite
old to her, at least thirty or thirty-five. She would have to
ask someone one day.

He surprised her by asking, "Do you want to come
to my house, Mistress Jessica?" He had probably
forgotten about Herbert already.

He lived on his own, his mother having died some
months before. Fortunately, she had left him the cottage
they had lived in since his father's death, and neighbours
rallied round, taking it in turns to cook extra for him. He
would have to go to the workhouse, otherwise, but he
wouldn't last long in there, they all said. They couldn't see
him assigned to that fate.

But go inside his house? "No, thank you, Wilson, I
still have my chores to finish." Actually, she told the
truth, and should return to the smallholding.

She expected to see her aunt going crazy as she

glanced back up the lane but could see no sign of her, so the constable must still have been there, having his ear bent. Once her aunt started, she could talk for England, so Uncle Will often said.

Wilson turned and shambled off with droopy shoulders towards his cottage, as she made her own way to the barn. Her aunt wouldn't know she had skived off, if she caught up with the jobs she should have done half an hour earlier. If only the blinking spot on her face would stop itching, and she still hadn't found out anything about Herbert Grant, having not trusted Wilson.

* * * *

The horse pulling the plough seemed particularly jittery, making it difficult for Ronnie to control it with one hand. His mother had eventually returned the previous day, and had smothered his cut with one of the ointments—he couldn't remember which—and wrapped a bandage around it. He had never known anything like the excruciating pain, not even when he had caught his finger in a door at the age of ten. The tip had almost been cut right through, but it hadn't hurt as much as his hand. Not only his hand, but his whole body ached, the muscles throbbed, and extra bruises appeared every few minutes.

He had not let on that he had fallen down the gully, he could not admit that. He had merely fobbed her off with some lame excuse, which had seemed to satisfy her, although she had given him an odd look from under her eyebrows.

"Whoa," he shouted as the old mare plodded onwards. He had wanted to turn the corner and go back to plough the next furrow, but hadn't pulled hard enough on the reins and she had carried straight on. "We'll end up in the hedge, you stupid mare," he yelled.

With one more yank, he managed to line her up, and started on the next row. The milkmaid occupied his thoughts and he almost fell when the mare shied at a large hare bounding across the field directly in front of them. The rein dug into his hand. He had automatically used both. "Ye gods," he screamed at the pain. Gritting his teeth, he pressed the bad hand with the good one as new red blood seeped through the thick bandage.

The horse whinnied and turned her head to look at him. "Move on, girl," he ordered. Black clouds scudded across the sky from the west, and he didn't feel like adding to his miseries by becoming soaked.

He managed the next furrow without any further interruptions. One left. He took a fleeting look upwards. The sky had completely clouded over. He would have to make haste if he wanted to finish it in time. "Gee up, old Doris," he called. "Can't you go any faster?"

A strong wind blew his cap off and, as he leaned over to catch it, he lost his balance. Thump. He landed with such force the breath was momentarily forced from his lungs. He lay there, unable to move. The mare bent down to eat some tufts of grass protruding from the unploughed, baked earth, as rain pelted down on his prostrate body. Once his breathing had returned to normal, he tried to stand, but swore as his leg gave way. He hauled himself up and tried again. By clinging onto the bridle, he swung his leg over the horse's back and latched on to her mane, gripping it as pain seared through his body. With a click of the tongue and enough pressure from his right leg, he turned her to face the farm, and through the gate into the yard, the plough clanking behind them.

With his hair plastered to his face and his coat sodden, he offered up a quick prayer that he'd made it, but then felt himself falling, and landed on the mucky farmyard in a heap.

Someone ran out of the barn, yelling.

Opening his eyes, he saw the one person in the world he wouldn't want to see him in such a state. He squeezed them shut again.

"Master Ronnie, you're hurt."

That's an understatement, he thought as he felt Charlotte lean down.

His mother hurried over, pushed the horse out of the way and bent down to him. "Oh, Ronnie, what on earth have you done now?"

He sat up. "I fell."

"Well, obviously, son, or you wouldn't be lying there."

"No, I fell in the field. I think my leg might be broken." It did seem to be bent at a peculiar angle.

She ran her hand down the length of it. "Yes, son, it looks as if it might be." She turned to the girl. "Run and find the master, Charlotte, and anyone else who might be around who could help us carry him into the house."

Charlotte turned to go but he called, "No, don't fuss, Ma. I'll just hold onto you two." With his mother's help he stood on one leg. Putting his arm around her shoulders, he hopped.

"Grab his other side," his mother told the girl.

He closed his eyes as she pulled his arm around her. Oh, how he had dreamt of having her so close. Not in his wildest imaginings had he ever thought it would happen. How ironic that it had taken a calamity for her to touch him. A faint whiff of sweat emanated from her and he breathed it in deeply.

Before he knew it, they had arrived in the kitchen.

"Lower him gently onto the chair," his mother instructed.

The girl's green eyes showed concern as she pulled away. He didn't want her to let go and grabbed her hand. "Thank you," he whispered.

His mother pulled up his trouser leg. "Bring that other chair over here and we'll lift his bad leg onto it," she said, smiling when Charlotte looked away as if embarrassed. "Haven't you ever seen a man's leg before?"

She laughed, but then looked worried. "Oh, dear, it is bad. We'll have to call the doctor."

Faith stood in the doorway, wringing her hands. "I...i...is he going to die?"

"Nay, nay, lass, it isn't that bad. Don't you worry. Fetch your uncle, if you would. I think he said he was going down to the lower field to check on the calves."

"A...a...are you sure he isn't going to die?" She came in further and peered at Ronnie's leg, then into his face.

"No, I've just hurt my leg," he explained patiently. "I'll be fine. Just find my pa, please."

She smiled and her almond-shaped eyes lit up as she turned and went out, seemingly satisfied.

"Should I return to the barn, ma'am?" asked Charlotte. "I was in the middle of—"

He grabbed her arm, assuming a pained expression. "No, please don't go yet, miss. Don't leave me."

His mother gently untangled them. "Now, now, son, she has to finish her jobs. The dairy won't operate on its own, especially now we're a milkmaid down."

With a weak smile, Charlotte left.

Ronnie closed his eyes. That smile would stay in his mind so he could remember it.

I'm in love, he thought, *and the feeling deadens the pain. It's delicious.*

His mother touched his leg and his eyes opened wide.

Well, maybe not all the pain.

* * * *

Charlotte almost ran out of the house and into the barn. She took some deep breaths. He had touched her hand. Held it, even. Had it changed in any way? No, she could still see a scar on the back. What about her palm? The line running down from her thumb seemed to have grown longer into her wrist.

That means I'm going to live a long life, she thought. *Maybe with him. Oh, wouldn't that be wonderful? Just think, married to him.*

With her arms wrapped about her midriff, she twirled around, revelling in the blissful thoughts.

Then reality struck home. It wouldn't be possible. What would be the point in even considering it?

Continue with your work, she told herself, *and stop daydreaming.*

She tied a white paper label, showing the date and the amount of milk, to the lid of the next wooden milk churn, and rolled it to the entrance to be collected on a cart and taken to the customers, many as far away as Ashbourne. Then, she churned some more milk into butter, and wondered if she would be asked to do Mary's job of going around the local villages, carrying pails of milk on yokes, and ladling it out to the villagers. It hadn't been mentioned, so they must have forgotten about it.

I'd better go back in and ask the mistress, she thought. That would be a good idea, for then she could check up on Master Ronnie. Catch another glimpse of him. Maybe he would touch her again, sending tingles down her spine.

Faith came in as Charlotte pushed a stray curl back under her brown hat. "How's Master Ronnie?" she asked, trying to appear casual.

"I…I…I hope he isn't going to die." The girl looked at her with tears in her eyes.

"No, I'm sure he isn't."

"Ou…ou…our Herbert did."

"Yes, but that's different."

"Wh…wh…why? 'Cos he was murdered?" Faith's eyes blazed.

"We don't know that yet. He might have just fallen."

"But Ronnie fell."

"Yes, but not down the gully." How could she persuade the simple girl that the two circumstances weren't at all the same? And she wanted to see how he fared. She patted the girl's shoulder. "Look, we're really behind with our work, and I need to find out who's taking the yoke today. Would you finish this off, please?"

"A...A...Auntie Lily is."

"I beg your pardon? Auntie...I mean Mrs Grant's doing what?"

"T...t...taking the yoke. She just said."

"Oh." That idea was out of the window, then. "Oh," she repeated. "Well, I need to speak to her about something else. I won't be a minute." She ran out, almost losing her hat in her haste. What excuse could she give? Her sister, Jessica? Yes, she hadn't spoken to her yet about taking Mary's place.

She peeped around the doorjamb of the open farmhouse door. Empty. Drat. They must have taken him up to his bedroom. That meant she probably wouldn't see him for weeks, not until he would be able to walk again, if his leg had broken.

With pursed lips she turned and slouched back to the dairy.

Several hours later, exhausted, she wiped her hands down her apron. Faith had left earlier, in tears again, fearing that her cousin would die, so she'd had to finish the work on her own. Subsequently, much later than usual, she dragged her weary legs to her Aunt Elizabeth's house.

"Come in, my dear," said her aunt. "You look shattered."

She nodded. "It's our Jessica I actually came to see. Is she in?" She slumped onto a chair.

Her aunt went to the stairs and called, "Jessica, your sister's here to see you."

Hurried footsteps could be heard running down the stairs. Jessica appeared, only half dressed, in her white petticoat and drawers, her mousy-coloured hair tied up in rags. "What do you want?"

Charlotte had expected a warmer greeting than that. But had her sister been crying? Her eyes looked red. "Good day to you, too," she said flatly. "What have you done to your face?"

Jessica twiddled her hair as she looked down at her feet.

"She's feeling out of sorts," explained her aunt, "because…" She directed her gaze at her younger niece. "Actually, I don't blinkin' well know why. Something to do with Wilson. I couldn't make any sense out of her. Maybe you can."

Charlotte really didn't have the energy to delve into her sister's woes. She just wanted to return home, have something to eat and fall into her bed.

"I'm sorry, maybe some other time. I just came to see if you wanted to come and work at the farm. Mary's left. She's been sacked, actually, and they need another milkmaid."

Jessica's eyes lit up. She grabbed hold of her aunt's hand. "Please, Auntie, may I? I could earn some money and repay you for all your kindness. Please, say I may."

Aunt Elizabeth raised her eyebrows. "But what about your chores here?" Charlotte could tell she was trying to look severe, but the little smile hovering on her lips betrayed her.

"Um. Maybe I could do some before I went. Feed the hens, at least, and collect the eggs."

Aunt Elizabeth turned to Charlotte. "I suppose they realise it wouldn't be for long. They do know your sister's expecting, don't they?"

"Oh, yes." Charlotte stood up, clinging onto the table. "They know that, all right." She didn't add that they tarred her with the same brush, that the dishonour affected the whole family. What would be the point?

Jessica put her arms around Charlotte. "Thank you so much, our Charlotte. Thank you. When do I start?"

"You'd better come up to the farm first thing in the

morning. They can tell you, then. I'm sure they'll want you to start straightaway. We were rushed off our feet today, at least I was. Master Ronnie had a nasty accident, and Faith—did you know she's Farmer Grant's niece?" At the shakes of their heads she continued, "Well, she hardly did any work, she was so upset."

"Well, she is…what is a nice way of saying it?" Her aunt hunched her shoulders.

"Feeble-minded."

"Yes, that's it. You have to take extra special heed of feeble-minded lasses. It isn't their fault."

"I know. But it doesn't help… Anyway, I'd better be off. Farewell."

* * * *

Charlotte had hardly left the house when Jessica wrapped her arms around her aunt.

"You've perked up, lass. It'll be flippin' harder work than you're used to, you know. It won't be a little bit of this and a little bit of that."

"I know, Auntie, but I'll be earning a wage, actual money. I might be able to save a bit for when the baby comes. Thank goodness that horrible Mary has gone. I wouldn't have even considered it if she'd still been there."

"If she hadn't left, you wouldn't have been offered the job." Her aunt patted her arm, shaking her head. "You'd better go up to your blinkin' bed. You'll need to be up with the cockcrow in the morning. And don't worry about feeding the hens. I'm sure I'll manage. I did so before you came, and I'll do so again."

"Thank you again, Auntie. But don't forget you're not getting any younger." She ducked out of the way as her aunt made to cuff her round the head.

"You cheeky blighter. I could change my mind, you know."

Jessica escaped up the stairs, her aunt's laughter

ringing in her ears, and lay spread-eagled on the bed. Oh, the joy—to have money in her pocket, even if only a shilling or two for material or wool. Some of the neighbours had already donated a few of the baby clothes their babies had outgrown, but she considered them shabby. Cast-offs and hand-me-downs were fine, but not what she wanted for her baby.

She had already started knitting a little matinee coat with some pale yellow wool her aunt had dug out from her knitting bag. She hoped there would be enough to finish it, so jumped off the bed and lifted the lid of her stool and took it out. As she held it out in front of her she noticed a dropped stitch. Damn. And another. The light had begun to fade, and she hadn't brought up a candle, for it hadn't been dark enough when she had come up, so could see no point trying to put it right.

The jacket carefully folded so the dropped stitches would not run any further, she replaced it in the tissue paper. *I don't know when I'll have a chance to finish it,* she thought, *not if I'm going to be working all hours God sends.*

But she should have an afternoon off once a week. She could do it then. Or maybe she would earn so much money she would be able to buy loads of new clothes. Wouldn't that be a turn-up for the books! That would show all the busy-bodies and nosey parkers who talked about her behind her back. She had seen them whispering to each other as she passed them in the village. Hadn't she done it herself, the year before, when that Howard girl, Mary's sister, had found herself expecting? She had been even younger than Jessica—only fourteen. She had lost the baby, though, in an unexplained fall, and had gone off to work in one of the mills near Cromford, or Matlock, somewhere miles away, soon after.

Her cheek did not irritate as much, but she still could not sleep. To be her own mistress, and have money. It would be hard work, she knew that, but she couldn't wait.

Martha dislodged something as she dusted the skirting board behind the dresser in the front lounge. It fell down and stuck fast. She tried to move the dresser forward, but it was too heavy, and made the blue plates rattle. She couldn't afford to break any of them. They had been Charlie's mother's, and his grandmother's before that. She had been a wealthy woman, his grandmother, so he kept telling her. So, what had gone wrong? He wouldn't explain that. Oh, no, just kept harping on about how the family had fallen into bad times. She blamed his drunkard of a father. The whisky had finished him off, in the end. He'd probably drunk away all his mother-in-law's money.

At least her Charlie didn't drink until he became inebriated. Well, not very often. Not like his father. She remembered one time, when they had lived with his parents in the early days of their marriage, she had found the older man under a hedge in the lane leading to their house, intoxicated, completely oblivious to anything. She had tried to help him home, but he had only groped her, telling her what a lucky man his son was, so she had left him there, hoping he would rot.

He was probably rotting in hell that very minute. Good riddance.

She couldn't reach the piece of paper. It couldn't be anything important, or she would have missed it, or Charlie would have. She left it. It wouldn't be going anywhere. If she found something missing, one of the butcher's bills or some other payment that hadn't been made, she would make a concerted effort, and find a knitting needle or something similar to poke it out. She racked her memory to think of anything else it could be, but nothing came to mind.

Children's voices rang in the lane. They were arguing again, Amy and Tommy. What a pity the schoolhouse wasn't open on a Saturday. But she could hear a different voice joining in, one she could not place. Through the back door she could see her son swinging a stick backwards and forwards as if beating hay, or separating grain from chaff.

"Mam, can Wilson have some lunch with us?" he asked, pushing the man forward. "He says he hasn't had anything to eat today."

"Oh, I wondered who could be with you. Yes, of course. Come in, Wilson. Take off your coat."

The man pulled his coat tighter around his midriff and shook his head.

"He's probably scared someone will pinch it." Amy picked up the newspaper from the chair, and pushed Wilson gently onto it. "We won't steal it, Wilson. It wouldn't fit any of us."

He still clung onto the tattered brown coat as if his life depended upon it.

"Never mind, you may keep it on if you wish." Martha placed a cup of tea in front of him. "Two spoonfuls of sugar and a little milk, just how you like it."

He took off his cap, put it on the table and slurped the tea, with one hand wrapped around the cup, the other gripping his lapels.

"Grand," he announced, as a huge smile spread across his cheeks.

"Would you like a cheese sandwich?" Martha asked slowly, standing right in front of him, as if he was deaf.

"Mam, you don't have to shout. He can hear perfectly well."

"Yes, of course. I don't know what made me do that." She had known the man all her life. He had been a boy of fifteen and her about five when she had first become aware of a difference, but, seventeen years later, she still didn't know how to treat him. Her children seemed to know better than she. "Anyway, wash your hands. I'll make some lunch."

Tommy sat down at the table.

"That means you as well, young man, even more than your sister. Show me." He opened his outstretched hands for her perusal. "Just look at the state of them. What do you think, Wilson? Do they look clean to you?"

Wilson gave a deep laugh. "Dirty," he declared. "Dirty."

"See, Tommy, even Wilson can see you haven't washed them. Now, over to the sink. I want them spotless."

With a deep sigh, he stood up and obeyed her. "We saw a robin's nest today, Mam," he called over his shoulder as he ran his hands under the tap. "It had six little chicks in it, all with yellow edges on the side of their beaks."

"I hope you didn't touch them."

"No, I didn't, but Jimmy…"

"I hope you're not going to say what I think you are."

He rolled his eyes from side to side. "I don't know what you think I'm going to say, so I better not say anything."

"Don't be cheeky, Tommy." His sister whacked him over the back of his head. "Just answer Mam."

"Ouch." He lunged at her and water sprayed them both. "It isn't up to you. You can't tell me what to do. You're only seven."

"And you're only six, so that means I can. Mam, tell him."

"Amy, leave him alone, if you please. He has enough with his pa and me telling him what he should and shouldn't do. He doesn't need you as well."

"But, Mam…"

Martha lifted her finger and pointed it at her daughter. "Just do as you are told, for a change. This constant bickering will be the end of me one of these days." She spread a tiny amount of butter on the bread and placed it on the table.

Wilson grabbed a slice before she had given him a plate, and stuffed it in his mouth.

"Don't you want anything on it? We have jam or honey or…" She showed him the jars.

He shook his head as he picked up a second wedge.

"I love honey." Tommy spread lashings of it on his bread. "It comes from bees, you know, Wilson."

"Go steady, save some for other people." Martha grabbed the jar from him. "But you are quite right. It does come from bees. Well done."

He stuck out his tongue, covered in half-chewed food, at his sister. "Nah."

She stuck her nose in the air, then spread a small amount of jam onto her own slice without replying.

"Anyway," continued Martha, "what were you saying about Jimmy? Surely he knows better than to disturb the birds. He's almost seven. Haven't his parents taught him better than that?"

"Well…" Bread sputtered out of the boy's mouth and landed on Wilson's hand. The man squealed and jumped up.

"Tommy, please don't speak with your mouth full. Now you've frightened the poor man. Apologise." Martha tried to make Wilson sit back down, but he grabbed some more bread, stuffed it in his pocket and ran out.

"I'm sorry, Wilson," Tommy called after him but the damage had been done. "Please don't tell Pa." He gathered up the crumbs and scooped them onto his plate.

She shook her head. Her husband didn't need any further ammunition with which to berate the boy.

"Mam might not, but I will." Amy stood up, tossing her fair hair behind her.

"No, you will not, my lady. It wasn't that dire that you need to bother your father with it. Now sit down, and let's finish this meal in peace."

"I have finished. I'm going back out. I heard

someone say we might hear this afternoon if Herbert was murdered."

"What about your manners, lass? You haven't asked if you may leave the table. Now sit down, please, until we've all finished."

With a dirty look at her brother, she sat down, her hands in her lap.

Martha finished chewing. "Have you had enough, Tommy?"

"Yes, thank you, Mam."

"So have I. You may both go now."

They jumped up and ran out the door.

"Let me know as soon as you hear anything," she called after them.

"Aye, Mam, we will," replied Tommy.

Probably still out of sorts for being scolded, her daughter did not reply.

Chapter 6

In a world of her own, Charlotte sat on her stool and pulled at the cow's udders. She had not seen the farmer or his wife, so had not been able to inquire after Master Ronnie. She imagined him lying in his bed, writhing in pain. Oh, to be able to go up and ease some of that pain, to mop his face with cool flannels, to wipe the sweat from his brow, to…

"Farmer Grant told me to come in here." Her sister, Jessica, entered. Charlotte had not been sure if she would make it. "He said you could show me what to do."

Charlotte moved the bucket out of harm's way, handed Jessica a large apron, and helped her tie it at the back. "You'll need this. And one of these." A stool. "Have you ever milked a cow before?" At the shake of her head, Charlotte sighed.

"No, Aunt Elizabeth was going to show me, but there never seems to be enough time. She said Uncle Will would, but…" Jessica shuddered.

Charlotte could understand why. She would not want her uncle close either. "Your cheek isn't quite so inflamed today."

"No, thank God. Aunt Elizabeth's ointment worked wonders."

"Good. Right, we'll start you on old Bessie, she's the most placid. They all are really, but she more than most." They went over to the cow. She looked up at them with large brown eyes, as if to say, 'Please don't hurt me'.

"Y…y…you'll like Bessie," Faith called from the other side of the byre. "Sh…sh…she's lovely. You look just like Charlotte, don't you? Ex…ex…except…" She gave a pointed look at Jessica's belly and turned her head away.

Charlotte glanced at it also. "You'll have to accustom yourself to that, the bigger you grow."

Jessica shrugged. "I know. I can take it. Just show me what to do." As Charlotte explained how to pull the udders downwards and aim the milk into the bucket, she retorted, "It sounds as easy as pie. I'm sure I'll manage."

"Let me watch you, before I go back to my cow. The poor thing probably thinks I've abandoned her." The black and white cow did, indeed, have an air of neglect.

"How can cows feel like us humans? Don't be so silly." Jessica sat on her stool and reached forward.

"You need to open your legs wide and sit closer." *That's been her trouble, though. She should have kept her legs firmly together,* thought Charlotte, but kept her counsel. They needed an amicable relationship if they were to work side by side for the next few weeks.

Jessica shoved her dress down between her legs and reached forward, her head back.

"Not like that. You have to rest your forehead on the cow's flank, feel her heat."

"But it'll wipe muck all over me." Her sister's mouth turned down.

"Yes, it more than likely will. But that's part of the job. One of its drawbacks, I admit."

With a grimace Jessica leaned forward again.

"Oh, and make sure your hands are nice and warm. You don't want to shock her."

Her sister rubbed her hands together and took hold of an udder. "Nothing's happening. Why isn't the milk coming out?"

"Pull. Pull downwards like I told you." After a few seconds the milk started to flow. "Make sure you aim it into the bucket. That's it. Just carry on until nothing more comes out, and then continue with the next one."

"How will I know which one I've already done?" Jessica sat back.

"Don't stop now you've started."

She bent forward once more and began again.

"You just have to remember. Use your loaf. You're supposed to be an intelligent girl."

"I am, I just… Oh, now look what you've made me do." As she shifted her bottom on the stool, she knocked the cow's leg and it kicked the bucket over, spilling the milk.

"Don't blame me, sister."

"If you hadn't…"

Faith jumped up and grabbed Charlotte's arm. "P…p…please don't argue. I can't stand arguments, they make me cry."

"I'm sorry. Of course we shouldn't." She patted the girl's shoulder and steered her back to her stool. "You ignore us. It's just our way."

Jessica picked up the bucket and started again.

Let her get on with it, thought Charlotte as she went back to her own cow. Maybe it was not such a good idea to have her sister working there. But she would just have to accept it and make the most of it.

Mrs Grant came in, shooing a chicken out of her way. "How are you settling in, child?" she asked Jessica. "Has your big sister shown you the ropes? I'm sorry I couldn't. My dear Ronnie's so poorly, although the doctor says his leg might not be broken, after all."

"That's good news, ma'am," replied Charlotte. "He shouldn't have to spend so long in bed, should he?" Good news, without a doubt. She wouldn't have to wait so long to see him again.

"No, indeed." She blew out the candles. "It's practically daylight. You shouldn't need these now."

As she poured milk into the churn, Charlotte watched her younger sister. "Are you picking it up?"

"Yes, I think I am. It isn't too bad, is it?"

"I…I…I enjoy it," said Faith, pouring in her milk as well. "W…w…watch out." She yanked Jessica out of the way. She had moved to stand behind the cow and would have been kicked.

"Oh, thank you. I should know better than that, shouldn't I?"

"You'll learn, when you've had a kick or two, especially if it's on the shin." Mrs Grant lifted up her petticoats and showed them a scar on her leg. "That's from a particularly vicious cow we once had. Her name was Mabel. If you went anywhere near her rear end, she would lash out. Most strange, they are usually such docile creatures."

"I…I…I have one too." Faith raised her frock well above her knee and showed them a barely visible mark on her thigh.

"Yes, dear, you don't need to show all the neighbourhood your…" Her aunt pushed her frock back down. "Maybe I shouldn't have done that. It gave the wrong impression."

"I…I…I…that was when I lived with my other aunt in Bakewell." The girl put her arm around the farmer's wife. "Sh…sh…she's not nearly as nice as you, Auntie Lily. I…I…I am so pleased you let me come to live here."

"You're a good girl, my dear. It's a pleasure to have you around." She turned to go out. "Come in for your breakfasts when you've finished."

Jessica's eyes lit up. She smiled across at Charlotte. "Breakfast? I didn't realise food was included."

"Yes, some days, when Mrs Grant has time."

"My belly is already rumbling, and I'd been thinking I would have to eat the sandwiches Aunt Elizabeth made me for my lunch. Now I can save them." She bent back towards the cow, humming quietly.

Maybe it wouldn't be so bad after all. They had been close as children. Martha, five years older than her, had seemed more aloof and had not wanted to play their childish games, so they did not have such a tight bond, and when she had married Charlie, pregnant at fifteen—

just like Jessica, in fact, although they had been courting for several months—any bond they might have had, had snapped. Especially as Charlie... He seemed nice enough, but Charlotte could sense an underlying tension whenever she visited, which she did not do frequently. Maybe she should make an effort and visit more often in future. She could ask her older sister for some tips on how to handle her new feelings for the farmer's son.

As they walked into the farmhouse an hour later, she wondered if she dare ask if she could go up... But no. A respectable girl would not enter a man's bedroom. It just would not be allowed.

"Will sausages be acceptable?" Mrs Grant asked.

"Oo, yes, please, Mrs Grant." Jessica grinned. "I love them."

"M...m...me too. Much nicer than bacon." Faith waited for Charlotte to wash her hands and sat down next to her.

"Which do you prefer, Charlotte?"

"Anything will be most welcome. Thank you." She raised her head to one side, listening for any sound from upstairs. "How's Master Ronnie?" There, she had said it. She had told herself she would not, but it had come out of its own accord. It didn't hurt to be concerned, anyway. His mother would surely not read anything untoward into her enquiry.

"He's sleeping. The doctor gave him some laudanum to dull the pain."

She continued to eat her breakfast, her head bent. She did not want Mrs Grant to notice the flush she could feel welling up on her cheeks whenever she thought of him. *But why am I thinking of him? There's no point.* She knew that, but the thoughts came unbidden into her mind. She seemed to have no control over them.

"When is your baby due, Jessica?" she heard the farmer's wife ask. Her head shot up in surprise. Respectable folk did not speak about it in public.

Her sister didn't seem bothered. "In about ten or...no, I think it's nine weeks now." She put down the bread she had been about to eat. "Oh, my goodness. It's creeping closer and closer. It's down to single figures."

"And do you have many clothes for him or her?"

"One or two. Everyone has been so kind, giving me their cast-offs... I mean..." She shovelled another sausage into her mouth, looking rather sheepish.

"You have to be thankful for small mercies, young lady. You can't be too choosy. I was going to offer you some of my grandchildren's old clothes, but if 'cast-offs' are not good enough for you, I might not bother."

"Please, ma'am, I would be grateful for anything. I didn't mean to sound as if I'm not, please believe me."

"The baby will go naked if you can't accept charity." Charlotte did not want to lecture, but sometimes her sister set her sights too high. She had always been like that, wanting the best, had never willingly accepted what she deemed to be inferior things, although, because she was the youngest, she'd had to make do with hand-me-downs, and had never had a new dress, made just for her. Perhaps that was why.

"I know, I know. It's just sometimes, I wish..."

"You should have thought about that before you..." Mrs Grant's head jerked up and down in quick succession, "you know...laid with... Who is the father, anyway?"

A gasp came from all three milkmaids, amazed that she should make it her business to question the girl so intimately.

"Y...y...yes, I wondered that." Faith peeped out from under her eyebrows, clearly unsure as to whether she should be included in the conversation.

"That's my personal affair." Jessica stood up and scraped her chair along the wooden kitchen floor. "And I'm not divulging the answer. Not to anyone. Thank you for the breakfast." With that, she walked out.

Charlotte quickly swallowed her last piece of sausage and also stood up. "Yes, Mrs Grant, we had better not take up any more of your time. Thank you for the meal. Are you coming, Faith?" With her hand under the girl's elbow, she tried to help her stand, but she resisted.

"B...b...but I haven't finished." Faith remained seated. "A...a...and I want to know whose baby Miss Jessica has in her belly."

"Well, I'm afraid you won't find out today." Her aunt stacked up the plates and took them to the sink. "Maybe I went too far with your sister, Charlotte. Please accept my apologies. I really do have her best concerns at heart. You understand, don't you? It's just that with your mother having passed away, God rest her soul, and you being so young..." She went across and touched her arm. "Do you think she'll accept the clothes?"

"Please don't worry yourself, ma'am. I know you're only doing what you think best, and yes, she will accept them. I shall make sure she does."

"I...I...I would take them, if I was having a baby."

"Thank you, Faith, but I don't think..." Mrs Grant looked at Charlotte and shrugged.

Charlotte knew what she meant. Unless someone took advantage of the dim-witted girl while nobody was looking out for her, there would be no chance she would ever have a baby of her own.

"Come on, let's continue with our work. Duty calls, as they say." She ushered the girl outside. Where could Jessica have gone? Had she run off or would she be waiting in the byre?

The byre was empty. Surely she wouldn't have given up the chance to earn some money, just because someone had asked her the question that was on everybody's lips, money being her be all and end all? As a child she had run errands, done anything, to earn a farthing or two. Once she had received a whole halfpenny. Charlotte had never found out to the reason for such a fortune.

"M...m...maybe she's in the barn. There's a baby lamb in there. I...i...it was born during the night."

"Yes, let's look in there."

Sure enough, there she sat in the corner of the barn, cuddling the lamb, her face the picture of happiness, not at all how Charlotte had expected to find her. "Just look at this, our Charlotte. Isn't it the cutest thing you ever saw?"

"Where's its mother?"

"Sh...sh...she died, giving birth." Faith went over and stroked it. "Uncle Ed says I can name it, but I can't decide on one."

"What about 'Faithful', after you?" suggested Jessica.

"F...F...Faithful, yes, I like that."

"That's decided then. Faithful it is. But we must carry on with our work, or we will be here all night as well as all day. Put the lamb down, Jessica."

"Ugh, it's pooped on me. I shall have to go home and change my frock now."

"You won't have time for that. It'll take you a good ten minutes to reach home, five minutes to change, and another ten minutes to come back, that's not allowing for any time stopping to speak to folks on the way. No, you'll just have to wipe off as much as you can and cover it with your apron."

Jessica grabbed a handful of hay, and scrubbed it down her dress. Most of the mess came off, leaving a small yellow stain.

"You'll do, come on. The cheese will be curdled."

"Isn't it supposed to?"

"Only cottage cheese. We're not making that today. Maybe tomorrow."

"Will I be able to take the yoke and pails around the village? I'd love to do that."

"That's up to the mistress. I haven't been asked to do that yet, so I shouldn't think you will."

They worked together. Charlotte showed Jessica

what to do, and tried not to become exasperated when she did it wrong.

"But it would make sense for me to go, because you know what you're doing here. I wonder if I'll ever pick it up," Jessica moaned after spilling whey all over the barn floor.

They both looked up as Faith made for the doorway. "I…I…I need a pee. I won't be long."

Back at their tasks, Jessica asked what usually happened to the whey.

"It goes to feed the pigs," replied Charlotte. "They love it, and it helps to fatten them ready for market."

"Have you ever taken them?"

"To market? No, that's not my job. Ronnie usually does it." Charlotte twiddled with a curl, then tucked it behind her ear.

"I think you're sweet on him."

"Who?" she asked innocently, as if she didn't know what her sister meant.

"Ronnie. Master Ronald Grant."

"Why do you say that? Of course I'm not."

"It's just the way you say his name. Sort of slurry, and whispery. Oh, Ronnie!"

"Don't be silly." She cuffed her sister's arm, pretending to hit her.

"Your secret's safe with me. I shan't tell anyone."

"There's nothing to tell, I assure you. I hardly know the man."

"At least he's not like his awful brother. I wonder if anyone's heard the coroner's verdict." Jessica stood up, arched her back, her hands on her hips, and made circling movements with her head. "It makes your back ache, doesn't it?"

"You become accustomed to it after a while." Charlotte copied her. "But this does help."

"Do you think Herbert was murdered?"

"How would I know? I didn't even see the body."

"I couldn't see much blood, no stab wounds or anything like that, but maybe his neck was broken by strangulation, or he was suffocated by a pillow. I wonder how long it takes to die with a pillow over your face."

"You can put your gory imagination away. You'll scare Faith. I can see her on her way back, now, so hold your tongue, if you please. Don't forget, he was her cousin."

"Oh, yes, I'd forgotten. She's…"

"What?" Charlotte raised her eyebrows. Her sister could be quite outspoken at times. She hoped she wouldn't say anything untoward about the girl.

Jessica shook her head. "It doesn't matter."

"Good. I should hate you to embarrass yourself by speaking out of turn."

"Have you had a nice pee?" Jessica called over to Faith as she came in. "Do you feel better?"

"Wh…wh…what? I mean pardon?"

Charlotte gave her sister a warning glare.

Jessica whispered. "I'm only giving her a friendly greeting. What harm is there in that?"

"There is friendly and friendly." Charlotte lowered her voice. "Please do not overstep the boundary."

Jessica stalked over to the other side of the barn. "I can't win with you."

"Come back, don't be such a mardy beggar. I'm only looking out for you."

Faith began to sing. "Mardy beggar, mardy beggar," with no sign of a stutter.

"Please don't do that, Faith. It's not mannerly."

Shamefaced, the girl looked down from the vat where she had been turning the blocks of cheese. "S…s…sorry."

"Maybe you should sing all the time, Faithful," suggested Jessica, leaving the corner she had snuck into. "You didn't stammer at all just then."

"Uh?"

"Jessica, just leave her alone. And don't call her that. We've just named the lamb Faithful, so she will become muddled." Charlotte combed the curds. "But you were right. She didn't stammer at all, did she?"

"No. Is it worth mentioning it to her aunt?"

"Maybe. Anyway, are you helping me with this, or not?"

Chapter 7

Martha peered through the darkness of her bedroom window as she drew the curtains. The rain sheeted across the village green opposite, obliterating the woods she could usually see in the distance. The trees she could just make out down the lane swayed precariously in the strong wind, their boughs bent over.

"Shut those curtains and come to bed," called Charlie. "I need a cuddle."

"Yes, darling, I'm coming."

Letting loose her hair, she picked up the candle, ready to blow it out.

"No, don't do that, I want to see you in your full glory. Take off your nightgown as well." He lay on the bed, completely naked, his arms behind his head.

"But I have only just put it on."

"All the more enticing, to watch you take it off."

I might as well play up to him, she thought. It would probably be over quicker. Slowly and seductively, she drew the pink cotton nightgown over her head, swivelling her hips until it was off. Playfully, she threw it at him, covering his head.

He jumped up and cast it aside. "Come here, you witch, tormenting me like that. You know how to turn me on." He grabbed her waist and kissed her belly. She dug her fingers in his black hair, moaning, as his tongue licked at her soft flesh.

Just as she lay back to enjoy the sensation, he turned her over and laid her on her back, spreading her legs open.

Two minutes later, he rolled over, spent.

That didn't take long, she wanted to protest, but knew he would only become enraged if she complained. His prowess could never be criticised. She curled into a ball. His snores soon indicated he had already dropped into a deep sleep. She wished she could do so, as thunder rattled the jug in the washbowl, and lightning illuminated the picture of his mother on the wall, giving her an eerie, evil appearance, more so than usual. She had never had a high opinion of Martha and had always criticised everything she did. Thank goodness she had moved away to the next village when she had remarried after his father had been killed.

The following morning she went downstairs, while Charlie still snored. Sunlight had already begun to stream into the kitchen. The storm of the night before had vanished, leaving a clear blue sky.

She went into the front room. One of her neighbours ran past the window as she opened the curtains. Then another. What could be happening? She pulled up the sash window and called out as a third man hurried past, "What's going on?"

"A landslide," he called back, "over at Doveledge."

"A landslide? Oh, my goodness! Has anyone been hurt?" But the man had already disappeared.

She could not very well go out in her yellow dressing gown but if she went up to put on some clothes, she might wake Charlie—although, he would probably want to be in the know, anyway.

Tommy came downstairs, his fair hair sticking up on end. He yawned and scratched his bottom. "Folks are shouting outside. They woke me up." He yawned again.

"Yes, I heard them. Apparently there's been a landslide."

His eyes opened wide. "Oh, golly gosh. Can I go and see?"

"No, it might be treacherous. I don't want you caught up in anything dangerous."

Amy also came down, her thumb in her mouth. Martha had tried to coax her to stop, ever since someone had told her about a friend's daughter who had to have her hands tied down to her sides at night-time to make her stop. It seemed she had been pulling her jaw out of shape.

"I'm going up to put on some clothes. Put the kettle on, please, Amy, and make us a cup of tea."

"What's going on outside?" Amy bit at her lip as she filled the kettle.

"It's a land…what did you call it, Mam?" Tommy's animated face peeped through the window.

"A landslide, at least I think that's what the man said."

"Can I go outside and see what's happening?"

"Not in your nightshirt, no, and it's over at Doveledge. You wouldn't be able to see anything from here. Wait there, make yourself a butty or something while I nip upstairs."

Taking the stairs two at a time, she opened her bedroom door. Charlie turned over and reached out to her. "What's all the commotion? Can't a man have some peace on a Sunday morning?"

Evading his outstretched arm, she sidled to the chair where she had left her clothes the previous night, and took off her nightdress that she had put back on during the night when the howling wind had woken her. She told him about the landslide.

He pushed back the covers and grabbed his trousers. "I'd better go down there, to see if they need any help. Do you know how bad it is?"

She shook her head. "No, I was about to go myself."

He pulled on his trousers and a shirt, pushed past her, ran downstairs, and out of the front door. *He must be in a hurry,* she thought, *to use the front door.* They only opened it on rare occasions, for speed, rather than going out the back, across the neighbour's yard and down the entry.

With the last button on her frock fastened as she

went down, she saw her children on the front step. "Come on in, you two. You're not dressed."

"Everyone else is out here. Most of them don't have clothes on, either," called Tommy. He scooted past her and ran upstairs. "Where's me clean shirt, Mam? I spilled gravy down the one I wore yesterday."

She began to tell him, but he had already charged back down in the dirty one. "Don't matter. This one'll do."

"Now, our Tommy, I said you weren't to…" He pulled on his shoes and run out of the door. She ran after him. "Tommy, come back here." His retreating back disappeared around the end of the row of terraced houses.

Amy pulled her dressing gown around her. "You may as well save your breath, Mam."

She sighed. Her daughter was right. "I'm going after him. Heaven knows what mischief he'll find. You be a good girl and stay here."

"Aren't you going to drink the tea I made you?"

"Oh, yes, thank you." She hurried into the kitchen, poured some cold water into the tea and drank it down in one go. "You may as well prepare yourself for school while I'm gone."

"Mam, it's Sunday."

"Of course." Hadn't Charlie just said that? "Well, you can go back to bed, if you like. We may have to abandon going to church today. It depends what we find." She gave her daughter a hug.

"I might come down and find you when I'm dressed, or I may just go and see what my friends are doing."

"It is up to you. I know you'll be sensible." She gave her a kiss, hurried out and joined other people, some pulling on their coats, others buttoning up their shirts, or tying the ribbons on their bonnets, and remembered hers. Too late to go back for it.

Lily Grant could be seen farther along the mile-long lane, so she hastened to catch up with her. "I didn't expect to see you here, Mrs Grant. I heard your Ronnie had a nasty accident. How is he?"

"He's bearing up, the lad is. But you know how men are. The slightest ache and pain and they're convinced they're going to die."

"Aye, you're right there. Is he...I mean...how's he coping with his brother's demise?"

The farmer's wife shook her head. "To be honest, there never was any love lost between the two of them. I think, in a way, he's relieved. Well, our Herbert did torment him, goad him, like, at the slightest opportunity."

"Um, I had heard. Word spreads, doesn't it? There aren't many secrets in these parts. Oh, talking about secrets, thank you for taking on our Jessica, by the way. She's a flighty girl. I hope she's knuckling down and working hard. I should hate for you to regret it."

"She's doing fine. Your Charlotte keeps her in check. She's a nice girl. I hadn't realised that before."

"Who, Jessica or Charlotte?"

"Well, both, of course. Charlotte is much quieter, more mature, isn't she? Do you not have any notion of who the baby's father is?"

"No, her mouth is firmly closed on that subject. I didn't know she was seeing anyone."

"Well, she's not the first lass to find herself in that situation, and she won't be the last. That's for sure."

A man hurried past them, back in the direction of Lea Croft. Martha called to him, "What's happening?"

"It's chaos down there," he replied.

"Oh, dear. It sounds bad."

Loud shouts and screams emanated from the throng of villagers gathered near the top of the cliff called Doveledge. This crag, like the other one, typical of the Derbyshire scenery, rose behind them, trees and plants growing out of the stone.

"Oh, my goodness, where are the buildings? They've all gone," gasped Martha.

A man at the back turned to her. "Yes, every last one. The old barn just went a few minutes ago." One or two rundown cottages had stood near the edge, and some old barns. Fortunately, they had not been inhabited for several years, not since part of the cliff had fallen away during a violent storm a few years previously. "It's to be hoped there weren't any tramps or vagrants holing out in them." It had been known for them to do so at times, especially during thunderstorms.

They tried to push their way closer to the edge. Martha spotted Tommy with his friend, Jimmy, precariously near the crumbling overhang. "Where's Charlie? Why isn't he looking after him?"

The people fell silent and cleared a way through for her as she made her way to the front. Why were they looking at her in such a sympathetic fashion? It had not been her cottage.

"Tommy," she called, "come away."

"But, Mam…"

"I said, come away. You'll fall down. Now, do as you're told." She moved closer. Someone pulled her back. "Mrs Holloway…"

"Yes?"

"It's your husband."

"What's my husband? Where is he?"

Tommy ran and buried his face in her skirt. "He fell."

The friendly faces all seemed to be staring at her. Surely he didn't mean…? Her eyes open wide, and mouth agape, she looked at the man. He nodded. "No, not my Charlie! It couldn't have been. You must be mistaken." She searched the crowd, sure she would be able to see her husband among them. When she couldn't, she inched to the edge of the precipice, which was what it had become, and peered over. Rocks, boulders and small trees still shifted downwards, as if they had a life of their own, but she could see no sign of a person.

"He can't be down there." She stepped back.

"But I saw him, Mam, I saw him fall over the edge," Tommy howled.

She bent down to him. "You aren't telling me fibs, are you?"

"No, Mam, honest to God. He just…" He burst into loud sobs, his body shaking.

Martha picked him up and walked back.

Lily Grant came across and put her arm around her. "They might find him. It doesn't mean he's…"

Much as he had made her life a misery at times, Martha still loved her husband. What would she do without him? "Yes, you're right. We must remain positive. He could have caught hold of a tree root, or anything. I bet, in a short while, he'll come climbing over the top, as bold as brass." Who was she trying to kid? But she had to give her little boy some hope. "You'll see, our Tommy. Your pa is indestructible, isn't he?"

He lifted his head from her shoulder, nodding.

"We mustn't give up hope until…" Her voice broke as she spotted a magpie land nearby. Known to be harbingers of doom if seen in the singular, she dared not say any more, for it could tempt the fates and make the unspeakable come true.

She turned to some of the men with ropes and ladders. "Are you going to climb down after him?"

"We don't know, ma'am. It's too dangerous to attempt anything at this stage. The cliff's still falling away. We don't want to lose anybody else."

"So, you do think…?"

He patted her arm. "Anything is possible, ma'am, until we know for certain."

"Our Amy, should I go back and tell her?"

Lily pulled at her. "Not until something has been found. There's no need to upset the lass unnecessarily."

"Oh, what should I do? I'm all at sixes and sevens. Should I stay here? Yes, I can't just go and leave him. He might need me if he's injured." She jiggled from one foot to the other.

Tommy had quietened and wriggled to be put down.

"Stay here with me, darling. Don't go wandering off. I don't want to lose you as well."

His friend, Jimmy, came over with his mother who said, "I'm so sorry, Martha. Our Jimmy saw it all with your Tommy."

"Did anyone else go?"

Tommy shook his head, his gaze on the wet ground.

"I don't think so," replied Mrs Howard.

"He were trying to save a dog," Tommy whispered.

"A dog? He's lost his life for the sake of a dog?"

"Yes," Jimmy explained when his friend could not continue. "It went right close to the side, and he ran over and reached out to grab it, and the ground just…" He blew out his breath in short gasps "…it just…" Another puff "…went."

Martha felt sick. How wretched for the boys to have witnessed such a scene. With a sharp intake of breath she drew them both to her side and caressed their heads.

The crowd had become even larger. The sound of their chatter grated on her nerves. They were probably all talking about her husband. She couldn't blame them, though. A catastrophe always brought onlookers. Nothing much happened in the sleepy neighbourhood to raise excitement, so an occasion such as that brought them all out.

The second thrilling incident in one week.

One of the men came across to her. "Some of us are going to scoot down that way." He pointed farther down the lane, where trees anchored their roots into the cliff edge that gradually sloped downwards after a mile or so to ground level.

"It will take us a while 'til we reach the bottom end,

but we might be able to find something down there. I suggest you go home, ma'am, and wait for news." He urged her towards the direction of the village.

"But I can't leave. What about those men? Can't they do something?" She indicated some people with ladders who seemed unsure what to do.

"It's too unsafe for them to try anything. I would suggest, ma'am, that you go."

She had been brought up with most of the sympathetic faces around her, but not the strangers. Evidently, word had spread to the neighbouring villages, and folks being nosy creatures, they had all come to find out what had happened.

"What do you think, Lily?"

"Well, I need to be back at the farm, so I'm willing to accompany you, if you wish."

Tommy tugged at her skirt, with a pleading expression. "I want to stay here, Mam, and wait for Pa. He'll need someone when he comes back."

"But it's beginning to rain again." She stuck out her hand. The clouds had been looking ominous, and raindrops started to fall on her face. "You'll soon be wet through, and then you'll catch a cold, and what good will you be to your pa, then? Eh?"

He opened his mouth as if to speak, as the monotone dong of the church bell drifted across the darkening atmosphere.

"Has someone died?" asked Jimmy. "Isn't that the bell they ring when someone dies?"

"Is it for Pa? Do they think he's dead?" Tommy grabbed her hand. "I thought you said he was indestruc…indister… You didn't say he would be dead."

"We don't know anything, Tommy, Jimmy. Someone must have the wrong end of the stick. They're being premature."

Tommy yanked away his hand and ran to the edge before she realised his intention. "Pa!" he yelled. The sound echoed around them. "Pa, where are you?"

The ground beneath him began to shift. She ran forward, screaming his name, her heart in her mouth. Just as she thought she would lose her son as well, someone grabbed him and pulled him to safety.

"Oh, thank you, thank you," she gasped as she dropped to where they had fallen with the impetus.

The mass of crowd had all moved forward. Some of the men tried to push them back. "The ground is very unsafe. Please go back," one of them yelled. He came to Martha. "You, too, ma'am, please move away. I can feel the earth trembling, even this far back."

She pulled Tommy to his feet as his saviour stood as well. Once out of danger, she shook his hand. "Thank you so much. Your quick thinking saved him." She took a closer look. "You're one of the Howard twins, aren't you?"

"Yes, ma'am."

"Well, thank you again."

The Howard twins, brothers of Jimmy and the milkmaid, Mary, were notorious for finding themselves in bother. They had been in prison more times than a little. They couldn't be all bad, though. She would be eternally in his debt. The next time anyone berated him, she would tell them of his heroic action. After all, he had put his own life in danger to save her son.

He walked off, back into the crowd. She didn't even know which twin he was. They were so alike, not many people could tell them apart. Rumour had it that even their own mother muddled them up at times.

The rain pelted on her head, and her frock had become wet through. With no shawl or bonnet to protect her, she gripped Tommy's hand and they ran back. Most of the crowd had already gone, the rain dampening their curiosity.

The church bell had stopped. Why on earth had they rung it? Maybe for someone else. Maybe there had been another death. It might not have been for her Charlie at all. Highly unlikely, though. Someone would have broadcast the fact. They wouldn't have been able to keep quiet something as important as that.

Amy ran towards them, her hair splayed out behind her. "Mam, Mam, is it true? Is our Pa really dead?"

"We don't know, child." She enfolded her in her wet arms. The girl felt warm. She must have only just come out.

"I was playing up at the top copse, looking for birds' eggs, when it began to rain so I came home. Mrs Howard just came in and told me what happened." She looked up as tears streamed down her cheeks. "Please say it isn't true, Mam."

"Let's go inside. We're all soaking wet." They ran the rest of the way and tumbled through the open front door.

Martha hurried into the kitchen and grabbed some towels from the overhead airing racks. While they rubbed themselves down, they heard the church bells ringing again—the usual call to morning service. "Is it that time already?" She looked up at the clock on the wall. "We had better make haste if we don't want to be late."

"Aw, Mam, do we have to go today?" Amy put down her towel and scraped her hair back off her face.

"We need to pray for our pa." Tommy's head appeared from under his towel. "If he's dead, we need to pray extra hard, don't we, Mam?"

"Yes, son, we need to pray for him, whatever's happened. Go and find some dry clothes, quickly." She ushered him upstairs then turned to her daughter. "You'll do, Amy, your frock is only slightly damp. You weren't out in it as long as we were. Just find a shawl and bonnet. We still need to look respectable."

Martha ran upstairs to change into her Sunday best frock, hoping her wet, muddy petticoat would not show. Her hair scraped back into a bun, she found the nearest bonnet, and ran back downstairs.

"Where's our Tommy? Hasn't he come down yet?"

Amy stood ready. "No, Mam."

"You look very pretty, my darling. That's your new shawl, isn't it? The one Mrs Thingamabob gave you? It really suits you. What's Tommy doing? Run up, would you, and hurry him up."

As she adjusted her bonnet in the mirror, Amy's voice came from upstairs. "He says he can't find his best shirt."

"Oh, tell him to keep his other one on. It won't matter for once. He can cover it with his jacket." They didn't have time. She hated entering the church if the service had already started. Everybody turned to stare and the older members of the congregation glared disapprovingly at the latecomers.

"Where's your cap?" she asked him when he eventually came down. He shrugged. "Never mind, let's go."

They hurried out, noticing they weren't the only latecomers. Maybe the vicar would delay the start when he saw so many had not yet arrived. No such luck. He had already begun his sermon. As she had expected, the elderly parishioners frowned, but most of them with sympathy, she noticed. About to sidle into a back pew, the vicar beckoned them forward to sit at the front.

She tried to concentrate on his words of wisdom during the service, but her mind would not keep up. Thoughts whizzed around her head like demons on Halloween night. What if her husband *was* dead? How would she feed the children?

Amy nudged her. She realised the vicar had addressed her personally.

"And we must all pray for a safe deliverance for our neighbour, Mr Charles Holloway. We pray he will be found safe and well. Amen."

The congregation all repeated, "Amen."

Martha heard Tommy say it extra loudly, looking

around for everyone to copy.

"Amen," she whispered again.

As everyone stood up, the door at the back opened with a loud clang and they all turned to see the verger opening it for them to leave. She slumped back onto the pew. Jessica and Charlotte came up to her. She hadn't seen them during the service. They both took her hands, giving her encouragement to keep brave and hope for the best. Several other villagers also crowded around her.

Leave me alone, she wanted to scream, but she knew they were only trying to help.

"If there is anything we can do, just let us know." Charlotte gave her a kiss. "Me and Jessica have to return to the farm. We were only allowed to come because of…you know. Mrs Grant stayed behind. Someone had to."

"Yes, just say." Jessica kissed her also. They hurried up the aisle, whispering to each other.

The vicar came over to her. "I shall pray for your husband. Do not despair. The Lord will—"

"Will He save him, Vicar?" Tommy interrupted him. "Will He really save our pa?"

"Well, I am not in a position to say He will. But I shall do everything in my power to try to sway His decision." He ran his fingers under his dog collar.

Tommy sat down, his hands in his lap. "That means no, then, doesn't it?"

The vicar tousled his hair. "Do not give up hope. The Lord works in mysterious ways His wonders to perform."

"May I go now, Mam?" Amy asked, looking towards the back of the church. "My friends are waiting for me."

"Yes, of course, dear. We had all better leave." She turned to the vicar. "Thank you for your kind words."

"You know where I am if you need me." He adjusted his cassock and hurried off to the vestry, probably eager to start preparing his dinner.

Should she cook dinner for Charlie? And he was supposed to be going to work. Should she notify them? But they would have heard, surely, and would already know.

With a deep breath she walked out, a semblance of a smile forced onto her lips. Tommy clung onto her hand. Most of the parishioners had already left and the few remaining looked hesitant, as if they weren't sure whether they should speak to her or not.

She smiled, hoping it wouldn't resemble a leer, like one of the gargoyles adorning the walls of the old church.

Chapter 8

The following day, Mrs Grant pulled back Ronnie's faded blue curtains and told him he could leave his bed.

"Aw, thank goodness for that. I've been going crazy."

"Have you finished the book I gave you?" She helped him onto the chair.

"No, I can't concentrate." He daren't admit the only thing he could think of was the pretty, petite milkmaid with the long, auburn tresses and green eyes. He had not been able to catch a glimpse of her in the farmyard, but he had imagined her going to and from the dairy. He had even heard her voice when she had come into the farmhouse for some breakfast the previous day. How tantalising it had been not to see her in the flesh. How soft and pink her flesh would be. How smooth to the touch.

His mother's voice interrupted his reverie. "Do you think you would be able to come downstairs for your breakfast?"

"Yes, Ma, most certainly." He ground his teeth.

"Must you do that? You know how I hate it. I shall leave you to put on some clothes. Give me a shout if you need any help." She went out, carrying a pile of dirty sheets.

As he tried to fasten his shirt buttons, he prayed the milkmaids would be coming in for their meal. What time had it been the previous day? He picked up his clock. Nine o'clock. Maybe they had already been. He had not heard them, though. But he had slept later, having spent most of the night tossing and turning, for the pain in his leg had kept him awake, and he had only eventually fallen asleep in the early hours.

He put his left leg in his trousers, but his right one proved painful to bend, so he took the trousers off, sat on the bed, leaned forward as far as he could, dangled them under his right foot, then manoeuvred it inside. Lathered in sweat, he finally pulled them up and fastened the buttons with shaking hands. A tie or a cravat? A tie would be too obvious as they were only worn on special occasions, so a cravat would have to do. He had no mirror in his room, so smoothed down his unruly hair and hoped his moustache looked neat, just in case she came.

The banisters on the landing provided support to the stairs, but every step jarred his back. With only one handrail—fortunately on the right side so he could use his good hand—he had nothing to hold onto on the other side, and lost his balance. His foot slipped off the first stair and he thought, for a heart-stopping moment, he was going to fall to the bottom, but he landed halfway down.

Racked with pain, he debated whether to give up. Was it worth the effort? But yes. He would make it, no matter what. With his good hand as support, he bumped down on his backside to the bottom, but then he had the problem of how to stand. Could he reach the umbrella stand at the end of the hall, and pull himself up, or should he call his mother? But he wanted to do it himself, so he twisted his body, pressed the backs of the knuckles of his left hand onto the bottom step, gripped the handrail and, victory! Next the kitchen. If he pressed himself against the wall he could take tiny steps until he reached the door. He slumped, exhausted, onto the nearest chair.

Where could his mother be? Probably in the outhouse, doing the washing. Ah, yes, he could heard her singing. She loved to sing, and had a beautiful voice, as good as any opera singer in those fancy halls. Not that he had ever been in one.

"Ma," he called, once his breathing had recovered.

She came in, her face red and sweaty. "Oh, hello, dear. Are you down already?"

Already? It had taken him a good half hour. "What do you fancy today?" She picked up the frying pan.

"Is it just me, then?"

"Oh, yes, we had ours ages ago."

Damn and blast. Too late. His appetite vanished. "Whatever's quickest," he mumbled.

She put down the frying pan. "How about a couple of boiled eggs, done just how you like them, the yoke slightly runny? And I could cut your bread into little oblongs for you to dip in, like I used to when—"

"Ma, I am not a child any more. I am a grown man."

She sighed and dropped two eggs into a pan of water. "Yes, yes, you are, and one day you'll be the man of the house." She cut some bread and buttered it, musing, "You were such a sweet child, so obedient. I've never regretted, for one single day, taking you in. You've been more of a son to me than Herbert ever was."

"And I am eternally grateful that you did. Thank you, Ma. There's no telling where I would have ended up if you hadn't."

"Probably the workhouse, or, at the very least, one of those orphanages where they're fed gruel. I shall have to look out that book of your father's called 'Oliver Twist'. That tells you all about orphans and how they were treated."

They both shuddered. That would have been the worst place imaginable.

He ate his breakfast alone, his mother having returned to the washhouse. What could he do? Not a lot, with his bad leg. Maybe he could sit outside in the sunshine and watch the goings on, and maybe…maybe a certain milkmaid might come along. But how to make his way out there without falling down, and being seen by her in a precarious predicament?

His mother began singing again. He didn't want to

disturb her, so, holding onto the backs of the chairs around the table, he hobbled to the back door as his father came around the corner of the dutch barn that housed the remains of the hay. Clinging onto the door with one hand, he waved.

The farmer ran across to him. "Hello, son, how are you doing?" He took hold of his arm, trying to steer him back into the house.

"Well, not too good, Pa, so I thought it might be pleasant to sit out here for a while, and enjoy the good weather after the horrible storm we had the other day."

"Good idea, son. Here, let me find a comfy chair for you." He released him, and Ronnie almost toppled over, but saved himself by clinging onto some ivy growing up the wall.

A chair and some brightly-coloured cushions brought out, he lowered Ronnie onto it. "I'll just find a footstool, then you'll be set up for the morning."

"Thank you, Pa."

"Can I bring you anything else?" he asked as he came back out with a stool. "A cup of tea or…"

"No, really, Pa. You're much too busy. You have my work as well as your own. Please do not concern yourself." Ronnie adjusted himself into a more comfortable position.

The farmer looked across at the washhouse. "Your mother sounds happy."

"Yes, she does. Nobody would think her elder son had…" He left the sentence hanging in the air. Saying the word made it real. Not that he was too upset. Nor his mother, or so it seemed.

"Um, well…" Farmer Grant walked across the farmyard. "I had better finish the ploughing."

Ronnie raised his face to the sun's warm rays. Not a cloud marred the blue mantle overhead, only a v-shaped flight of honking geese as they winged their way over the tops of the trees down the lane.

He closed his eyes but, moments later, a voice alerted him. Was it…? No, only her sister, Jessica.

"I heard you hurt your leg in a nasty accident, Master Ronnie."

"It's on the mend." The disappointment was palpable. "Thank you," he added as an afterthought.

She had a pretty face, but his taste did not run to tall, mousy girls with loud voices. She could not hold a candle to her sister, Charlotte. Should he ask about her? But what would he ask?

"I should be returning. Our Charlotte will be on my back if I am out too long. Good day." She skipped off around the byre.

He wondered with whom she had lain to become pregnant at such an early age, feeling sure her sister had not done so. But what did he know? Maybe Charlotte had lain with dozens of men. A pain knifed through his insides at the thought. He wanted to be her first, her first and only. Even though he didn't really know her, he knew he wanted to marry her, and spend the rest of his life making babies with her. But would his parents permit it, her being only a lowly milkmaid, and him the heir to the farm? But he would cross that bridge when he came to it. No point putting obstacles in his way before he had even spoken to her.

* * * *

Charlotte grabbed Jessica as soon as she came into the dairy. "You've been gone ages. What took so long?"

"I've been talking to Master Ronnie."

"Oh, where?" Her heart began to flutter. How come her sister had been able to speak to him?

"He's sitting outside the farmhouse." Jessica pointed back out of the barn, as if Charlotte could see around corners.

"And…what did he have to say for himself?"

"Nothing, really." She shrugged. "Nothing of any consequence, anyway."

"How does he seem?" She turned her face away, so her sister could not tell how her heart beat so furiously. *Stop being silly*, she told herself. *As if he would look twice at you.* "I am just...um..." she wiped her milky hands down her apron. "I am just going to the lavvy."

She almost ran out, but slowed down when she turned the corner. He sat there, his head back, oblivious to her. As she walked towards him, his mother came out of the washhouse. "Oh, our Ronnie, how long have you been there?"

She didn't wait to hear his reply, but scooted back the way she had come, before she could be seen. Bother! A missed opportunity. But, maybe she could try again later. She went to the lavvy, to give herself time to calm her beating senses.

On her return to the dairy she asked Jessica, in what she hoped sounded a casual voice, "Were you in love with...?" But what would a fifteen year old girl know of love?

"I beg your pardon?" Her sister bent over the vat, concentrating.

"Nothing." She could ask Martha. She had been jealous of her oldest sister when she courted Charlie. She seemed to remember they had been very much in love, then. Maybe not so much now.

"I...I...I was in love, once." Faith came across and looked into her eyes. "Th...th...that was why I was sent here."

"You, in love?" Jessica's head jerked around. "How could someone like you...?"

Her words tailed off when Charlotte glared at her, saying, "Were you, Faith? Who with?"

"A boy. He lived next door."

"And did he love you?"

"Y...y...yes. I used to sit on his knee. H...h...he

was nice." Faith wiped a tear from her cheek.

Jessica stopped stirring. "So why weren't you allowed to carry on sitting on his knee? Why did your aunt send you here?"

The girl shrugged and walked back. "I...I...I don't know. She just did."

Maybe he acted inappropriately, thought Charlotte. She did not consider the girl to be capable of marrying and raising a family, so her aunt probably deemed the safest option would be to separate them before anything happened. Faith would not realise if he overstepped the mark.

All of a sudden, Jessica squealed, her skirts caught up in her hands. "Oo, my goodness, there's a rat."

"Is that the first one you've seen?" laughed Charlotte. "There're all over the place. You become used to them."

"I don't like it. Get rid of it."

"The farm cats will catch it, sooner or later. They're very good at that."

"Well, find a cat now." As it came closer, she screamed again and ran into a corner.

Faith grabbed a broom and chased it around the dairy, finally shooing the animal out. "I...i...it's gone."

"What if it comes back?"

"You'll just have to learn to live with them, if you want to continue working here." Charlotte did not want to seem sympathetic towards her sister, or she would never grow accustomed to the vermin, although she remembered how scared she had been when she had first encountered one. She had reacted in exactly the same way.

"If you find a nest, you must report it straight away, either to me or to Farmer Grant or his wife."

"A nest, you mean like a bird's nest?"

"No, not made out of moss and twigs like birds' nests. Rats use soft bits of fluff and wood shavings. But they can breed like crazy, having hundreds of babies in a year."

Jessica put her hand on her belly, then set to work once more. "One baby will be more than enough for me—too many, in fact."

"Well, you…" She had been about to say, 'made your bed, now you must lie in it' as the saying went, but what would be the point in going over it again? Her sister had already been reproved so many times, especially by Martha and Aunt Elizabeth. She didn't need Charlotte on her back all the time as well.

"I…I…I wish I was having a baby," Faith muttered.

"You can have mine."

Charlotte spun around. "Our Jessica, how can you say such a thing?"

"Well…I don't really want it."

"Ooooo, c…c…can I?" Faith ran across and hugged Jessica.

"No, Faith, she didn't mean it. She was only jesting." Charlotte turned to her sister when the other milkmaid sloped off, crying. "Now look what you've done. You've upset her for no reason."

"Well, she *can* have it for all I care. What do I want with a baby? I want to—"

"It matters not what you want, my girl."

"You can't lecture me. You sound just like Aunt Elizabeth. I've had enough of her rantings, as well."

They both turned when Mrs Grant came in. "Do I hear raised voices?"

Faith ran up to her and wrapped her arms around her ample midriff.

"What's the matter? Have they been upsetting you?"

"Ch…Ch…Charlotte says I can't have Jessica's baby."

The farmer's wife pulled her away, her face full of astonishment. "I should think not. What on earth put that idea into your head?"

Jessica looked sheepishly at her. "I'm afraid it was me, ma'am. I said... I'm sorry." She burst into tears.

"Oh, for goodness sake!" Drawing a deep breath, Charlotte put her hand on her sister's shoulder. "Can we just forget all this nonsense and do some work?" She turned to Mrs Grant. "I'm sorry for all the palaver."

"I'll just take this one and make her a cup of tea." The farmer's wife steered her niece out of the dairy. "If you two girls could continue with your work?" She gave Jessica a cold stare as she went out.

Sniffing, Jessica wiped her face with her sleeve. "Do you think I'll be in her bad books?"

"Well, you haven't helped ingratiate yourself into her good ones. Hopefully, she'll realise it was just a single occasion, but you had better watch your tongue around Faith in future. She doesn't understand the ways of life. She's simple."

"Yes, I know. I shall apologise to her. Should I go now?"

"No, let the matter drop for the time being. Maybe later. We're too far behind for you to leave now." *And I still haven't had chance to see Master Ronnie,* she thought, but of course, didn't say aloud.

The following morning Charlotte found Jessica already in the byre when she arrived.

"Just look at this," her sister exclaimed before she had hardly walked through the door. "It couldn't be the rat, could it?" She showed her one of the milking stools. Its legs had been broken off.

"No, a rat wouldn't have caused that. How odd. I'm sure it wasn't like that yesterday when we left."

"No, it definitely was not. Should we tell Mrs Grant?"

"Tell me what?" The lady in question appeared at the door. "I've just come to tell you Faith won't be working today. She was very upset."

"I can only apologise again, ma'am." Jessica looked down at the floor. "I didn't mean any harm. I was just feeling sorry for myself, and didn't consider how she would take it."

"My niece is what they call a mongoloid. She doesn't understand that some people say things they don't mean. I shall forgive it this one time, but if she does come back, I shall expect better behaviour from you if you want to continue working here."

"Yes, ma'am. I'm sorry, ma'am."

"You don't have to call me 'ma'am'. Mistress will do. I cannot be doing with all this high-fallutin' language. Anyway, what were you talking about when I came in?" She came inside the byre and noticed the broken leg in Jessica's hand. "Oh, how has that happened?"

"I found it like this when I arrived."

"Well, we don't have time to worry about it now." She took the stool and put it in a corner. "We still have two good ones."

The farmer herded the cows inside and they began their milking.

"How's Master Ronnie?" asked Charlotte as the mistress turned to go out. She had missed him the previous day. He had already gone back into the farmhouse by the time she had found time to go out again.

"He's bearing up, bless him. Can't wait to be back at work. He says he might even help his father with something light today. I'll tell him you were asking after him."

"Oh, no, please don't go to any trouble." She didn't want him thinking…what? That she thought of him day and night, even dreamt about him?

"It's no trouble." She went out, leaving Charlotte trying not to blush.

"You look rather red, our Charlotte." It evidently had not worked. "You do fancy him."

"Who?"

"Master Ronnie. I've noticed you go all coy and silly whenever his name's mentioned."

"Don't be so silly. Of course I don't." She would have to try harder if she wanted to hide her feelings from her astute sister. That was the second time she had said something. Even though she was two years younger, she had always been more worldly, more up to date with things like the latest fashions. Not that they had ever had the money to buy such fripperies, but Jessica had hankered after them, whereas Charlotte could not care a jot what she wore, as long as it was practical and suitable for the weather.

Her sister put up her finger and tapped it against her nose. "Don't worry. I shan't tell anybody."

"That's because there's nothing to tell. Now, milk that cow before she develops udder rot."

Ignoring the knowing look in Jessica's eyes, she tried to concentrate on her own milking. Ronnie probably wouldn't be sitting outside if he intended helping on the farm, so she might not have the opportunity to see him or speak to him. Maybe it was just as well. What would be the point in pursuing her aim?

Chapter 9

Martha climbed out of bed. There seemed little point staying there any longer. She had hardly slept all night, and had been awake since the crack of dawn. After plodding downstairs, she prepared the children's breakfasts, and made their sandwiches to take to school. Tommy had not wanted to go the previous day. He had wanted to stay at home because his pa would expect to see him when he walked in, but she had eventually persuaded him to go, by telling him it would make his pa proud of him, and that he would want him to continue doing well in his lessons. He could write his name already. Amy had not learnt to write until she had been over six years old. She had lovely handwriting now, and, in fact, their teacher, Miss Ewart, declared her to be one of the cleverest girls in her class, and Tommy could do well to follow her.

A welcome mug of tea in her hands, she tried to make sense of what had happened. Her husband's body—for she was certain he must be dead after such a long fall—had not been found. They had searched all day—some with their bare hands—until it had become too dark, and continued at daybreak the following day. But nothing had turned up. Only horses could squeeze through the valley at the bottom of the cliff, so they tied implements to their harnesses to dredge through the mud and silt, but still nothing.

Tommy came down, yawning. "I forgot to tell you, Mam, Freddy says he'll take me to the seaside when they go."

"You what? The seaside? With Freddy? I didn't know you were particular friends with him."

"Oh, yes. He's mine and Jimmy's new friend. I think

he called it the seaside. What's that?"

"It's the coast, where the sea meets the land. When did he say this?"

"Yesterday. We was talking about boats in school, and he said his pa were going to take him, and I could go as well."

"We shall have to see what happens."

He looked directly at her. "You mean…with Pa?"

She nodded. She dare not tell him that if he were not found they would have to move out. She only had the few shillings she had put aside from Charlie's wages the previous Friday after she had given him his spending money, as he called it. More like his beer money. He never spent it on anything else. They would have nothing to live on once that ran out, unless she could take in work of some sort, or maybe find a job in the village. She had not had to work since Amy had been born. What could she do? That had been one of the problems that had kept her awake.

If Jessica had not been offered the milkmaid's job up at Home Farm, she could have asked there. But she shouldn't begrudge her youngest sister the chance to earn some money. Not in her condition. Maybe she could find a job in the village in one of the shops. She would make a special journey and ask around.

"Is your sister up yet?" she asked as she patted down his unruly mop of hair.

"I don't know. I didn't hear her. Um…Mam?"

"Yes, dear?"

"You know that man, the brother of the dead man?"

"Ronnie? Yes, what about him?"

"Um…no, nothing. What's for breakfast?"

She heard him go to the back door and try the latch. It didn't open.

"It's still locked," she called behind her. The clang of bolts being pulled back made her stand. He wouldn't be able to reach the top one.

"How would Pa have come in, if he'd come home in the night?" Opening the door, he stepped out into the bright sunshine.

"He…" Innocent little Tommy still would not accept the fact his father had gone. Should she disillusion him? But maybe he was right. She shouldn't give up hope. "I would have heard him knock, darling." Her arm around his shoulder, she took in deep gulps of the warm spring air. If Charlie happened to be alive, at least the weather would be favourable for him. But if so, where on earth could he be? He would have come straight home. He had to be dead. She needed to find a job.

"There's Jimmy." Tommy waved to his friend, standing at his own back door. "Can I go and play with him?"

"Tommy, lad, you aren't even dressed and you need to start sorting yourself out for school."

"Oh, do I have to go today?"

"Well, Jimmy will be going, and Freddy. You'll be able to play at break time."

He trudged back into the house, his mouth turned down, his hair still stuck up. She just wanted to cuddle him so she bent down level with him, enfolded his little body in her arms, and kissed his head, breathing in the little boy smell of…

"Phwah! Have you trumped?" She pulled back.

He laughed. "Didn't you hear it?" He wafted the air behind him. "It's a good 'un. Lovely and whiffy."

"I think you had better scoot off to the lavvy, young man, while I go and wake your sister."

He went outside, still chuckling. At least it had taken his mind off school.

She went to the foot of the stairs and called her daughter, listened until she received a faint reply, and returned to the kitchen to put a pan of water on for their porridge. She usually made it with milk, but hoped they wouldn't notice. Then she sliced some bread. Bread…she could make some of that to sell, cheaper than the bakery in the village. But she wouldn't have the money to buy the flour and yeast, not to make enough. She spread some jam onto the slices, not bothering with butter. They had almost run out, and butter was a luxury they would have to manage without. After she'd parcelled them up in paper, ready for the children to take to school, she stirred the porridge.

Tommy came back in at the same time as Amy, who had already dressed. She sat down at the table and asked "Any news on Pa?"

"No, dear, I'm afraid to say."

"Has anyone heard about that man we found down the gully, that…Herbert Grant person?"

"No, I think we should hear today." She didn't want to think about him, let alone talk about him. She placed a bowl of porridge in front of them. "Eat your breakfast."

Tommy sat down opposite his sister and put a spoonful in his mouth. "It's hot."

"Well, it has just come out of the pan, so what do you expect?"

Amy blew on hers to cool it and tasted it. "Ugh, what have you done to it? It isn't like the usual stuff. It's horrid."

"Here, put some sugar on top. It'll be fine." Martha spooned the soft, brown sugar over it, and poured a little milk on as well.

"It tastes all right to me," said Tommy. "But I'll have some more sugar."

Before she could stop him, he had taken a heaped spoonful and spread it on his porridge. Goodness knows how long the sugar would have to last. She grabbed the bowl and put it behind her on the sideboard.

Amy screwed up her nose. "It still doesn't taste right."

"Well, I'm sorry, but it'll have to do. I don't, we don't…" She couldn't tell them why. She couldn't saddle them with her monetary problems. "Please, just eat it."

"I'll have your'n if you don't want it." Tommy was not so fussy. He reached over to grab her plate but she pulled it back.

"No, you won't. I'll finish it." Screwing up her face, she ate the rest as Tommy watched every spoonful in case she changed her mind.

Martha hauled him out of his chair. He couldn't really still be hungry. "Up you go and pull on some clothes, young man, and then you can call for Jimmy on your way."

He came down ten minutes later, his shirt buttons in the wrong buttonholes and his brown trousers not buttoned at all.

"Tommy Holloway, you can't go to school looking like that. Come here."

"I couldn't find two socks the same, so I put different ones on." He pulled up his trouser leg to show her. On one leg he wore a brown sock and, on the other, a black one. With a smile she shook her head and hugged him before running upstairs to find either another brown or black one. Neither found, she grabbed a blue pair from the bottom of his tallboy and hurried down, to see the back of his brown jacket and cap disappearing out the door.

"Goodbye, Mam." He waved.

"But your…socks…" She looked at the ones in her hands and shrugged. Never mind. Who would notice? It wasn't as if the weather permitted short trousers. It would soon be warm enough for them, though. She hoped they still fitted him. He had grown upwards during the winter but not outwards and, although quite small for a six year old, he still might not be able to fasten them.

"I hope he put his boots on properly. Did you notice, Amy?" she asked her daughter as she stood from buttoning her own boots.

"Yes, Mam. I helped him."

"Oh, thank you. You're a good girl."

Amy walked towards the door.

"Don't forget your snap." Martha picked up her parcel and held it out, praying the butterless sandwiches would not be too unacceptable.

"Oh, yes, thank you."

"I see our Tommy took his."

"He isn't likely to forget food." Amy reached up and gave Martha a kiss. "Bye, Mam." She stopped. "Do you think they'll find our pa?"

With an attempt at seeming hopeful, she replied, "I don't know, child. I really don't know. Pray that they do, eh?"

"We all said a special prayer for him yesterday in school. Surely that'll help?"

She gently urged her daughter out the door. "I'm sure it will." She wished she meant what she said, that she had a glimmer of hope in him walking through that door as bold as brass, demanding his dinner, but she knew little chance of that existed. "Goodbye."

With every last oat scraped from the saucepan, she licked the spoon clean, ate the dry crust that remained from the loaf, and washed it down with her cold, milkless tea, trying to decide on a course of action for the day. The village seemed the most sensible place to start. She would need her best frock if she wanted to give a good impression.

With a determination she didn't really feel, she put the dirty pots in the sink to wash later, and went upstairs before she had a change of mind or heart.

Half an hour later she took a deep breath and stepped outside, pulled on her best pink bonnet and wrapped her grey shawl around her shoulders. The sun felt warm on her face. Should she take her parasol? She decided not to, it would only hinder her, and she didn't want anything to prevent her achieving her purpose. A clear mind and clear hands were what she needed. But perhaps her reticule would be sensible. Not that she dare take any money. The rent man would be calling the following day. If she could not pay him, they would be out on their ears. No point taking a reticule, then.

Her head high, she strode down the street, trying to hum, but sounded more like a banshee's wail, so she gave up.

Lily Grant came towards her, carrying her milkmaid's yoke, accompanied by her niece. "Good day to you, Martha. Where are you going, all dressed up like a dog's dinner?"

"Actually, I'm going to the village to…" Should she admit her purpose? Would the farmer's wife think her premature in assuming her husband might be dead?

Lily carefully put down the yoke, so as not to spill the milk, and looked at her with sympathy. Her head to one side, she put her hand on Martha's arm. "Is there any news of your husband?"

Her former effort at being brave dissipated as she shook her head and her shoulders crumpled.

"What will you do?"

Tears threatened as she took a deep breath and forced her voice to speak calmly. "That's why I'm going to the village. To see if anyone will take me on. I don't have any experience but someone might be desperate."

"If I hadn't taken on your sister, you could have come to work for me."

Faith tugged at Martha's sleeve. "I…I…I work on the farm."

Lily appeared to have an idea. Her face lit up. "Actually, Faith is not very…how shall I put it? She's having a day or so off, so if you wanted, you could take her place until the end of the week."

"It's very good of you, Mrs Grant, but I need something more permanent. If Charlie…" Her voice broke and she could not continue.

Lily understood. She waited until Martha had control

again and repeated her offer. "So, if you cannot find a position in the village, don't hesitate to come to us. I'm sure we could find something, especially with Ronnie being out of action."

Martha brightened up. "That's a thought, but, no. I haven't ridden a horse for years, or…"

"There must be other jobs Ed could find you. We wouldn't be able to pay you very much, but as long as it's enough to cover your rent and food."

"I worked on my uncle's farm when I was a child, doing odd jobs, looking after the animals, that sort of thing. I loved it. Oo, Lily, do you really mean it? Do you think Farmer Grant would agree?" She looked down at her pretty blue frock. "I wouldn't need to wear this. I would look rather overdressed."

Faith giggled and covered her mouth with her hand.

Lily picked up the yoke. "Wait until I've finished my rounds. I shall come for you and we'll face him together. I cannot let you…" She stopped as milk slurped out of one of the pails. "You must need milk, so go and fetch a jug. I won't charge you."

Martha wanted to kiss the middle-aged woman. She ran back to her house and picked up a small jug from the table, then put it down again and exchanged it for the largest one she could find. If the farmer's wife was willing to make her a gift, she might as well go the whole hog. Not for herself but for the benefit of her children.

With a spring in her step, she hurried back to find them.

As she walked to the farm with Lily Grant two hours later, having changed into her oldest frock and apron in case they asked her to start work straight away, she asked about Herbert. She had felt guilty at not doing so earlier. Too wrapped up in herself, she had not given a thought to the anxiety the farmer's wife must have been going through.

"The policeman said we should have the results of

the autopsy soon. It might be today."

"If he was murdered, I wonder who could have done it." Martha hoped her tone did not betray her inner emotion. She had her own ideas about the matter but would not voice them aloud.

"There's plenty who would have wished him dead, I'm afraid to say. But it's one thing to wish it, and another actually doing it."

"Yes, you're right. It's a rum do."

"I...i...is your husband dead as well?" Faith asked.

"We don't know, dear," Lily intervened. "Mistress Holloway does not wish to discuss it."

Faith hung her head for a moment, and then looked up with a grin. "We...we...we have a baby lamb in the barn. It's called Faithful, after me."

"Ah, lovely. You'll have to show it to me when we arrive."

"I...I...I like baby lambs."

"Yes, they're cute."

"I...I...I know a song about lambs." Faith began to sing. "'Mary had a little lamb, it's...' Oh, I...I...I can't remember any more. What's the next line, Auntie Lily?"

Lily looked across at Martha as if to gauge if she would mind if she continued the song, and received a smile, so finished it.

Martha joined in. She had loved singing nursery rhymes to the children when they were little.

"A...a...and we have some chicks," continued Faith when they stopped. "They're all soft and yellow. I like yellow. I...i...it's my favourite colour."

"Mine too, although I don't have many yellow dresses. In fact I don't have any at all, come to think of it." Martha smiled at the girl who grinned back. She found her childish manner endearing. She had heard of mongoloids but had never known one, always imagining them to have two heads or something equally abnormal, but this girl did not seem any stranger than Wilson. In fact, she resembled him quite a lot. Maybe he shared the same affliction. Nobody had ever questioned it before. He had always just been known as the village idiot.

Once they arrived at the farm her courage deserted her and her stomach turned somersaults. What if the farmer didn't want her? And, even if he did, what if her sisters resented her being there? She brushed her sweaty hands down her sides and straightened her back as Lily told Faith to take her into the farmhouse while she took the now-empty pails back to the dairy.

Drumming her fingers on the table while she waited for Mrs Grant's return, she felt as nervous as a bride on her wedding day. What an ironic similarity! She had come because she was, more than likely, no longer a wife, more than likely a widow, without having the funeral, or even the body of her husband to mourn. Hopefully they would eventually find him so she could do so.

"W…w…would you like a cup of tea?" Faith picked up the kettle and placed it on the range without waiting for a reply. Martha wondered if the girl would be capable of such a task and was about to refuse, but one would be so welcome. She ran her tongue round her dry lips, and took some short breaths.

The tea—made just as she liked it, weak and milky— had already been placed on the table by the time the farmer's wife returned. "I've been looking for Ed but he must be out in the fields."

Martha began to stand up. "Shall I come back later, then?"

"No, no, finish your drink." She flopped onto a chair and turned to her niece. "Is there one for me, dear? I'm fair parched."

"S…s…sorry, Auntie." The girl took a large mug from the side of the sink and poured her some. It looked much stronger and Martha wondered if it would be unacceptable, but Lily put it to her lips and drank it without taking a breath.

"I was ready for that," she exclaimed as she took off her bonnet, shook out her long grey hair, scratched her head and stood up. "That's annoying me today. I don't know why. I'll just go upstairs and give my hair a good brushing. Please excuse me."

Now what do I do? wondered Martha. *I can't just sit here all morning.* Would her friend be offended if she washed the pots she could see on the side of the sink? She picked up her cup and approached the sink. Faith jumped up also and grabbed the cup from her as if she realised her intention.

"I thought I'd wash up," Martha explained slowly, miming the actions, in case the girl did not understand. Although, she had understood everything she had said before, so why should she not do so then?

"N…n…no, that's my job."

"Oh, fair enough. I don't want to tread on your toes."

Faith looked down at her feet. "M…m…my toes?"

Martha flapped her hands. "I didn't mean…literally." How could she explain what she meant? Perhaps she should leave. "I think I shall go and see my sisters. Will they be in the dairy?"

"Y…y…your sisters? Who are they?"

"Charlotte and Jessica."

"J…J…Jessica's your sister?"

"Yes."

Exasperation welled up inside her as Faith pulled a face, and she decided it would be easier to find out the wherabouts of her sisters for herself. About to go out, she heard Lily's steps on the stairs, so waited for her.

"That's better." Lily had put on a different hat. Her round face looked haggard as she tied the ribbons. "Shall we go and see what your sisters are up to?"

Faith pulled her aunt's sleeve. "I…I…I didn't know they were Mrs Holloway's sisters, Auntie. Y…y…you didn't tell me that."

"Didn't I, dear? That was remiss of me. Do you want to come, or would you rather stay here?"

"Wh…wh…where's Ronnie?"

"I'm not sure, but he can't be far. He can barely walk."

"I…I…I thought he might play cards with me."

"Well, if I see him, I shall tell him. Perhaps you could sweep the floor while we're gone?" Lily opened the pantry door, took out a besom and handed it to Faith. She stared at it for a moment, before accepting it with a smile.

As they walked across the farmyard, picking their way through the geese that wanted to surround them, Lily took off her shawl and folded it. "It's too hot for this. I should have left it behind. But Faith would probably only have hidden it somewhere. She calls it 'tidying up', but I can never find anything in its right place after she's done so. She's a simple girl, but very likeable."

"Yes, she is. I was only thinking that earlier." Martha ran her hand across her wet brow. Should she take off her shawl also, but where would she put it? Easier to keep it on, even if made her sweat.

They found Charlotte and Jessica arguing in the dairy.

"Now then, girls, I have someone to see you," said Lily.

"Our Martha, what are you doing here?" asked Jessica as she glanced at Charlotte as if to see if she knew.

"She's going to help out whilst Ronnie's unable to work, and to give Faith a break."

The girls pulled a face at each other.

"There's no need to look like that," continued their employer. "She'll be working more on the farm, and merely assisting you as and when required."

"I shan't tread on your toes, so don't worry about that." *They* would know what she meant.

Lily clapped her hands. "Back to work, then. I hope

you weren't arguing over anything serious."

Both girls looked down, shamefaced. "No, Mistress," replied Charlotte. "It was just—"

"I don't want to hear what it was about. I just want a good job done. I cannot afford to have my staff bickering when they should be working. Is that understood?"

"Yes, Mistress," they both sang as they returned to their respective tasks.

Lily turned to Martha who had kept silent, not wishing to interfere between her sisters and their boss's wife. "We'll have another search for Ed, and see what he'd like you to start on."

With a glare at her sisters over her shoulder, Martha protested to Lily, "But I didn't think you'd asked him if I could stay."

"Oh, don't worry about that. I shall tell him in such a way he'll think it was his idea all along. That's the best way to deal with men, don't you find?"

"Well…" She had never been able to do such a thing. If Charlie had a notion on anything it would be gospel. If she ever tried to come up with an idea, he might consider it for a fleeting second but, unless he really entertained it, it would be a no-no, so she usually didn't bother making suggestions. Occasionally, he would moan that he had to make all the decisions, but what would be the point in her trying to propose anything? He would only do the opposite.

They found the farmer in the top field, checking on the ewes to see if any were about to give birth. He lifted his cap and swept his hair over his brow. "Good day, ma'am."

"Good day, Mr Grant."

He turned to his wife. "To what do I owe this pleasure?"

"Isn't Ronnie with you?"

He looked under the ewe he had been holding and pulled up the sheepdog's tail. "Well, I can't see him. Can you, Mrs Holloway?"

She laughed. "Oh, call me Martha, please."

Lily glanced around, a worried look on her face. "I don't know where he is, if he isn't with you."

"He won't be far, me duck. Don't fret. He's a grown man." He put his cap on, and they started walking down the field. "Anyway, you haven't answered my question."

"Oh. Well, you were only saying you needed help and they haven't found Charlie yet so, here's your solution—Martha Holloway."

His eyebrows lifted.

He doesn't like the proposal, Martha thought as she held her breath. *And how can I blame him? What a stupid idea, to think a mere woman could do heavy farm work.*

"Oh, right you are." He took his cap off once again, scratched his head and looked her up and down. "Can you lift a bale of hay or—?"

"I'm very strong, Mr Grant," she quickly cut in. "I used to work on a farm in my youth. I'm hard-working and diligent."

She tried to think what other attributes she could attest to, but no more were needed, for he rubbed his chin and pronounced, "Well, then, welcome to Home Farm." He put out his hand, then wiped it down his trouser leg, before offering it again.

She shook it and gushed, "Oh, thank you, sir. You won't regret it, I promise."

"We may as well make it a family affair, have all the Bridge girls working here. You don't have any other sisters hidden away, do you?"

"No," she laughed. "Only the three of us."

"What about brothers? Perhaps some male help would...?"

"No, no brothers, I'm afraid. My father would have loved a hoard of boys, but they didn't happen."

"Sons don't always measure up to what their parents would have wished." The farmer looked wistful as he stared over the rugged hills into the distance.

His wife took his arm and nestled her face in the rough cloth of his sleeve, silently sympathising with him.

Chapter 10

As Martha and Lily reached the farmyard, having left the farmer back in the fields, the policeman cycled in.

He pulled up and raised his hat. "Good day to you, Mistress Grant and Mistress Holloway."

Lily rushed over to him. "Do you have news on our Herbert?"

"Yes, ma'am." He glanced pointedly at Martha. "Shall we go somewhere more private and... Is your husband at home?"

Lily looked at Martha, then replied, "He's in the fields. Do you want me to fetch him? But you can say what you have to in front of Mrs Holloway. I don't mind."

Martha patted her arm. "Mrs Grant, it's fine. Why don't you take the nice constable inside while I run back for Ed?"

"Well, if you're sure."

"Of course, it's no trouble." She hitched up her skirts and hurried back the way they had come, all sorts of thoughts racing through her mind. He must have been murdered. The constable would not have been so secretive had it been a case of accidental death, or whatever they called it.

She soon found the farmer, and regaled him with the news. He rushed ahead of her, for she was puffed out, and had to take a breather. As she made her way down more slowly, she deliberately dragged her feet, not wanting to hear the result, and went directly to the dairy, where her sisters were making butter in large conical casks made of staves bound with wooden hoops.

"Hello, our Martha." Jessica rubbed the small of her back.

She replied in a soft voice, "The policeman's here."

Jessica looked at Charlotte and back to Martha. "Oh, does that mean…?"

"I don't know. He wanted to speak to Farmer Grant and his wife in private, so I assume so."

Charlotte did not look up or speak. Maybe the result would not affect her. But everyone else wanted to know. The whole village had been humming with people expressing their opinions of who could have killed him, if that was what had been decided, of course.

"Don't you want to know, Charlotte?"

She shrugged and continued with her task.

Jessica was not so reticent. "He deserved it, whatever happened."

A sudden thought came into Martha's head. "He isn't the…?" She pointed to her sister's large belly. "Is he?"

Her sister looked shifty. "What, the father? Of course not." She pretended to stack some pieces of cheese that looked neat enough already. "What gives you that idea? I wouldn't want that reprobate for the father of my child. No thank you, not in a million years."

Martha thought her sister protested too much, but didn't want to cause an argument, so kept her thoughts to herself.

"Good riddance." Charlotte had found her tongue. She stood, hands on hips, a look of defiance on her pretty face. "Good riddance to bad rubbish, I say. He was a rat, a mean, stinking—"

"Our Charlotte, don't let anybody hear you speak of him like that." Martha looked around furtively, in case anyone might be lurking in the shadows. "You could find yourself in trouble, especially if they have decided he was murdered."

"I don't care. I would gladly hang."

Jessica and Martha both gasped. "What on earth did the man do to you to bring on such an outburst?"

Charlotte merely pulled a face and shuddered.

"I know I didn't like him," started Martha. "He…" Should she admit anything? But no, Charlie could become implicated. Best to keep quiet, even to her sisters who she knew would never speak up against her, but you never knew with those lawyers and legal people. She had heard they could twist your words around to make them sound the exact opposite to what you had meant to say. "I mean," she continued, "not many folks did, did they?"

Jessica signalled to her and she turned to see the farmer's wife standing in the doorway behind her. By the look on her face, she had heard. Should she apologise? With a grimace she took hold of her friend's arm. "I'm sorry, I…"

Lily's face crumpled. "It's only what everyone thinks, I know, but he was my son, for all his faults."

Wretched, Martha looked to see if the constable or the farmer had followed, but Lily had come alone.

Lily wiped her nose on a har.dkerchief and then asked, "Has anyone seen Ronnie in the last hour?"

The sisters all looked at each other and shook their heads.

Martha thought Charlotte's face had become red but, as she had turned away from her, she couldn't be sure. She hoped the girl had not developed a fancy for the farmer's son. Nothing could come of it. She did not want her sister to experience heartache over something she could not have.

"No, I'm sorry. Has the policeman told you anything?" she asked, her eyebrows raised in question.

Lily cried into her handkerchief. Had that been a nod? Martha waited for the answer, but the farmer's wife did not elaborate. How frustrating, not knowing. But should she prod the wretched woman? She put her arm around her and held her until her sobs subsided and she blew her nose.

"I don't know why I am crying. It's just that, when

it's spoken out loud it becomes a reality." Lily dabbed her eyes with the corner of her apron. "And, like I said, he was my son, after all is said and done. He may not have been the best son in the world, but I still loved him, deep in my heart."

"Yes, of course." *But tell me what the constable said,* Martha wanted to scream. She couldn't bear the suspense.

"So he was murdered, then?" Jessica spoke with the innocence of youth. No refinement, no subtlety with her.

Lily nodded. "That's why he wants to speak to Ronnie—the policeman, I mean."

"He's still here?"

"Yes, and he'll want to speak to all of you."

The sisters stared at each other in fear. "What, today?" asked Charlotte. "But why us?"

"He'll have to speak to everyone in the village, unless someone owns up."

"Yes, now it's out in the open, somebody might do that, hopefully, to save the poor constable having to interview everybody," Martha said, thinking, *At least he'll be spared having to talk to one possible suspect.*

The farmer's wife turned to go. "I need to find Ronnie."

But I haven't been given anything to do, yet, thought Martha. She wouldn't earn any money idling the day away, gossiping about Herbert.

She followed Lily out. "Would you like me to go and find him, or are there any tasks or jobs I can do instead?"

"Oh, my goodness, of course. Let me think." Lily tapped her fingertips on her chin, her hands still visibly shaking. "You could sweep out the yard. That would be a start."

Martha glanced around the mucky yard, with its piles of cow manure and goose droppings. What a lovely start!

"There should be a large broom in the barn. And then, the pigs will need feeding and the barn, where any sickly lambs are to be brought in, could do with cleaning out."

"I shall start straight away." The tasks she had been given did not appeal to her but she straightened her back. If it had to be, then she would try her utmost to do it with perfection, even if it meant soiling her hands, and most probably her clothes, in the process.

Three hours later, covered in slime and sludge, she wandered back to the dairy. It would not be advisable to enter in such a state, so she stopped at the door. "Where's Charlotte?" she asked Jessica.

Her sister swivelled round and burst into laughter. "Oh, our Martha, what a sight!"

She looked down at her clothes. "It isn't that comical!"

"Oh, but it is. The clean and tidy Martha looking like a…what can I call you? Oh, it's so hilarious." She burst into more peels of hilarity, bent over double clutching her sides.

Her laughter proved infectious and Martha soon saw the funny side of the situation. Her own mouth turned up at the sides and, before long, she chuckled as much as her sister.

"What on earth…?" Charlotte came in. "Oh, my goodness! What have you been doing? You look as if you've been living with the pigs for a week."

"Well, I was trying to feed them when I slipped. Ugh, that pigsty is grotesque. One of them even stood on my hand, when I slipped and slid as I tried to stand up." She reached out to show her the hoof print.

Charlotte jumped back. "Oo, don't touch me. I've never seen such a state. Don't you think you'd better clean yourself up? There's a horse trough over there." She pointed over to the other side of the farmyard.

"Thank you for your concern, sister dear. That's about what I have sunk to, washing in a horse trough."

"Well, you can't go home like that, and Mrs Grant wouldn't want you in her kitchen, so what else is there?"

"Oh, our Charlotte," began Jessica, now recovered from her fit of hysterics, "she can't wash in there. That water's probably as dirty as she is."

"I shall have to go down to the river. It would be preferable to using that thing. If Mrs Grant comes looking for me, please tell her where I am." After a few steps she turned back. "Oh, by the way, have you had to speak to the constable yet?"

"Yes, that's where I've been," answered Charlotte. "He said he wanted to have a word with you next, but…" A grin covered her face from cheek to cheek as she glanced once more at Martha's filthy clothes, as if she couldn't believe her eyes.

In a bid to ignore the jibes, she asked her younger sister, "Have you been, Jessica?"

"Yes, but I couldn't tell him much."

"What did you say to him, Charlotte?"

"Don't you think you'd better hurry down to that river before anyone else sees you like that?"

"Yes, I'm off." She hurried away. It didn't take her long to reach the stream where it opened out into a large pool. After a quick look around to make sure she wasn't being watched, she stripped off her apron and frock, and then decided to go the whole hog, so took off her stained underwear and jumped in, as naked as the day she'd been born. Oh, what bliss! Delightful cool water on her heated skin.

After rinsing the dirt and mire from her hair, she lay back and luxuriated in the pure water. Then, anxious that the policeman might come looking for her, she climbed out, rubbed the dirt as best she could without any soap from her frock and petticoat, and dabbed the stains on the frilly white breeches in the shallows.

As she lifted a leg to put them on, a hand snaked around her waist. She screamed, but her scream was cut off by another hand being clamped over her mouth. A familiar voice hissed in her ear, "Be silent, my lovely one."

It can't be, she thought. *He's lying dead at the bottom of the cliff.*

He released his hold and turned her to face him. Twin emotions raced through her—relief that she wouldn't have to work on the filthy farm but, on the other hand, a sinking feeling that life would not become any easier.

"Where…?" she began to ask, but he stopped her words with his mouth, and his hand smoothed over her silky skin. Feelings of desire she had not experienced for a long time spread through her from her toes to the top of her head. He laid her down gently on a patch of grass and nuzzled her neck, before latching onto her breast, his hands caressing her body in circular movements. She gripped his hair, her whole body on fire with passion. She didn't need any persuading as he brought her to the brink of ecstasy within minutes. Ignoring her moan of protest, he pulled away, ripped off his shirt and trousers and resumed. Her fingernails raked down his back as she sucked his nipple, knowing how much he loved it. Rhythmically, they moved as one until, with a yell of triumph, they reached their goal together.

Satiated, she lay in his arms, but then remembered the policeman. "I must go back," she told Charlie, explaining why. She tried to stand, but he pulled her down.

"I don't want anybody knowing I'm still alive. You mustn't tell anyone."

"But why? I can't let everybody think you're still dead. I have to tell."

"If this policeman is sniffing around, it's better if I stay low for a while."

"But where will you stay? Where have you been living? And why haven't you let me know sooner?" Overwhelmed by the emotion of the moment, she burst into tears.

He cradled her in his arms. "I have my reasons. One day you'll understand."

She began to shiver. "Let me dress and return to the farm. I can't take all this in." She quickly flung on her damp clothes. "But how am I going to pretend you're dead? You know I'm no good at lying. It's second nature to you, but not to me. And, anyway, why are you doing this at all?"

He kissed her, long and passionately. "Remember, I love you."

She made no reply. How could he love her, if he could subject her to such misery?

He sidled behind the trees and disappeared. With her bonnet in hand, she made her way slowly towards the farm. How would she be able to act as if nothing had happened? As she had told Charlie, she could not tamper with the truth. It wasn't in her nature. And she would have to continue on the farm, filthy and tired, and for what? For how long? He hadn't even said when he would be in touch again. Did it mean he had murdered Herbert? She hadn't thought to ask him that. But would he have told her? Probably not. Better if she didn't know. She would probably only blurt it out if the constable asked too many probing questions. It would be difficult enough supressing the knowledge that he was alive, but, at least nobody would ask her that. They all assumed he had died, unfound.

* * * *

"What did the constable ask you, Jessica?" Charlotte patted the butter she had just made, still smirking at the state of her older sister's filthy frock. Neat and tidy Martha, with her house always so spick and span. How good to see her in a state of disarray for a change. Not so perfect, after all.

Her sister stopped working and gave her a quizzical

look. "Oh, he didn't ask much. What about you?"

"The same. What did you tell him?"

"Well, I had nothing to tell."

Charlotte piled the butter up in the corner, wishing she had not started the conversation. She shrugged. "No, me neither." Nothing she could admit to.

"I wonder where Master Ronnie is."

Her ears pricked up when Jessica mentioned that certain man's name, but she averted her face. "Um, yes, I wonder."

"I'm sure you do. It's a good job you haven't been outside for a while, or I might have thought you had an assignation with him."

"Don't be ridiculous."

"Maybe that's where our Martha's gone. Perhaps she fancies him an' all."

Charlotte's head shot up. That hadn't occurred to her. "Don't be silly. She's a married woman."

"So, that doesn't stop some people. Anyway, she's probably a widow now, and looking for a new husband."

"Don't talk nonsense. In any case, Master Ronnie wouldn't have wanted her in that state. She was absolutely ditched. Even that randy husband of hers, if he isn't dead, wouldn't have."

Jessica walked over to her. "What makes you call him randy? He hasn't tried anything on with you, has he?"

"Um, that's not what I meant, of course not. Why? Has he with you?"

"Me? I'm only fifteen, I mean…sixteen."

"What does that have to do with anything? Somebody clearly has."

Jessica took off her loose bonnet, swept her hair over her shoulder and stalked off to the back of the dairy.

"If you won't tell me who the father is, then you must expect speculation, our Jessica," Charlotte called after her. "You are your own worst enemy, keeping silent about it."

"Just cease, will you. I am not divulging the information to anybody, not even you. So shut up."

"Please yourself." Charlotte rolled a large, conical churn over to the other side of the dairy and straightened as she wiped the sweat from her brow. "I'm going out to the lavvy. Make sure the cheese is finished by the time I return."

Jessica didn't reply. From the set of her stubborn mouth, she was still sulking.

Let her, it's no odds to me, Charlotte thought as she walked across the farmyard, her eye cocked in case a certain person might be hovering nearby. But no such luck. Where could he be? It couldn't be true what Jessica had inferred, could it? He wouldn't have gone after Martha? He had disappeared a long time before her sister had come in, looking like one of the urchins she had seen in the gypsy camp. Poor Martha. How humiliating for her.

The constable came around the corner as she opened the door to enter the primitive privy. She couldn't go inside while he might see her. Pretending to examine something on the wall, even though bursting for a pee, she waited until he had gone by.

He stopped, however. "I shall have to return later to see your sister."

She turned. "I beg your pardon?"

"Pray, forgive my bad manners, miss. I was miles away." He took off his helmet and bowed slightly. "Good day. Please excuse me, I do not have time to wait any longer for your older sister."

"Good day, Constable. I shall inform her when she returns." As he climbed onto his bicycle, she added, "Do you have any suspects yet?"

He shook his head. "No, miss. Well, we have no substantial evidence as yet. But do not fret, we will solve the matter. Good day."

She waited until he had cycled out of sight and raced

into the lavvy. She couldn't have held out much longer. Thank goodness he hadn't kept her talking too long. As she adjusted her frock on her way out, she saw Martha hurrying up the lane leading from the river. She looked flustered. With a wave she called, "You've just missed the constable."

"Oh, good." She stopped, panting.

"Good? Why don't you want to speak to him?"

"Oh, I didn't mean that."

"You look slightly cleaner than when you went. That was so funny, our Martha. I have never seen you in such a state."

"I'm glad to be a source of mirth." She looked around. "I'd better find Lily and see what other delightful duties she wants me to perform. Do you know where she is?"

Charlotte shook her head. "No, probably in the farmhouse, unless she's still out looking for Master Ronnie."

"Oh, hasn't he been found yet?"

"Not as far as we know. You didn't see him, then?"

Martha gave a start. "Who?"

"Master Ronnie? You didn't see him?"

"No. I wouldn't have asked, would I, if I had?"

Charlotte thought her sister seemed shifty. Had she been telling the truth? She didn't seem herself. But maybe the extra work and, of course, the worry of her Charlie being missing had overcome her. She held out her hand. "Are you well, our Martha? You don't seem to be."

"Me? I'm as fit as a fiddle. Couldn't be better. I'll just go and find someone." She hastened away, leaving Charlotte pondering.

Chapter 11

The following morning Martha sat up as soon as she awoke. Her clock told her she would be late. Her body told her to go back to sleep. She had scarcely slept a wink all night. Noises and sounds had creaked through the cottage, making her start more than once. Had it been Charlie? At one point she had thrown back the covers, intent on going downstairs to find out, but had thought better of it. If it had been a burglar out to steal the family silver—not that she had any to steal—she had not fancied a confrontation in her nightgown, so had lain down and covered her head with the blanket in a bid to blot out the sounds.

"I suppose I had better go and see if anyone has been," she murmured to her old rag doll that sat on her tallboy, a keepsake from her childhood that she could not bear to throw away, even though it had one hand missing, the stuffing stuck out, and no hair.

As she jumped out of bed, her muscles protested from the hard work the day before, but she popped her feet into her slippers, and grabbed her dressing gown from the back of the door. The sun felt warm through the window already. It promised to be another hot day.

Just what I need with all that tough work ahead of me.

A quick look around the kitchen showed the loaf of bread she had baked the evening before standing on its end on the sideboard, only half its size. Had she even left it there? She couldn't remember. Exhausted, she had crawled up to bed as soon as the children had been settled in their beds, not caring to put things away as she usually did. She couldn't even recall locking the back door. She tried it. It opened straightaway. Clearly not.

The pantry next. As she opened the meat safe she

caught her finger on a sharp piece of the wire door, cursing as it began to bleed. The remains of a cooked ham hock she had intended to have for dinner that night had gone missing.

Sucking her finger, she scanned the shelves at the few remaining jars of preserves and pickles. During the winter they had gradually been used up, and she had hoped they would last until the new crop could be grown in the summer. She couldn't be sure, but felt some of them had gone missing. A few other items also, including the last piece of the seed cake she had baked the day Charlie had gone. A smile crept over her lips. One of his favourites, seed cake.

"Oh, well, at least he won't starve," she muttered.

"Who won't starve, Mam?" Tommy came up behind her.

"Um, sorry, son?" She couldn't let him know. But she felt so cruel, keeping it from him. He would have been ecstatic.

"You said, 'He won't starve'."

She ruffled his hair. "Did I, son? I must be going mad in my old age."

He laughed. "I thought you were always telling me you weren't old. You're only twenty-four."

"You cheeky monkey. I'm twenty-two. But, at the moment, I feel forty-two."

He sat down at the table. "Shall I have the day off school, so I can come and help you on the farm?"

She took down some plates and gave him a hug. "No, my darling, you need your lessons. They're important."

"But it ain't fair you should have to do all the work." He looked up at her with such a mournful expression, her resolve almost melted when he added, "Why isn't Pa here? Why can't they find him?"

"Don't give up hope. One of these days he might come walking through that door." She had to take a deep breath and hide her face. But at least she had not lied.

Charlotte came downstairs, dressed for work. "Good day, Martha. Are you coming to the farm today?" Her sister grabbed the slice of bread she had just cut. "Slap a bit of butter on that for me. I'm starving."

"What about your manners?" Tommy glared at her and grabbed at the bread.

"What?" His auntie gave him a disbelieving look.

"You didn't say 'please'. Just because my pa ain't here don't mean you should forget."

"Oo, how dare you, our Tommy? You're the one who usually leaves his manners behind when he leaves his bed," Charlotte retorted.

Martha took the crushed bread, put it on a plate and spread a meagre amount of butter on it. "Please don't squabble. My head is already splitting. And yes, if I need to earn some money, I shall have to return to the farm. Are you going now?"

"Yes." She stuffed the bread into her mouth, pulled a face at Tommy, and opened the back door. "See you later."

Tommy muttered under his breath, "Not if I see you first," causing Martha to grin. How like his father he looked, from his little upturned nose to the small cleft in his chin. Although his blue eyes did not mirror Charlie's brown ones, they were large and fanned by long, dark eyelashes.

"You shouldn't speak to your auntie like that, you know. It's naughty. Your pa wouldn't let you wriggle out of it if he were here."

"But he ain't. That's just it. He ain't here."

She longed to tell him, but even though she had not actually promised not to say a word to anyone, she dare not betray Charlie. To distract herself, she went to the door leading to the stairs. "I had better wake your sister, or she'll be late." She called up the stairs, "Amy, are you awake?"

No reply, so she wiped her hands down the apron she had put on over her dressing gown and started up the stairs. Her daughter appeared when she had reached half way. "Oh, you are up. Why didn't you answer me, save me having to climb Mount Everest when I'm so stiff?"

"Sorry, Mam, but I have a headache. Could I stay at home today?"

"Let me see." She continued up and felt her daughter's forehead. "It doesn't seem hot to me. Open your mouth." Amy stuck out her tongue. "You're fine. Go and dress for school."

"But, Mam…"

"I know why she doesn't want to go," Tommy called from the foot of the stairs.

"No, you don't. Mind your own business," Amy screamed at him in a voice that clearly had nothing wrong with it.

"Has someone been saying nasty things again?" asked Martha. Something similar had happened a few weeks before, and she had been off for a few days before the truth had come out. "Is that why you don't want to go?

"No. I really do have a headache."

Martha didn't know what to do. Should she give her daughter the benefit of the doubt and pander to her so-called illness?

"Well, come downstairs and have some breakfast," she conceded, "and then we'll see how you are."

If Amy genuinely felt ill, she wouldn't be able to leave her alone while she went to the farm, and if she didn't go to the farm, they would have nothing to eat by the following week.

While she wondered which neighbour she could call on to pop in and check on her daughter, Amy reluctantly preceded her down the stairs. But would it be fair on them if Amy had some infectious disease? Most of them had children of their own, and they wouldn't want them catching anything. Old Mrs What's-her-name, right on the end, a Polish lady, or Norwegian, or some such nationality, who had a right peculiar name nobody could pronounce, would sometimes look after other people's children. Martha had never needed to call on her services, so could not be sure of her.

Tommy opened his mouth to speak, but Amy gave him such a glaring look he closed it again.

She needed to unravel the matter. "Please tell me, Tommy. What's going on?"

"It's nothing, Mam," cried Amy before he could reply.

"Tommy?"

He looked at his sister. Amy shook her head vehemently, her face screwed up in pleading. He turned to Martha. "I think it's…"

"No, our Tommy, don't bother Mam with it, not when she has so much to put up with."

"Amy." Martha took her hands and pulled her towards her. "Please tell me. I shan't be cross. If you're having trouble, I need to know about it."

"Jimmy's brother." Tommy spoke up for his sister.

"What about Jimmy's brother? For heaven's sake, tell me." All matter of horrible possibilities raced through Martha's mind.

"He said it was Amy's fault our pa's dead."

"How could it be her fault?"

"'Cos she doesn't, I mean didn't, love him enough."

"Of course she loves him." She turned to her daughter. "Why on earth would he say something like that? And, anyway, we don't know he's dead." Oh, why couldn't she just tell them?

"It was something I said about him hitting you once."

"Me?"

"Yes, I was only… I'm sorry…" Amy buried her tear-streaked face in Martha's bosom.

"I'm going round to the Howards' now. We'll sort this out once and for all."

Tommy yanked at her arm. "But, Mam, you aren't dressed."

"I don't care. I'm not having my daughter berated like that. Come on."

Amy pulled away and ran to the other side of the room. "No, please don't."

"Look, my darling, the world is full of bullies and if we let them escape without any punishment, they'll never stop. We have to stand up to them." Not that she ever stood up to hers, but that was different.

"I will, I promise. I don't want you involved, though. Please. I'll go to school."

Martha drew in a deep breath. "Well, if you're sure."

"Yes, Mam, honest."

"Run up and put on some clothes then, while I make your breakfast."

Tommy sat down with a thump. "I told Jimmy to tell him he was naughty saying those horrible things. I did try, Mam."

"Yes, I'm sure you did, my darling. No matter how much you and your sister argue, you're both there for each other in times of trouble. I know that. You're good children."

She had been about to add that their pa would be proud, but didn't want to mention him again. She found it hard enough keeping it from them, without putting her foot in it and bringing him back into the conversation.

Guilt-ridden that her daughter had to face being bullied, she prayed it would blow over, and that Amy would be able to avoid the boy. If she did not work, though, both children would starve, or they would all end up in the workhouse.

She hurried to the farm, dreading what chores would be in store for her. She had scrubbed her petticoat until her fingers had become sore the previous evening, but the stains had not come out. Her frock fared better and, fortunately, the weather being warm, they had dried on the line overnight, enough to put them back on without much discomfort. She couldn't afford to spoil any of her other clothes. She only possessed two other frocks, one of them her best which she wore to church or to weddings.

Before she had reached the end of the lane, she spotted Lily Grant, alone, her yoke over her shoulders.

"Good day, Lily," she called. "I'm so pleased to have caught you before you start your rounds. Do you still need me today?" She held her breath, in case of a negative reply.

"Oh, yes, Martha. Faith's abed with a bad head, and Ronnie…well he didn't come home until late evening, in a right state, but he wouldn't tell me where he'd been, and now he's also in bed, too tired to leave it."

Ashamed that she had forgotten Ronnie had been missing most of the previous day, Martha caught her breath. "Oh, Lily, I'm so sorry to hear that. Is he well, though?

"I think so. He…anyway, could you start…let me see. Ed's taken the cows up to the higher field today and he's hoping the rest of the ewes will lamb. Check, when he returns, if he needs any help. If you could feed the chickens—I forgot to do that before I came out. I'm all at sixes and sevens. I don't know my arse from my funny bone, or whatever the saying is. I must rush, or this heat will curdle the milk before I can sell any." She dashed off, milk slopping from under the lids of the pails.

Locating the farmer in the lambing barn, she asked if he needed help. The ewe he was attending seemed to be having trouble parting with her offspring. His hand up her insides, he twisted it, and out shot a slimy lamb, covered in membrane. He wiped straw over its little body to clear most of it away, and placed it at its mother's head. She immediately began licking it as he delved in and pulled out another, then a third.

"Have a look at that ewe over there," he called, pointing to a black-faced one. "She looks about ready."

She could take a look, but how would she know? What signs would she need to be aware of? She went across and stroked its head. "Are you ready?" she asked, feeling somewhat foolish. The sheep raised its head and bleated. "Is that a yes or a no?"

Ed came and joined her. "I think she's telling you she is. Whoa, here it comes." Before he had time to check, another little lamb was born.

"Do you bring them all inside?" she asked.

"Oh, no, only those we consider to be at risk. We would be here all day and all night, otherwise."

"That's what I thought," she answered as she lifted up another one that had dropped at her feet. "Isn't Mother Nature wonderful? I never cease to marvel at her."

"She sure is, with the help of God, of course. Although, I sometimes think they are one and the same thing."

"Yes, I suppose they are. I hadn't thought of it in that way." A loud bleating from the other side of the barn caught her attention. "Oh, that one over there looks in trouble," she called to Ed.

"Here, I'll nip across if you can finish with this one. She's had one so the second shouldn't be so difficult."

She worked solidly, rushing from one to another, until peace reigned for a moment. She arched her back. "It's hard work, but so satisfying," she exclaimed when Ed came across to her. "I can tell you love your job."

"Most of the time it really is rewarding, seeing new life appear each spring, not only in the livestock but also in the fields. The corn and barley's already coming up, showing little green shoots to the sun. I just hope we have some more rain before long, or it will shrivel. We rely on it to see us through to next year."

"I never put you down as a poet, Ed Grant."

"Oh, I have my moments. Our Ronnie writes poetry you know, but he wouldn't thank me for broadcasting the fact. He says it's for namby-pambies."

"Oh, surely not? That fellow…what was his name? Shakes…something or other. Didn't he write poems? Not that I've ever read any of his stuff. Have you?"

After a quick look to check none of the ewes that had not yet lambed looked imminent, they went outside. "No, can't say that I have. I expect our Ronnie has, though. Our Herbert could hardly read at all, or write for that matter. He never took the slightest interest in it."

The farmer took his pipe out of his pocket and filled it with tobacco from a pouch. Then he struck a match on the heel of his boot and lit it, sending puffs of smoke in her face.

"Is there any news yet on whether they've found his murderer?" she asked through the smoke.

"No, not that I know of. The constable said he would be in touch as soon as they know something." After another puff, his hand cupped the bowl of the pipe. "He didn't actually say, but I had the impression he had quite a few suspects in mind." He gave her a peculiar expression, as if about to say something else, but turned away.

My Charlie probably one of them, she thought he had more than likely been going to add, but, being the lovely, kind gentleman that he was, he didn't voice it.

He replaced the pipe in his pocket after banging it upside down against the wall. "Better be seeing if any more lambs are ready. Lily should be back soon."

Does that mean he would rather I did something else? she wondered. "I haven't fed the chickens, yet," she remembered. "Where will I find their food?"

He had turned into the barn, but called over his shoulder, "Lily usually saves the potato peelings and mixes them with some meal. But she would have fed them earlier."

"She told me she'd not had time."

"Oh, look in the kitchen then."

She hurried over to the house. The back door stood open so, after a soft knock in case Ronnie or Faith were up, she had a look inside. A bowl of something resembling what the farmer had described stood next to the sink, so she picked it up and took it outside. Where should she put it? The chickens scratched at the ground, all over the place.

"Cock-a-doodle-doo," a large cockerel right next to her raised its head and called, as if he knew what she held, and wanted to summon his harem to come and eat. Several of the hens ran over to her.

"Clever man," she muttered. "Here you are, then." Should she pour it all in one place? She tried to remember what Aunt Elizabeth did, but she only had a small amount of hens compared with those at the farm, so it didn't really compare.

She scooped out a handful, scattered it, and moved farther along, surrounded by hoards of brown and black hens, many with furry-like tufts of feathers on their legs. Some tried to peck at her skirts. "There's no need for that." She tipped the remaining contents of the bowl into the grass under a large spreading chestnut tree and retreated, although some of the birds followed her. "It's all gone, look." She showed them the bowl, then put it down on the ground. "You may as well lick it out."

Their beaks made little tap-tap noises as they pecked at the metal bowl, and she didn't hear Ronnie sneak up behind her until his voice spoke in her ear. "Good day, Mrs Holloway."

She jumped back. "Oh, it's you, Ronnie." For a second she had thought it might be Charlie, who would occasionally call her by her married name, usually when in a good mood. "How are you, today?" Bloodshot eyes and his pallid complexion gave her the impression he had been drinking, which did not seem like him at all.

"I'm fine, thank you," he replied, although he looked far from it. "Do you have any news on your husband?"

"Um…no." Charlie was the last person she wanted to discuss, for the lad might pick up on her lies. "What about your brother's murderer? Have they found him?" When he pulled his jacket around him with his bandaged hand, she exclaimed, "Surely you can't be cold? I'm fair lathered, myself." She wiped her brow and continued, "Do you want me to take a look at your hand? How is it healing?"

He stared down at his wound. "Oh, no, thank you," he murmured before looking towards the dairy for the second time. "It's fine." Had he expected Charlotte to come out? Maybe she had been correct in her assumptions. Maybe they had already started courting, although, surely someone would have seen them and spilled the beans?

Jessica came out, her hand on her belly. For a split second, Ronnie jerked upright, but then his body drooped. He had clearly been expecting the other sister.

"Hello." Jessica waved and pointed to Martha's clothes. "You look slightly cleaner than yesterday, our Martha."

"Cheeky madam. But yes, thank goodness, I have not had to do anything dirty yet." Her apron already looked mucky, covered in spots of blood and new-born lamb, though.

"Where did you go to yesterday, Master Ronnie? Your ma was going frantic."

Martha shook her head. Sometimes her younger sister could be too outspoken. "That's none of your business, my lass. You shouldn't be asking questions like that."

"Well, it's not me who wants to know. Our Charlotte tried to pretend she paid no heed, but she didn't fool me."

An animated look came into his eyes as they lit up. "Oh, tell her I'm really sorry to have put her to any bother."

"Tell her yourself. She's in the dairy...on her own." Jessica's face took on a joking quality. "On her very own." Jessica had clearly not seen them together, or she would not be teasing him so.

He bowed and walked in the direction of the dairy, then hesitated. "No, it is not appropriate to visit a young lady on her own, not without..."

Jessica cuffed his arm, playfully. "Go on. We won't tell anyone, will we, our Martha?"

Martha didn't want to be a part of her sister's matchmaking. "If he thinks it is inappropriate, then so be it. *Some* people know how to behave with decorum. Leave it be, our Jessica, and carry on with whatever you came out for." She gave her sister a shove, almost knocking her over. That had not been her intention, but she needed pulling down a peg or two, for being too forthright. Perhaps she should have a word with Aunt Elizabeth, although, in her opinion, she was a strict disciplinarian, so what else could she do?

"Spoilsport," Jessica mumbled as she went towards the privy.

Martha turned to Ronnie who was still staring at the dairy door. "I apologise for my sister, Master Ronnie. She's still young and, having no mother to put her in her place, I am afraid she's rather flighty."

"There's no need. Pray, do not fret. I didn't take offence." He tugged his eyes away from his target, and walked off down the path, in the same direction Martha had gone towards the river the previous day. Should she call him back? What if Charlie expected her, and laid in wait? Ronnie might see him. Oh, how she hated all this subterfuge. It just wasn't in her nature, being a simple, honest, God-fearing person, who never committed sins— well, maybe a small offence, occasionally, but nothing serious. Why did he have to stay away? He must be guilty. There could be no other explanation.

As Ronnie disappeared out of sight Martha turned back, unsure what to do.

Lily came along the lane from the village with her empty milk pails. "I saw the constable earlier," she called as she approached. "He wants to speak to you when you have a minute." For a second, Martha's heart almost stopped. She hoped she had escaped without seeing him when she had missed him the previous day, but she breathed a sigh of relief when Lily continued, "I told him he would have to come here as you're busy, so he said he would try when he had finished interviewing the rest of the villagers."

"Thank you." She tried to keep the relief from her face. She didn't want the farmer's wife becoming suspicious. With the widest grin she could muster fixed to her face, she asked, "What would you like me to do next?" Hopefully, Ronnie would not bump into Charlie. Surely he would keep well hidden.

Lily glanced around, then patted her arm. "Put the kettle on, would you? I am so parched, I could drink the river dry. I'll just wash these out, and I'll be with you in a moment. Make one for yourself."

"Oh." That could not be counted as a money-earning task. She couldn't expect to be paid for mashing tea. "Right you are. Then what?" Lily had already walked into the dairy, so didn't hear her.

As she entered the large farmhouse, Faith came through from the sitting room in a pink dressing gown, a decidedly unwell sheen on her face. "O...o...oh, I th...th...thought you were Auntie Li...Li...Lily."

"Are you sure you should be up, Faith? You look proper poorly to me. I think you should go back to bed. I'll bring you up a nice cup of tea." Martha didn't want to catch the illness, whatever it was. The previous year many of the villagers had died from a disease called dipther—

something or other. She couldn't quite remember its name, but she hoped the girl next to her didn't have it. "Do you have a sore throat?" she asked. Apparently all those people had started with a sore throat.

"Y…y…yes." She opened her mouth wide to show her. At the smell of the girl's bad breath, she didn't even look, but shooed her away.

"That needs bed," she said, turning to the kettle. "Up you go."

"B…b…but I w…w…want to see Auntie Lily."

"I shall send her up to you as soon as she comes in. Now be a good girl and go and snuggle up in your comfy bed."

Faith hung her head, but did as she had been bid. Although younger than her, Martha felt years older. Being married with a child at the age of fifteen gave a body an experience and wisdom that unwed maidens could never gain.

Lily still had not returned by the time she had poured out the tea and taken one up to Faith, though she left the young woman's room as fast as she could. She went to the back door, her own drink cupped in her hands, to see if she could see her.

In the distance, up near the copse, she thought she saw a movement. She squinted, shielding her eyes from the fierce sun, and saw it again. A person? She couldn't be sure. Perhaps Ronnie. But, she remembered, he had been wearing a green jacket, and this man wore a brown one, similar to Charlie's, in fact. But it could be Ed. No, she could hear him talking to Lily in the barn. It had to be Charlie. Should she go and meet him? Would he be expecting her to?

She had better go, so she rushed inside, placed her cup in the sink and hurried back out. Lily came out of the barn as she was halfway across the farmyard. "Where are you off to in such a hurry?"

Dash it. What can I say? Think quickly. "A sudden urge

for a pee." As she ran to the privy, she called over her shoulder, "Faith was asking for you." Then she pulled open the door and slammed it behind her.

Full of indecision, she leaned back against the door, then, after a moment, pulled down her drawers and sat on the wooden seat and tried to work out a plan of action. Could there be any jobs she could volunteer for out in the field? Maybe she could check on the ewes that had not been brought in? Yes, she would do that. She pulled up her drawers, dashed out, avoiding the geese that seemed always to be in her way, and ran into the barn to ask the farmer, rather than his wife.

"Um, yes," he replied, after she had told him her intention, "unless Lily has more pressing chores in mind for you." He sat back on his haunches and wiped his hand across his face. Martha didn't like to tell him he had just smeared blood down his cheek. He would find out soon. He should be used to it, anyway.

"She didn't say so. I won't be too long, anyway."

He opened his mouth as if to say something further, but she scampered out, her petticoats in her hands so as not to fall over them. After scanning the horizon for any movement, although she could no longer spot anything, she made for the place she had seen Charlie. Brushing aside the bracken and saplings in the copse, she scratched her hand on a particularly vicious bramble. "Ouch," she cried as she sucked at her finger. Another cut to add to the one from that morning.

"Psst," she heard from her left. She peered through the dense undergrowth. "Psst," he repeated.

"Is that you?" she whispered.

"Of course it's me. Who else would it be?" A very dishevelled Charlie stepped out from behind a tree and looked about furtively.

"It could have been anybody."

"Oh, you have assignations with a number of men, do you?"

She sighed. It seemed he would start an argument, already. She shouldn't have come.

"Just tell me what you want, Charlie. I don't have time for a spat. I have to earn a living to feed your children, and, anyway, Lily will wonder where I am."

"If you're going to be like that, I might as well go." He turned and began to slope away.

She pulled at his jacket. "Charlie, don't be so mardy. Why can't you just come home and admit to whatever it is that's preventing you from doing so?"

"You wouldn't understand, Miss Lily-White Hen who has never done a wrong thing in her life."

Except find myself in the pudding club, and have to marry you, she thought.

"What can be so wrong to keep you from your son? Please, young Tommy cries for you at night. Surely it would be better to face up to whatever it is." With open hands, she lifted her shoulders.

"No, I can't," he uttered and vanished into the interior of the copse.

What had been the point in that? None the wiser, she shook her head and hurried down to the farm. As she crossed the farmyard once more, she remembered she had not even seen a sheep, let alone check on the ewes. She had better keep out of Ed's way in case he asked, which he would be sure to do. It would be better to rely on Lily for her next instruction.

Chapter 12

Ronnie limped up the lane, his hands in his trouser pockets, kicking at stones with his good foot. Why had he not taken the opportunity to see his sweetheart when it had been offered him? So close to going into that dairy to grab hold of her, lay her down amongst the milk churns, and kiss her beautiful face until she surrendered to him. He had wanted to do the same thing the previous day, but had gone off, instead, and stayed at the inn, drinking until he could barely stand. He could not remember how he had returned home. Vague recollections of being dumped out of a cart flitted through his brain.

Blowing his breath out in short pants, he raised his face to the sky. "Thank you, God, for stopping me, for not letting me succumb to my devilish wants," he cried. "I am a bad man, having such wicked thoughts. She is a pure, sweet girl. It would be a mortal sin to have my evil way with her."

A young faun attracted his attention as it leapt over the thistles at the top of the field. Its mother followed, and then three others. He stopped to watch them. So carefree. The clear sound of a bugle carried through the air. That meant the hunt must be near. He jumped back and almost lost his footing as a rider in a red coat came over the hedge, not ten feet in front of him, then several others. The bugle sounded again. A fox must have been sighted. Some of the riders continued over the hedge opposite, but a few stopped, circling their horses in the lane.

He did not want to be trampled so took several shaky steps backwards towards a gate leading into a field, opened it and squeezed through as the pack of hounds caught up. He spotted the fox running across the bottom of the field. The huntsmen must also have seen it, for, with a cry of, "Tally ho," one of the runners pushed the gate further open, and they all careered down the field after it. Ronnie felt a moment's chagrin for the animal, but recognised it as a pest that killed chickens and geese, so their numbers had to be culled. He hoped it was not a vixen with cubs, for it would surely be caught in the next minute or so.

Several more runners chased by him. Should he go after them? He had often wanted to join a hunt, but had always been too busy. His bad leg would hinder him, though, so he searched in the hedge bottom and found a stout stick with a large knot on the top and just the right height to support him if he extended his arm. Another horse and rider rode by and he could see several more runners behind it. Excited, he hurried down the field, hobbling in pain, but caught up in the thrill of the chase.

"Come on, young Ronnie," the father of a lad he had known at school called from atop his chestnut mare as he rode past. "You don't want to miss the kill."

With no breath to speak he merely waved as, puffing and panting, he continued down the hill. The bugle sounded for a third time, the baying of the hounds loud on the still air.

The knobbles on the stick cut into his hand but, determined to carry on, he reached the site of the kill, where he could see the hounds fighting for the tiny remaining scraps of flesh.

His eyes opened wide with surprise. The person who had arrived first, the one who waved the brush, and had been daubed with its blood, was a lady. He knew her to be one of the daughters of the lord of the manor, but could not remember her name. Because he did not move in their circles he only knew the gentry by the snippets of gossip that circulated around the village. He had never actually spoken to any of them. Out of his depth, he turned to go home.

"You look a wounded soldier," a soft voice spoke in his ear. The most beautiful girl he had ever seen stood next to him. The bluest eyes imaginable looked at him from beneath a jaunty red hat perched on top of short blonde curls. Dressed in a dark pink jacket, she looked about his age, maybe a year or two older. His own clothes looked scruffy in comparison, his boots muddy, his trousers ripped at the knee.

Another young lady came across and touched her arm. "Aren't you going to introduce us, Filly?" she asked.

"I haven't been introduced myself." She held out her hand. "Good day, I am Felicity Burns, and this is my sister, Wilhelmina, known to everyone as Billy."

He could see a comparison, but the second girl's eyes weren't as blue. Completely out of his depth, he bowed then kissed each proffered hand in turn. "Ronald Grant at your service, ladies, but if you would excuse me, I must depart."

With a deep inhalation of breath, he turned to leave, but they would have none of it. "Oh, you cannot go, sir," crooned the one called Filly. "You must stay and entertain us. We are sorely lacking in diversions at the moment. This hunt is the first exciting thing to happen to us this year, is it not, Billy?"

"It most certainly is. You must come to our ball on Saturday. Some new young blood would be most welcome."

Ronnie looked down at his clothes again. Surely they must be making fun of him?

What was he thinking about, speaking to these young ladies while Charlotte slaved away at the farm? His loyalties lay with her. Even if he had the inclination to go to a ball, which he 'most certainly' did not, he would want to take her, not dance attendance on these two popinjays.

"Thank you for the invitation, but I must decline. Good day to you." That time he did walk away, uncaring if they thought him ill-mannered. He could hear them giggling behind his back. Let them giggle all they wanted. Filly and Billy! They sounded like goats or horses. But the first one's eyes were very beautiful.

The uphill trek taxed his leg. He could not put any weight on the stick, for the palm of his hand had blistered. What on earth had made him think it would be fun to follow a hunt? His intention had been to have another look at the gully where his brother had been found. He still felt awful for threatening that young boy.

Halfway up the field, he sat down. Hardly daring to peep down at the group below in case one of the ladies looked back, he could see them dispersing. Several rode past him, some perilously close, but he didn't look up, he didn't want to have to acknowledge them again.

He recognised one of the runners as the butcher's son, who had married the lord's youngest daughter, amidst huge opposition from her father. The man stopped and asked Ronnie if he required help. He shook his head. "No, thank you. I am just having a rest."

The man continued with the others, and soon Ronnie found himself alone. He stood and staggered on, the pain almost overbearing. He prayed Charlotte would not see him in such a state, and eventually made the farmhouse where he slumped onto a chair, his breathing ragged, barely able to hold up his head.

How stupid he had been, not giving a thought to the consequences of his rash actions. One part of him wished his mother would come in and comfort him, hold him in her warm arms and whisper soothing assurances in his ear like she had done when he had been a little boy, but the rational part hoped she would not see him so. As he kept telling her, he was a grown man. But occasionally a hug would be nice.

With his head rested on his folded arms on the table, he did not hear anyone come in, a gentle hand on his back the first indication he had company. He lifted his head and buried it in her warm bosom, fighting tears.

Something made him pull away maybe because she did not smell like his mother, or because of her shape. Jessica! "I am so sorry, Miss Bridge. I do beg your pardon. Pray forgive me." Oh, the humiliation! And what if she told Charlotte? How would he explain that away?

"Don't worry, Ronnie, I won't tell anyone. I only came in to look for your mother."

"She isn't here."

"Well, do you have any idea where she might be?"

"No, I'm sorry, I don't." Gripping the side of the table for support, he stood. "Maybe she's with my father in the lambing shed." Would she really not say anything? "Look, I am really sorry I touched you like that. If I had realised it was you…"

She patted his arm. "I told you, I won't tell. If it's our Charlotte you're concerned about, then don't be. You can't do anything wrong in her eyes."

"Yes, but…" He stared down at her belly. It seemed twice as large as the last time he had seen it. "She might think…"

A chuckle bubbled up as she raised her hands. "You mean she might think you're the father of my baby? Don't make me laugh!" Her expression changed as if she realised she had made a gaffe. "Not that…I don't mean… She just wouldn't think that, so don't go worrying yourself about it." She rushed out as he covered his head with his hands.

Could things become much worse?

* * * *

Charlotte dragged her body out of bed, dressed quickly, went downstairs, and gave her face a quick wash in the sink.

"Is that all?" asked Martha.

"It'll have to do," she replied. "I can't be bothered with more." And why bother, indeed? Ronnie seemed to be avoiding her. She had not spoken to him for days, and she had spied her sister coming out of the farmhouse the other day, looking smug. Had he been inside? Did he prefer Jessica? She still had not managed to wheedle out of her sister the name of the father of her baby. Maybe…

"You don't believe it, do you?" asked Martha from behind her.

How did she know what I was thinking? Charlotte spun round. "I beg your pardon?"

"That our Tommy's been invited to the seaside?"

She had not even realised her sister had been speaking to her. "Um…"

"You weren't listening, were you? Your head was up in those clouds again. I hope you are not hankering after Master Ronnie. He's out of your reach, my girl. His father would never condone such a match."

She tried to hide her blushing face. "I don't know what you mean."

"I've seen the way you look at him. But, mark my words, be careful." Martha poked her on the shoulder. Her face looked severe, but also sympathetic.

"I'm sure he would rather have our Jessica, anyway."

Her sister spluttered. "I don't think so. Who in their right mind would want to saddle themselves with someone else's baby? Tell me that."

Charlotte shrugged. "We don't know who…"

Martha had walked across to take the kettle off the range. She dropped it back, spinning round. "You mean…? No, I'm sure it wouldn't be him." She shook her head vehemently, picked up the kettle once more and emptied it into the teapot. "No. Has she said as much?"

"Oh, no, she won't tell me anything. I just thought…"

"Well, I'm sure you can drive that particular thought from your pretty little head. Now, drink this and be off with you. You don't want to be late." She pushed a mug of milky tea towards her and buttered a slice of dry-looking bread. "I shall have to bake some more before I go to work, or we'll have none for our tea."

Charlotte saw the drawn lines at her older sister's mouth, and put her arms around her shoulder. "It must be so hard for you, our Martha, trying to juggle the house chores as well as working up at the farm. You need to make our Amy and Tommy help out more."

"I know, but they're only children."

"I would do something, but…"

"I understand. You're shattered by the time you come home. I don't expect you to. Now off with you. Shoo."

Charlotte sucked the bread to soften it as she hastened along the lane, and then remembered she had not asked if there had been any news of her brother-in-law. Not that she particularly wanted him back, but at least he brought in a wage.

Something didn't seem right as she herded out the last of the cows. Milking had gone well and she and Jessica had worked together amicably, even having a laugh when one of the animals had turned its head and given her a dirty look when she had insulted it for staining her frock.

Maybe she should change her opinion about Jessica. Sometimes her over-active imagination led her down blind alleys. It didn't matter, anyway for, as Martha had said, she had no future in yearning for Ronnie, no future at all.

The dairy looked, as usual, neat and tidy, everything in its place. But something niggled at her. She couldn't put her finger on the problem, if there were to be one.

"What's the matter, our Charlotte?" asked Jessica as she followed her inside. "You seem pre-occupied."

"I don't know. I just have a feeling that something's…well…not quite right."

Her sister took a quick check. "It seems fine to me. Where do you want me to start?"

"I suppose we'd better begin with the curds and whey."

"I love that word, 'whey'," she pronounced it with extra emphasis on the 'wh', "don't you? It reminds me of that nursery rhyme Mama used to sing to us about Little Miss Muffet."

"Me, too. Our Martha used to sing it to Tommy, as well. He's too old for nursery rhymes now, so he says. Too grown up." She poured some milk into a churn. "I still miss Mama, don't you?"

"Every hour of every day. I probably wouldn't be...you know—" She wrapped her arms around her midriff "—if she hadn't died. I didn't know what to do with myself, how to cope with the grief. I just wanted someone to hold me in their arms and..." Tears began to fall down her cheeks.

Charlotte hesitated for a moment, and then enfolded her in a tight embrace, also crying. Her younger sister had always been self-sufficient, never seemingly needing hugs and cuddles as much as her, but, deep down, her vulnerability had cracks.

"I'm sorry. I should have been there for you."

Jessica pulled away and wiped her face with her sleeve. "It isn't your fault. You were only a child as well. That blinking illness."

"Um, consumption." Charlotte continued with her work. "I'd been about to say it could have been worse. She could have caught that other illness that half the village died from, but she died anyway, so how could it be any worse?" She rolled a churn over towards the door. "Can you smell burning?"

Jessica raised her head and sniffed. "No, I don't think so."

"Well, I'm sure I can." She peeped outside. "I'm sure it's burning. I'll just go and have a quick check."

* * * *

Ronnie grimaced as he pushed back the covers. He couldn't tell which hand hurt the more. The left one had almost healed, but still seeped slightly, and a mass of blisters covered his right palm.

"You stupid bloody idiot," he swore. "Fancy thinking you could join the gentry." His mother had dabbed his hand with butter the previous evening, but it had not helped much. He grabbed his dressing gown, pushed his arms inside the sleeves and, after a great deal of difficulty, managed to tie the belt to hide his modesty.

His mother turned from the range. "Ah, our Ronnie, just in time for a cuppa." She poured one out and set it on the table. "How's the hand?"

"Which one?" he asked sullenly. "I don't know which is worse."

She shook her head indulgently. "Well, if you will go careering off after the nobility, you only have yourself to blame."

"I know, I know, there's no need to rub it in." He picked up the mug with his fingertips and thumbs, and sipped the welcome drink.

"I suppose you'll be out of action even longer now. Just as I hoped you would be back in the reins." Hands on hips, she sighed.

"I didn't do it on purpose. You know I like to pull my weight." He looked up at her. "I suppose Pa's mad with me."

"Well…" With a hand on his shoulder, she kissed his cheek. "More like disappointed."

"I wanted to prove to him that I could take over the farm when he's gone, make him proud of me. Now, he'll just think I'm a wastrel, who can't even look after himself, let alone a business."

"Don't cut yourself up, son. Your father won't be going for a long time yet. There's plenty of time to make amends. Some breakfast inside you will make you feel better." She broke two eggs into the pan on the range and scooped hot fat over them to cook the yolk, saying, "Sunny side up, just how you like them," and placed the plate in front of him. "Would you like me to cut them up for you?" With a grin, she ruffled his hair and pinched his cheek. "Like I used to when you were an itty-bitty little boy?"

After breaking off a chunk of bread, he dipped it in the runny yolk. "Aw, Ma, I think I can manage that myself."

"Right you are, then. I had better be off on my milk round. Faith isn't up yet. I'm quite worried about her." Chewing her lip, she went out.

As long as she doesn't give me whatever she ails from, he thought uncharitably. *I don't want anything else to add to my list of woes.*

Wiping the back of his hand across his lips, he stood up. "I could eat them all over again," he mumbled, looking to see what else he could snaffle. "I'm still hungry."

A biscuit tin stood tantalisingly on the sideboard. Could he open it? He would give it a good try. To make sure his efforts would not be in vain, he shook it first and then prised open the lid. Mm, his favourites, ginger, just right for dunking in his tea, although he realised he had drunk it all. Maybe there would be some left in the pot. He took off the bright red knitted tea cosy, but could not pick up the teapot, so gave up and ladled some milk into his cup instead. It wouldn't absorb as much of the biscuit, but sometimes you had to settle for second best.

Shouts sounded outside, so he rushed over to the door. The smell of smoke assailed his nostrils. Where could it be coming from? One of the farm hands ran by, shouting, "Fire in the barn. Fire!" Dare he run out in just his dressing gown? Perhaps not. But he would be needed. Not a good enough excuse to be seen in public half-naked, though.

He ran upstairs, ignoring the pain in his hands, and pulled on a pair of trousers and a shirt. Should he wake Faith? If she was really poorly, though, it would be better if she stayed in bed. The shouting would more than likely wake her, anyway.

More people had arrived by the time he reached the barn. Smoke erupted from the door and oozed through the eaves, as well.

Jessica ran around like a headless chicken, yelling, "Where's our Charlotte? She came out to investigate the smoke. Where is she?"

Nobody had seen her. They all gaped at each other, shaking their heads.

"Maybe she's in the barn," someone cried.

"In the barn? I have to save her." Ronnie ran full pelt, ignoring his father's shouts of "Don't go in there. It's too dangerous."

If the love of his life were in trouble, he needed to save her.

* * * *

Martha packed the children off to school and hurried to the farm to start another gruelling day. A smell of smoke wafted through the air as she left the village. Loud voices came from ahead, and through the trees she could see black smoke billowing upwards.

"It must be the farm," she shrieked as she threw down her parasol and broke into a gallop. Charlotte and Jessica could be in trouble. As she rounded the bend, she had full view of the scene. Fortunately, she could see only a barn, not the house, on fire, but her sisters could still be involved. A row of men and women had formed a long line, passing buckets of water from one to the next, to pour over the inferno. Bright red and yellow flames pothered out of the roof. She spotted Jessica in the line. Thank goodness. But what about Charlotte? Sparks and burning pieces of wood dropped perilously close to the farmhouse.

Jessica ran over to her. "Our Charlotte's lost, Martha. She might be inside."

"No! Don't say that." In a frenzy, Martha looked about her. Surely her sister must be wrong, and Charlotte would be found amongst the throng of villagers who had come running up the lane.

"Ronnie ran in to find her, but he hasn't come out yet."

"Oh, my goodness. Please God, let them be safe." They both tried to approach the inferno, but were pushed back.

"Don't go any closer," a large man with a blackened face shouted.

"But my sister might be in there."

"She very well might be, but you are not going in. Please move back." As he tried to push the mass of people, a loud cracking noise split the air and more flames pothered out of the roof.

"Oh, my God," screamed Martha and Jessica together. "Charlotte!"

A dark figure carrying what looked like a body crawled out of the door. Martha ran towards it, pushing aside the man who had tried to prevent her going near. "Charlotte!" she screamed again.

The figure, unrecognisable because of the black soot covering his face, dropped to his knees and laid the body on the ground, far enough away to be out of danger. The whites of his eyes stared up at the people. "Is she still alive?" he whispered.

That's not Ronnie's voice, thought Martha. *I know who that is.*

Shoving him out of the way, she knelt down beside her sister, and stroked her smoke-filled hair away from her black face. "Someone fetch the doctor," she yelled. The girl's hand twitched. "Thank God," She exclaimed as she gently picked it up. "Charlotte, hang on, sweetheart. Don't give up. We're all here, praying for you."

Jessica knelt down beside her. "Please don't die, Charlotte. I need you," she sobbed.

The clang of the horse-drawn fire engine storming up the lane made everyone turn. The line of people continued passing the buckets although not a lot of water remained in them by the time they reached the barn.

"Where's Ronnie?" shrieked Lily, running up after the fire engine. "Is he all right?"

One of the men pointed to the hero who had saved the girl. "Isn't that him?"

Lily peered at the man and shook her head. "No, that's not him. Where is he?"

"I thought I saw him around the back." A woman pointed behind the barn.

Martha also peered at the man. "I thought you were in hiding," she hissed under her breath as Lily ran to find her son.

"Don't let on," he whispered.

Jessica turned from watching Lily. "Who's this then?" she asked.

"It doesn't matter, we have to save our Charlotte. Where's that blasted doctor?"

"We can't wait for him," a man said. "We need to take her to the hospital in Buxton."

"But how can we transport her there?"

"Ronnie will take her, won't you, son?" Lily came across, dragging her son by his sleeve. "Instead of snivelling that you couldn't go in to save her."

He bent down to the girl on the ground. "I'm so sorry, Miss Charlotte. I really wanted to, but I lost my nerve."

"Never mind that now," chastised his mother. "Rein up the horse."

"It's already been done, ma'am," called one of the helpers. "And we've laid clean straw from the dutch barn in the cart for comfort."

"I'll run and find some blankets and pillows, but be careful how you put her in." Lily ran off towards the house.

Several men stood each side of Charlotte and carefully lifted her onto the cart. Lily ran back out and they made her as comfortable as they could. She hardly made a murmur. Martha held her breath, praying it didn't mean she was past help. "I'll go with her, to make sure she doesn't wobble about." She climbed into the cart and knelt beside her sister, stroking her hand.

"Me, too. Please say I can come as well." Jessica tried to climb up with them but Lily pulled her down.

"There isn't room for you, lass. You stay here. She's in good hands with your older sister."

The cart pulled away. Everyone decided Ronnie's hands would be too sore to drive such a long journey, so one of the villagers took the reins as Martha made herself more comfortable for the long, rickety journey ahead, whispering soothing reassurances in her sister's ear. She didn't know if she could hear them, but felt sure they would help if she could.

As they rounded the bend in the lane, she saw her husband sneaking off up the hill. Where would he find clean clothes? He would have to wait for darkness and creep into the house. He could be burnt as well. Why, oh, why, didn't he just give himself up?

* * * *

Jessica turned to her Aunt Elizabeth, who had come running up the lane as the cart vanished around the corner. "She's not going to die, is she? Please say she isn't."

Her aunt wrapped her in her arms. "We shall have to wait and see. If it is God's will…"

Jessica pulled away. "But why would God want to

kill her?"

"God hasn't killed her, lass. The fire's done that. I mean, if she does die. Don't give up hope."

"Charlotte doesn't deserve this. It should have been me." Catching her lip in her teeth, she began to walk away.

Her aunt grabbed her. "Don't you say that. Don't ever say that."

"But that's what everyone will think. I'm the bad one. She never committed a crime in her life." Tears ran down her face. "It just isn't fair."

"Not a lot is in this life. We just have to bear it." Aunt Elizabeth drew her towards her, comforting her once more.

A shout made them look up, as a fireman struggled out of the blackened shell of the barn, carrying something.

"Don't tell me they've found someone else." Aunt Elizabeth nudged Jessica aside and, holding her hand, they moved closer. "Who can it be?"

The firemen pushed everyone back as the rescuer laid the charred remains of what looked like a person on the ground.

"It must be a lass, or a woman. It's too small to be a man," one of the neighbours said.

"That's for sure, unless bodies shrink when they're burnt."

Jessica shuddered, not wanting to think about it. Charlotte could have ended up like that.

Mrs Howard, the mother of the milkmaid Mary who had been dismissed, moved closer and began to cry.

"What's up with her?" Aunt Elizabeth asked the lady beside her. "Does she know who it is?"

"Well, I think I heard someone say…" The lady looked around and lowered her voice. "They said she had been asking if anyone had seen her daughter, you know? Mary. She had told her mother she was coming to the farm to see if she could ask for her old job back." She nodded, her chin back against her neck, her eyes open wide, as if she wanted Elizabeth to say she understood.

"So you think it could be her?"

"Yes. Who else could it be?"

"I haven't seen Faith this morning." Jessica lifted her head to see above the crowd that grew every minute. She breathed a sigh of relief as she spotted the girl, crying into Lily's bosom. "Oh, thank goodness, she's over there."

"But if it is Mary, how did the barn catch fire?"

Jessica remembered the milking stool, and several other things going missing over the past couple of days. Could the embittered girl have intended something more sinister? "Maybe she set it alight and couldn't find her way out through the flames?"

"Our Jessica, wash your mouth out. Why would she do that?" Her aunt's astounded voice cut her off.

"Nay, lass, why would you make such accusations?" asked the lady who had told them about Mary.

Jessica shook her head. "Nothing, I didn't mean…" Her and her big mouth. She had better keep it shut. She didn't want that policeman questioning her again.

The lady's brow furrowed. "But she was dismissed, wasn't she? And everyone knows she hadn't taken it kindly."

"Now, don't go putting ideas into anybody's head," replied Aunt Elizabeth. "It isn't fair on the girl, especially now she's dead and can't stick up for herself."

The lady moved away, and Jessica could see her whispering to two other ladies. They glanced in her direction, clearly talking about her. What had she done? The whole village would know what she had said within the hour. Her attention went back to the group near the person on the ground. "Maybe it's a dog or a sheep." She raised her voice so the women could hear her.

"Don't be silly. Look at the shape. It would have legs sticking out of the side," her aunt contradicted.

"Well, maybe they were burnt off."

"I don't think so." Another villager stepped towards her as someone laid a blanket over the black form.

The policeman stepped forward. "Did anyone see how this happened?" he shouted.

Everyone looked towards Jessica. "I didn't see it," she protested. "It was our Charlotte who went to investigate the smoke."

He stood in front of her and spat on the end of his pencil. Fearful of what he might write in his little book, she stared at it. "I didn't see nothing, I tell you," she repeated. "I was in the dairy."

"What about…?"

Lily and Ronnie hurried across, followed by Faith, still crying. "Please, Jessica, if you know anything, you must tell the constable."

"But I don't. You have to believe me."

"Someone told me you saw the former milkmaid—Mary, was her name?" continued the constable. "You saw her going into the barn."

"No, I didn't see anything of the sort. Who said that?" She searched the people around her, wanting to see a sympathetic face, but everyone, apart from her aunt, shook their heads or frowned at her.

"Well, miss, when was the last time you saw Mistress Mary?"

She racked her brain. Had she seen her since the girl's dismissal? No, she felt sure she hadn't. "She had already left when I started work here. That was why I came. I haven't seen her for months."

"Umm, a likely story."

"It's the truth. Why would I lie?"

He closed his book. "Who has seen the lady in question lately?" Without waiting for a reply, he turned to her mother. "Mistress Howard, you said your daughter told you she intended coming here. What time would that have been, ma'am?"

Mrs Howard pulled a handkerchief out of her apron pocket and blew her nose. "About six o'clock, just as her father went to work."

Pocket watch in hand, he continued, "Well, it's ten o'clock now, so where has she been all this time?"

Jessica shrugged as a voice shouted, "The farmhouse…there's smoke coming out of the roof."

Everyone gasped as they turned to face the house. Lily screamed and ran towards it, but was pulled back.

"Is there anyone inside, ma'am?" asked the constable.

"No, but my things…"

"Possessions can be replaced, ma'am. Life cannot."

The firemen aimed their hose at the roof and the bedroom windows.

"There aren't any flames so, hopefully, the fire hasn't taken hold." The farmer grabbed his wife's arm to try to comfort her. Jessica had not seen him in the scuffle of folks and wondered where he had been. His black face and clothes spoke for themselves, though. He must have been helping in the barn.

The doctor finally arrived and, after consulting with the policeman and Mrs Howard, the burnt body was placed into a cart and carried away. The crowd began to disperse, back to their drab lives.

"It isn't every day we have distractions like these, is it?" Jessica heard one of the elderly ladies say.

"Well, that's three in one week," replied Aunt Elizabeth. "So it's becoming quite usual. I think we could do without any more, thank you very much." She took Jessica's hand. "Do you feel up to staying, or do you want to come home now, with me?"

Jessica replied, "I had better see what Mrs Grant wants me to do. With Charlotte and Martha indisposed, she will need me more than ever." She leant back, stretching her muscles.

"Very well, if you're sure. That's brave of you. I'm

impressed by your maturity." Her aunt gave her a hug. Praise indeed. It wasn't often her aunt said anything favourable to her. "But if you don't feel up to it later, I'm sure Mrs Grant will understand."

Jessica looked across at the farmer's wife as her husband led her away, her face pale and lips pursed. She couldn't let her down. "No, Aunt. I'll be fine. You go home."

As her aunt walked towards the lane, two firemen went into the house, and Jessica saw Faith about to follow them. Nobody else seemed to be watching her, so Jessica ran and yanked her arm. "No, Faith, you mustn't go in there. It might still be on fire."

"B...b...but I need to go to bed. I...I...I'm tired." Her bloodshot eyes did, indeed, look exhausted.

Jessica steered her towards the lane and caught up with her aunt. "Could Faith come with you? She looks done in."

"Yes, of course. Come on, dear. I'll look after you."

"I'll tell Mrs Grant." She ran back and found the farmer and his wife.

"The firemen seem satisfied they've contained the fire in the house without too much damage," he said. "So that's one blessing."

"Blessing!" shrieked his wife. "You call this a blessing? All your fodder goes up in smoke, a girl is burnt to death and another one nearly so, our house almost goes up in flames, and you call it a blessing?"

A hurt expression flickered over his face. "You know I don't mean that, my dear. I was just trying to put a positive aspect on the situation."

Her head jerked in twitching movements and she clamped her mouth shut, as if she dare not say anything more.

Jessica touched her arm. "My aunt has taken Faith home with her, Mrs Grant, so you can put your mind at rest about her."

A look of horror lit up her eyes. "Oh, my goodness. I had forgotten about my niece. Is she all right?"

"Yes, yes, just a little tired."

"She isn't well, you know. I really shouldn't allow your aunt to be in contact with her."

"Why, what's the matter with her?" Jessica began to regret her impulsive gesture. She didn't want her aunt becoming ill.

"We don't know. Hopefully, nothing serious. It's probably just something to do with her condition."

She would have loved to find out what the girl's 'condition' meant. Surely not the same 'condition' she had? Somebody would have spilled the beans, if so. She daren't ask, just remarked, "As long as it isn't that awful disease that ravished the village last year."

"No, no I don't think so. Anyway, we'd better do some work. Are you able to stay?"

"Yes, ma'am. I told my aunt I would do whatever you need me to, and help out as long as it takes."

"Where do we start?" Hands on hips, Mrs Grant surveyed the scene.

"Shall I just finish off the job in the dairy?" Jessica suggested, not feeling up to anything too physical.

"Yes, child, that's a good idea."

About to walk in that direction, she saw two burly men bashing the sides of the still-smoking barn with planks. Scores of sparks jumped into the air as they fell, and the remains burst into flames.

The farmer raced over to them. "What the hell do you think you're doing?"

"We thought it would be safer to lie it all down. I thought I heard the fireman say so," explained one of them.

Jessica left them to it. She didn't want to become involved in any arguments. She continued with what she knew. Clasping her hands together, she offered up a prayer for her sister's recovery, unable to imagine life without her. Even though they often squabbled, she loved her dearly. And who had brought her out? Something about him had seemed familiar, but she couldn't quite put her finger on it.

* * * *

With a heavy heart, Ronnie scrutinised the ruins of the barn. How could he have been such a coward? His beloved Charlotte had needed him, and he had been found wanting, too scared for his own safety. He wouldn't blame her if she never spoke to him again.

He had run towards the smoky building, full of good intentions and ready to save her. Once he had reached the door, a flurry of smoke had puffed out and enveloped him, catching his breath. He had fought against it for a moment, but then looked down at his hands. How could he rescue her with one cut and bandaged, the other blistered? A moment's hesitation and he had been doomed, for someone had shoved him out of the way—he did not know who—and had charged inside and completed the task he should have done himself. Ashamed, he had wandered around the back of the barn, where his mother had found him, snivelling like a baby, afraid his love had perished, and all because of his faint-heartedness.

"Come on, son, give us a hand." His father's voice broke his reverie. Maybe he could be of some use. "Go and check inside the house, will you, to see what damage has been done in there."

That would not take too much effort. The sight of his cowardliness blocked from his brain, he entered the house. The kitchen looked fine. No damage there. The front lounge wouldn't have been affected, it would have been the rooms at the back. Upstairs, he opened the door of his bedroom. Flames shot out. He screamed and slammed it again, raced downstairs and yelled to the firemen packing up their hoses, "It's still alight. My bedroom's on fire."

His mother ran over to him. "Are you burnt, son? Your face is black."

"No, Ma, I'm fine." He wiped his sleeve across his face. "I shut the door before it had chance to catch me."

The firemen ran across and set their hoses up to the window. The glass smashed, sending flames pothering out, as the head fireman yelled to one of the others, "Who was supposed to check that room? I thought it had been declared safe."

His mother shepherded him across the farmyard. "Come away, son. We don't want to hinder them."

"Aw, Ma, I hope they can put it out. Our house. Where will we live?"

"We'll worry about that if and when. Why don't you bring in the cows? They'll need milking soon."

"But I won't be able to milk them, not with these blasted hands."

"No, I know you won't. But you can at least have them here ready. I shall have to help young Jessica."

"Yes, Ma. Oh, what have we done to deserve all this heartache?"

"I don't know, son. I really don't. Let's pray Charlotte pulls through. At least something positive will come of it, then."

"I have been praying. I really have. I…" He had been about to declare his love, but decided against doing so. It was not the right time or place.

He had plenty of time to ponder on his actions as he herded in the black and white cows.

"Steady, Marigold," he called to one with white legs and face, as she almost stumbled, catching her hoof in a rabbit hole. He knew the names of most of them, all named after flowers.

With the help of his stick, he steered them into the adjacent field and closed the gate behind him, because they would be in the way if the fire engine still stood in the farmyard.

He couldn't see any flames coming out of his bedroom window so, hopefully, the fire had been extinguished. He wondered what damage had been done. He didn't have many possessions, but he had a memento of Charlotte hidden at the back of his bedside cabinet—a handkerchief she had once dropped in the farmyard. He had thought about giving it back, but had kept it, taking it out whenever he thought about her in bed. Even though it was grubby, he slept with it under his pillow during the night and then hid it each morning, so his mother would not find it. She would only think him a milksop and tell him to give it back.

If Charlotte didn't pull through it would be the only reminder he would have of her, since he had been unable to retrieve the locket containing one of her hairs his brother had seen him kissing at the gully.

Herbert had taunted him and knocked it out of his hand, sending it flying over the edge. Ronnie had punched him and run off, uncaring if Herbert had fallen over the edge. He deserved to be dead.

Ronnie felt sure he had not, though, so could not understand why he had been found dead. He certainly could not tell anyone about it, especially that constable.

Jessica came up behind him. "Your poor mother!" She hugged herself. "As if she doesn't have enough to contend with."

"Yes, indeed. We must all pull together to help out. Can I do anything in the dairy?"

"Well, I've already done everything I can. I'm not sure how to make the butter. Do you know?"

"No, I'm sorry. I could, perhaps, roll the churns." Could he do that with his hands in such a state? But she shouldn't be doing it, not in her condition.

"I've already done them." A grimace twitched her lips. "They aren't too heavy." Tucking a curl into her mobcap, she began to walk away. "I had better see what your mother wants me to do now."

"I'll come with you."

They found his mother with a hen under her arm.

"What are you doing with that?" asked Ronnie.

"She's stopped laying, so we may as well have chicken for dinner tonight, that's if we can use the kitchen."

"I love chicken. We have it quite a lot at my Aunt Elizabeth's." Jessica smiled as she stroked the hen's head. "In fact, I think it fair to say we almost live on it."

"I suppose you do. You need to eat plenty of protein in your condition, I always say."

"Yes, Mrs Grant." Jessica turned to Ronnie and pulled a face.

He grinned. His mother liked to preach. It was one of her less endearing qualities.

They entered the kitchen, the chicken quite happily in the crook of her arm, not realising its fate.

"Oh, the range has gone out," she moaned as she passed him the chicken. "Wring its neck, will you? I shall have to light this if we want a meal tonight."

"Me?" The bird clucked as he looked at it, as though aghast.

Had it understood?

"Yes, you used to when you were younger."

"Would you like me to do it?" suggested Jessica. "I've done it loads of times."

With a straight back, he replied, "No, it's fine."

A slip of a girl would not better him.

Chapter 13

Martha sat beside Charlotte, trying to keep her eyes open. Would someone have fed Amy and Tommy? She hadn't had chance to ask anyone, but felt sure the neighbours would have done. They always rallied round in an emergency. When would the doctor be coming to examine her sister? They had been there ages and she did not know how much longer she could bear the stench of sick patients, all crammed in together. One woman coughed incessantly while a little girl, dressed only in a grimy petticoat, with no dress, let alone a coat or shawl, sneezed and spluttered. Other people had blood-soaked, makeshift bandages covering their heads or arms or legs. Fear that she might leave with some horrendous illness filled her with foreboding, even more than the worry that she had no money if anyone asked for a payment for her sister's treatment.

Charlotte stirred.

Martha jumped up. "Charlotte, are you awake?"

"Mm."

"Oh, thank God for that."

"Where am I?"

"You're in the hospital. Ah, at last, someone's coming to see to you." She stood aside as two men—doctors, she assumed—pushed their way through to them.

"How are you feeling, young lady?" asked the taller one. He looked several years older than the other. She thought the young one would probably be a trainee. He didn't look old enough to be out of short trousers. How could he know anything?

"My arm hurts." Charlotte lifted it up to show him.

"Mm, it's quite badly burned. Anywhere else?" He

felt along her body.

"Only my head."

"It looks as if you've banged it. Can you recall what happened?"

With a glance at Martha, she replied with a frown, "I seem to remember smelling smoke and when I went into the barn…" She began to cough, so the younger doctor passed her a glass of water. After a mouthful, she handed it back, leaning her head back on the pillows. "I saw Mary," she muttered, then became agitated, as if it hurt her to breathe.

The doctor wrote something on a sheet of paper. "Don't try to speak any more. We can find out later. The police will want to speak to you both."

Oh, heck, thought Martha. *They'll want to know who rescued her. I'll just have to say I don't know.*

"What do you think we should give her for the pain?" the older doctor asked the younger one.

"Laudanum?" The young man seemed as if he couldn't take his blue eyes off the pretty patient. Martha had done her best to wash Charlotte's grimy face while she had been waiting, so her beauty was evident.

"Yes, I agree, if the patient would like some?"

Charlotte nodded.

"Who is your next of kin?"

"Um…" a puzzled expression crossed her face. "I don't know."

"I'm her older sister. Both our parents are dead," volunteered Martha.

Apparently satisfied, he nodded. "If you could give your details to the nurse, ma'am…"

"Yes, Doctor." No nurse in sight, she assumed one would be along later, and gave a sigh of relief that neither of them had mentioned payments.

After they had gone, agog to find out what her sister had been trying to say—something about Mary—she opened her mouth to ask, but Charlotte seemed to have nodded off, so she tried to make her more comfortable in the hard chair. What would the former milkmaid have been doing in the barn? Surely she had not started the fire?

Her stomach rumbled. How long would she be there? She should have asked the doctor. While Charlotte slept, she thought she would go and find out.

A patient shouting obscenities at the top of his voice attracted her attention and she wandered towards the room, clearly the men's ward, and found a nurse administering an injection to him. The man quietened down as Martha went across. She had never been inside a hospital before so was unsure if she should enter a man's ward but, when nobody stopped her, she proceeded farther inside.

"Excuse me, Nurse. My sister, Charlotte Bridge, do you know how long she'll be staying? Only, I need to go home to my children, and I don't have the foggiest idea how I'm going to do that. I don't have any money for a hansom cab, and I don't know if the person who brought us is still around, I didn't think to ask him to wait…" Her ranting tailed off as another patient called the nurse, and she hurried across to him, giving Martha an apologetic smile.

The poor woman doesn't have time to listen to my woes, she thought. But she did need to know if her sister would have to stay overnight. Most probably, so she waited for a moment, glancing around at the crowded ward, every squashed-in bed taken up, some with men who moaned and writhed in apparent agony, others with no apparent injury, so most likely suffering from a disease. Like she had thought earlier, she didn't want to catch anything, so hastened towards the doorway.

Another nurse sauntered in, this one clearly not so busy. Martha collared her. "Excuse me…" She explained her predicament again.

"Which ward is she in?" asked the nurse, not

seeming interested. She looked tired. Maybe she had been working since the early hours. Martha didn't know anything about nurses' working conditions, but thought they would probably be harsh.

She indicated to the open door across the corridor. "That room over there where she's been since we arrived."

The nurse sighed but followed her. Martha pointed out her sister.

"I'll see what I can find out for you." The nurse walked away, her shoulders sagging.

Martha wanted to run after her and tell her not to bother, that she didn't want to be a nuisance, but she had to know. Though how would she find her way home, a good ten miles away? Dusk could already be approaching so she would need to start as soon as possible, and even then she wouldn't arrive until the early hours of the morning.

Charlotte's arm had been bandaged while she had been away, but she still sat in the uncomfortable-looking chair.

That was quick, she thought, watching her sleep.

Charlotte's mouth twitched and her eyes beneath her eyelids rolled from side to side, as if disturbed by a bad dream.

"I really ought to stay with you in case you have nightmares," she murmured as she stroked her cheek. "The nurses won't have time to comfort you. But I have to return to Amy and Tommy. They need me as well, especially with their pa…"

A sudden recollection of a busty barmaid she had caught him ogling a few months back in the village came into her mind. He had better not be with her! Surely not? He wouldn't do that to her, would he? But why hadn't he come home? Why pretend to be dead? There had to be another explanation.

"Ma'am?" The nurse who had gone off had

returned. "Yes, your sister will have to remain in the hospital for a while, possibly weeks, so we'll find a bed for her somewhere. I shall take your details and you'll be free to go."

"Thank you, Nurse." She kissed Charlotte's cheek. "She will recover, won't she? I mean…"

"Yes, ma'am, her injuries are only minor. She's a lucky girl." The nurse blinked, as if having trouble staying awake.

Martha felt sorry for her—all those sick and wounded people to attend to. She followed her to a side room and gave her all Charlotte's information. The woman did not mention if she would have to pay, so she did not bring up the subject.

"Thank you, Nurse. I'll be off, then." Much as she would have loved to wait and see her sister wrapped up in a clean, comfy bed, she had to leave, so tied her bonnet.

"Actually, it's 'Sister'."

What did she mean? "I know she's my sister. I told you that."

"I mean that's my title. Aren't you going to wait for the police?"

"No, as I told you, my children are on their own, and I need to…" She had already explained once, surely she did not need to repeat it? "Will Charlotte be fed while she's here? And what about clean clothes? I won't be able to bring her any. It's too far away. And how will we know when she's ready to come home?"

The nurse—or sister, whatever she called herself— patted her arm. "Don't worry, my dear. Everything will be fine. We'll tend to all your sister's needs, so off you go."

"Thank you. That's a load off my mind."

The sun had gone behind a large black cloud as she stepped outside. "Oh, no, that's all I need—rain," she murmured. "Without a shawl, let alone a coat."

It had been so hot when she had left home that morning, she hadn't needed one.

From the hospital entrance she could see the town below. A creamy-coloured crescent-shaped building drew her attention, and she wondered what it could be. Close by stood another large building with a glass extension on the side. Maybe one day, she would come back and investigate them if Charlotte stayed long enough.

Unsure which direction she should take, for she had never visited the town before, she stopped a smart, elderly gentleman and asked him.

He took off his hat and scratched his head. "Lea Croft? Cannot say as I have heard of it, ma'am. Is it near Ashbourne?"

"No, not really."

"Well, I am sorry, then, I cannot help you. Good day." With a curt nod, he replaced his hat and continued on his way.

Further along, she came to a signpost. One way indicated Ashbourne and the other Bakewell. Knowing she lived quite close to Bakewell, she took that route. Before long, the town of Buxton had been left behind, the black clouds had blown over and she could enjoy the beautiful countryside views. After a mile or so, she found a stream and stopped to take a drink of the cool, clear water. Cupping her hands together to form a bowl, she washed her face and, refreshed, but even hungrier, she continued on her way. Stopping wouldn't solve her problem. She needed to make a move.

Several people on horseback cantered past her. What she would give to have the use of a horse or a pony. Even the donkey she could see in the field ahead would do. Dare she? No, it would be stealing. But she could bring it back at a later date. It would only be borrowing. The donkey brayed and ambled over to her as she stood at the gate and scanned her surroundings.

"You want to come with me, don't you, old fellow? You want to help a tired, defenceless woman."

"Hey!" a voice shouted from the other side of the

hedge as she began to open the gate.

Drat! She had been discovered. As she refastened the gate, she smiled at the man. "Good day, sir. The weather is favourable, is it not?"

"Yes, ma'am, I agree. Good day to you. But why were you opening my gate?"

"Oh, just…" What could she say? "I happened to be passing and your donkey took a liking to me. What's his name?" She reached through the bars and stroked its mane.

"He doesn't have one."

"Doesn't have a name? That's awful. Every living thing should have a name. How about Tommy, after my son?" Why on earth was she wasting time here with this man? She needed to be on her way. Borrowing the donkey would evidently not be an option, unless… "You look a sympathetic man, sir. I don't suppose you would consider… But no, never mind. I wish you good day."

"I can be sympathetic, ma'am. What were you about to ask of me?"

"Well…" She explained what had happened, making it sound ten times worse. Exaggeration came easily to her on such occasions. She removed a handkerchief from her apron pocket and dabbed at her eyes, forcing a pathetic tone into her voice. "So you see my dilemma, sir."

He took off his cap. "I'm sorry, ma'am, but I can't afford to lend you this donkey. I need him to pull my cart. I'm a very poor farmer."

"I'm sorry to have bothered you, sir."

His eyes lit up. He looked her up and down and a lascivious leer crossed his face. "But I could see my way to helping out, if the lady knows what I mean."

His meaning dawned on her. "No, sir, I do not know what you have in mind, but whatever it is, I will not be a party to it. Good day."

Appalled, she gathered up her petticoats and hurried away, eager to put distance between them. How on earth could he have thought such a thing? She heard him cackle behind her, but daren't turn around to see if he followed her, in case he took it as an invitation to comply with his devilish plan. The journey would be more difficult then she had imagined, even though it had not grown as dark as she had expected.

After rounding a bend in the road, she stopped and drew in several deep breaths, bent over, her hands on her knees. A stunning view ahead of her caught her off guard as she looked up. Rugged hills, covered in purple heather and tall pine trees, growing from stone cliffs, interspersed with green fields, with cows and sheep dotted about, and a river meandering through the middle, fell away for miles, in fact, as far as the eye could see.

She dragged her eyes from the picturesque scene as hoof beats sounded, coming her way. She ran and hid behind a tree, in case it could be the vile donkey man. Through the low branches, she peeped out. Female voices drifted towards her. She could relax.

Two ladies came into view, one wearing a dark green coat and skirt, with a natty hat to match, the other in light blue. They both giggled at something one of them said and pulled up as Martha stepped out in front of them.

"Whoa," cried the one in green as her chestnut horse reared, almost unseating her. With a yank of the reins, she swivelled him around. "What the devil do you mean, ma'am, stepping out in front of us like that?"

"I'm so sorry, ma'am. I didn't think."

"You are not from these parts, are you?"

"No, I…" Should she explain what had happened yet again? No point. The ladies wouldn't be able to help her. She shook her head, repeating, "No."

"So what are you doing, skulking behind trees?" asked the one in blue, a pretty lady, about her age.

With a glance back the way she had come, to make sure the evil man had not followed, she decided to relate her story.

"How wretched for you." The lady cocked her leg over the pommel and slid down to the ground, saying to the other one, "We were just wondering what we could do today, weren't we, Agnes? Maybe we could help the lady."

Her friend did not look convinced. She stayed in her saddle, a frown creasing her brow. "Now, Emmie, don't you go getting ideas into your pretty little head. How can we do anything?"

"Don't be so hoity toity, there must be something." She pulled at her lower lip, then exclaimed, "I know. She could sit behind me."

"Don't be so silly," replied the one called Agnes. "How would she fit behind you, when you need all your balance to keep in your saddle?"

"I could...no... I was going to say I could straddle, but with the pommel in the way, it would be too awkward."

Martha looked from one to the other. "Please, ladies, do not put yourselves out. I shall be fine."

"No, no." The one called Emmie took hold of her arm. "We must look after the less fortunate in our society. It is our duty."

Well, thank you, ma'am. 'Less fortunate' could be her situation, but the lady did not need to express it with such patronisation. "Pray, ma'am, please do not worry about me. I don't want to impose." She yanked her arm away and started to walk off, still riled at the young lady's attitude.

"Now you have offended her," she heard the one called Agnes say. "I think you should apologise."

There was no time to listen to their arguments, for she needed to be on her way.

The one called Emmie ran after her. "Please, ma'am, I did not mean any harm. My mama always tells me I should bite my tongue before I speak. Please let us help you."

Inhaling deeply, Martha stopped.

"I could sit behind my cousin. She uses an ordinary saddle, and you could use my mare. She is very docile. You should not have any trouble riding her."

"Ma'am, I'm unused to riding, have not done so for years, and never in a saddle like yours, so…"

"But it is easy, is it not, Agnes?" The lady pulled her towards the brown mare that did look tame, as it chomped at the grass on the verge.

Her cousin turned her own horse about. It didn't seem nearly as amenable. "If the lady does not wish to be helped, then let her be on her way, Emmie. You cannot be in command of everyone, much as you would like to be."

Emmie looked offended. "I don't, I just want to be of assistance." She turned back to Martha. "Is it not worth a try? If you cannot manage it, then you will not have lost anything, will you?"

Only my time, thought Martha. *I could have been a mile closer to home by now.*

"See that log over there." Emmie took hold of the reins and steered her towards the log a few yards farther along the road. "Just lift your skirt. Nobody is looking."

Martha took a deep breath, convinced she would not manage to climb on. Surprised when she managed to first time, she sat on top of the horse, gripping tightly onto the pommel, as Emmie handed her the reins. Certain she would fall off as soon as the mare moved, she held her breath. She jerked, but held on.

Emmie clapped her hands in glee as she jumped up and down. "See, you can do it."

"I'm still not sure." Why had she agreed to play along with this caper? It would not help her cause, just delay her. Jessica would not have been led into something she didn't feel confident with. She would have just said a resounding 'No' and walked on. Oh, to be like her youngest sister sometimes. But, on the other hand, she would probably have been up for the experience. She would always be ready for new adventures.

They began trotting. Maybe she could do it, after all. She had not fallen off. Not yet, at any rate, although she still didn't feel safe.

Emmie climbed up behind her cousin and they soon caught up. "How are you coping...um...I don't know your name?"

"It's Martha, Martha Holloway, and I haven't fallen off yet, so I'm not doing too badly." Actually, once she had gained some momentum, she realised she could move rhythmically with the mare's steps, and found it quite a pleasurable experience.

"See, Martha, what did I tell you?" The cousins rode past at a faster pace, and were soon around the next bend. Martha daren't go too fast, so trotted along at a more leisurely speed.

They arrived at the town of Bakewell and the two ladies in front pulled up. "How far is it from here?" asked Agnes.

"Only a few miles, I can walk if you are eager to return home." To tell the truth, even though she had managed to stay in the saddle, her thighs chaffed.

"I think we had better. We have come much farther than we usually do."

Emmie slid down from behind her cousin. "Oo," she exclaimed, "I can't walk straight." She tottered drunkenly towards Martha, her legs apart. "I'm not used to riding in such a fashion."

Martha tried to keep a smile from her face at the sight of the aristocratic girl lolloping along like a clown she had once seen at a circus.

Agnes dismounted as well. Her laughter rang out. She obviously didn't have any qualms about upsetting her. "I knew you would have your come-uppance one of these days, Emmie. Your benevolence has just bested you."

Trying to stand up straight, Emmie stuck out her

tongue.

"That is not very ladylike." Her cousin laughed again as she offered her hand to Martha.

Martha wasn't sure what to do. "How do I dismount?" She didn't fancy dropping down in a heap.

"Just lift one leg over the pommel. We will catch you." Agnes pulled her cousin closer. "Won't we, Emmie?"

At the pain in the younger girl's eyes, Martha could not be too sure. She did as instructed, though, and slid to the ground. Her legs could hardly support her and she daren't move, let alone try to walk. No wonder Emmie waddled around in such a manner, she must have been in the same boat. Clinging on to the saddle, she gritted her teeth.

"You look in a worse state than me." Emmie smiled. "Whatever will your husband say when he can't—?"

"Ermentrude!" Agnes screamed. "Behave. Please do not disgrace yourself by saying what I think you were about to say."

Rather than focusing on what the girl had—or had not—intended saying, Martha hid her face in the mare's flanks, trying desperately to stop herself laughing. Ermentrude? What a name! No wonder she was called 'Emmie' for short.

"What?" The girl said innocently. "I had only been going to say—"

"We do not want to hear it." Agnes touched Martha's arm. "Do you think you will be able to walk now?"

"I shall try." She gingerly let go of the horse's bridle, shook one leg, and then the other. Straightening them was the problem, and standing upright. Her shoulders back, she took a few tentative steps, rather wobbly ones, but made it without falling flat on her face.

"I had better see if I can manage to stay in my saddle," declared Emmie, still looking rather shaky. Agnes cupped her hands for her to put her foot in and pushed her up. A grimace on her pretty face, she made herself comfortable.

Martha noticed one or two passers-by stopping to watch. She tried to ignore them, as she took several more tottery steps.

"I cannot thank you enough," she muttered, a smile pinned onto her face, "for helping me. You have saved me no end of time with your generosity." She wondered if she would have been better off walking, but she had to show her gratitude, had to appear mannerly.

"I hope you reach home before dusk," called Agnes as she waved and cantered away. Emmie, or Ermentrude, merely waved before following her cousin.

Martha wondered why she should be in so much pain, when clearly used to riding, but probably not bareback with a saddle stuck in her belly.

The sun had dipped low on the horizon. Would she make home before it set? A cool wind had blown up, ruffling her bonnet and already dishevelled hair, so she took off the bonnet and tucked the loose strands behind her ears. At least it took her mind off her sore legs.

By the time she reached the outskirts of the village, exhaustion almost overcame her. After the traumatic day, she just wanted to drop into her comfy bed. Too tired to even fancy any food, she hoped the children would be safely tucked up in their beds so she could retire as well.

Chapter 14

All seemed quiet as Martha opened the back door. "Thank goodness," she murmured.

"Where have you been 'til this time?"

She jumped at her husband's voice. "Blinkin' Ada, why are you sitting in the dark?" she exclaimed, her heart pounding.

"I'm waiting for my wife."

"I've been with our Charlotte at the hospital in Buxton. You know that. You saw me go in the cart. Anyway, how come you've dragged yourself out of hiding?"

He jumped up and grabbed her arm. "Someone had to look after our children, seeing as you deserted them."

"I didn't 'desert' them." She yanked her arm away. "I had to tend to my sister. She has nobody else. What did you expect me to do? Leave her to go on her own? She was barely conscious. How would you like to wake up in a strange place, not knowing where you were, or how you arrived there?"

"Couldn't your other sister have gone?"

"Jessica? In her condition? Don't be so stupid."

He slapped her face. "Don't you call me stupid, woman. I've laid my life on the line, coming here."

Fearful that her lip had begun to bleed, anger brewed up inside her. After all she had been through, the last thing she needed was her husband venting his spleen on her. "That's the last time you hit me, Charles Holloway." She grabbed his sleeve and thrust him with all her might out the door, slammed it behind her, and pushed the bolt in place before he could reopen it.

Leaning back against it, she crumpled. What would she do now?

He thumped on the door. "Let me in, you bitch. You'll suffer for this."

"Go away, Charlie. Go back to that hole you've crawled out of. Or that woman you've been shacking up with. We don't need you. Me and the children can manage quite well on our own."

"Let me in! I'll break down this blasted door if I have to." He whacked it again. She hoped the hinges on the old wood would hold.

Tommy came downstairs, rubbing his eyes. "Mam, who's that shouting outside? It sounds like our Pa."

She pulled him towards her. "Yes, darling, it is."

"But he's dead...well, I didn't think he was, but everyone said he was."

"I know..."

"He sounds really angry. Why? Why won't you let him in?"

"Is that our Tommy?" Charlie thumped again. "Tommy, lad, open the door. It's your pa."

Tommy looked up at Martha. "Mam?"

She shook her head. "No, son, don't let him in."

"Your lip's bleeding."

"Um, I know." She dabbed at it with the back of her hand. "Go back to bed, there's a good boy."

"But, Mam, what about Pa?"

"Leave him to me, sweetheart. Don't you worry your little head about him. He's gone too far this time." She nudged him towards the stairs and he reluctantly went back up, looking over his shoulder every other step. She nodded each time, gesturing for him to continue. "I'll be up in a few minutes. Don't worry."

The door rattled as Charlie banged on it again.

She shouted through it, "Go away, or I'll tell the police I saw you kill Herbert Grant."

"You wouldn't. You couldn't have."

Ah, she thought, *have I found him out?* He had almost admitted it.

"You can't have seen me, because I didn't do it."

"A likely story. So why have you been in hiding for the past few days? Just leave us alone."

The hammering stopped. She put her ear to the wood to see if she could hear him leaving. It seemed like it. A breath of relief released, she slumped into a chair, all feelings of tiredness vanishing.

All of a sudden, the door to the front room opened and he stormed in. She had not realised the front door had been unlocked. How stupid could she have been!

Her hands in front of her face, she cringed against the kitchen wall, but he wrenched them down and hit the side of her head with an almighty wallop, sending her falling to the floor. She curled up into a ball, expecting his boot, or at least his fist again, but neither came. Instead, she heard him rooting in a drawer. The sound of knives clinking against each other had her jumping up. She ran into the front room and hauled the armchair against the inner door, before running to lock the front one.

"Please, God, make him go away," she prayed as she leant against it. But perhaps it would be better to just leave the house, go as far away as possible, until he calmed down. But she couldn't do that. What about the children upstairs? Surely he wouldn't hurt them? In his present state, though, she couldn't be certain. She had never seen him that incensed before.

What should she do? For sure, she couldn't go back into the kitchen. Maybe if she waited, he would become bored and leave. She climbed onto the armchair she had moved and listened for movements. Could that be the boards creaking on the stairs? Tommy coming back down? If so, she had to stop him. As she shoved the armchair away, a scream rent the air. She opened the door and hurtled up the steep stairs, two at a time.

Charlie stepped out onto the landing, holding the limp body of her son.

"Nooooo," she screamed, "not my baby."

Tears fell down her husband's cheeks. "I didn't mean to do it."

She spat in his face, snatched her son from him, cradling him like a baby, and took him into the bedroom. Amy lay curled up in a ball on her bed, her thumb in her mouth, rocking to and fro.

His nightshirt covered in blood, she laid Tommy on the other bed, and touched his forehead. It felt warm, as did his cheeks. She pressed her cheek to his mouth to see if she could sense any breathing, but couldn't be sure.

"Is his chest moving?" The voice from the doorway made her cringe.

"What do you care, you murderer?" she sneered.

"I didn't mean to do it."

"So you said, but how can you stab your own son without intending to harm him? Why did you even take a knife up there? Just leave. I never want to see your ugly face again, except when they hang you."

He moved towards them.

"Leave us alone," she screamed, making Amy cry. Martha leapt up and scooped her up, sat down next to Tommy, her daughter on her knee, and crooned in her ear.

Charlie turned to go. "I'll go and fetch someone."

She didn't reply. She had spoken her last words to him, ever.

Her elderly next-door neighbour, Mrs Lancaster, rushed in and tried to prise Amy from her, but she clung on. She could see blood stains on Amy's nightshirt, and also on the front of her own dress. Were they her daughter's?

"Did your pa hurt you too, darling?" she yelled as she tried to disentangle her fingers. "Let me look. I need to know if you've…"

Sick to the stomach as the neighbour helped her lift the child's nightshirt over her head, she held her breath. Lily white. No sign of any wounds. A huge sigh of relief escaped her as she enveloped the little girl once more.

"What about the boy?" The neighbour bent down to touch him. "Is he dead?"

"No, no, he can't be, not my Tommy." She had to convince herself. She could not believe the unthinkable. She turned to the lady. "Did you see that?"

"What?"

"His hand moved."

Mrs Lancaster shook her head. "It's more than likely only a tremor. It happens, sometimes. It doesn't mean…"

"But there it is again." She felt sure that time. "Look."

More neighbours had appeared. Martha looked up, astonished at how full the little room had become. She gestured to them. "He's not dead. Look, he's moving."

She gathered him up in her arms and buried her face in his hair, whispering in his ear, "You can make it, my little Tom-tom. Please, for your mam, hang on."

A man, whom she recognised as the apothecary, prised him away from her. "Let me examine him, Mrs Holloway."

Her charge released, she pushed people out of the way so she could watch. Where had so many folks come from? She didn't recognise some of them.

"Well, Mrs Holloway, your son has had a lucky escape." The apothecary straightened his back. "I don't think the wound has severed any arteries or punctured any vital organs. He is a lucky boy."

"Oh, thank you, sir. Thank you so much."

"He will need complete rest and quiet." With a pointed look at the mass of people crowding the little room, he continued, "And he should make a complete recovery." He took out a bandage and padding from his case and wrapped it around the little body.

"Mam," whispered Tommy, his voice husky and weak.

"I'm here, son. You're going to be fine."

"Pa, he…" He raised his arms to her, and she gripped him in as tight an embrace as she dared.

"I know, son. I won't let him near you ever again. I promise."

The apothecary shooed everybody out and left Martha with her children. She sat humming to them, until Tommy began to moan. "It hurts, Mam. It hurts so much."

"I'll go and catch the apothecary and ask him for something to take away the pain, my darling." She didn't have any money, so could not be sure what he would say. Charlie had not paid the weekly penny to the public dispensary for ages. She had badgered him, but because they never had illnesses, he had insisted it was a waste. He would rather spend the money on beer.

As she stroked her son's hair back from his face she told him, "Just wait here."

"I will, Mam. I don't think I'll ever leave my bed again." His eyes closed as he screwed up his face.

Amy lay on her bed, still sucking her thumb, her eyes also closed. Martha bent down and gave her a kiss on the cheek, and the little girl snuggled under her blankets.

The apothecary stood talking to one of the neighbours in the kitchen. The others had gone.

"Please, sir, is there anything you could give our Tommy for the pain? I don't have any money for laudanum or anything like that. He's trying to put on a brave face, but I can tell he's suffering."

"He will be, Mrs Holloway, but, like I said, he is fortunate. I shall let his blood. That should help. Your neighbour was just telling me your husband stabbed him. Is that correct? I shall have to inform the authorities."

Before she could reply, a knock came on the door, and the constable poked his head around it.

"Oh, you've saved me the trouble, Constable. Come on in."

Surprised that the doctor should have the temerity to

invite the policeman in, Martha let it pass. He would have come in, anyway. She turned to the doctor. "About my Tommy, please, I would like him to be made comfortable before I speak to the law."

"Yes, of course. I shall go up and see to him now. What about your daughter?"

"She isn't in any pain, but she seems traumatised."

"Did she witness it?"

As she nodded, she saw the policeman take out his trusty notebook. "I shall start writing things down, Mrs Holloway, but I need to take a full statement."

"Yes, sir, in a moment. Pray, take a seat."

Martha accompanied the apothecary upstairs. Both children lay as she had left them.

Tommy tried to sit up. "Can I sleep with you tonight, Mam?"

Amy opened her eyes and whispered, "Me, too?"

"Yes, of course. Let me find you something to wear." She rummaged in the drawer and found them clean white nightshirts, before kicking the bloody ones under the bed. "I'll settle you both in my bed when the apothecary has finished with you, Tommy, but then I have to go and speak to the policeman. He's waiting downstairs."

The doctor took out his blood-letting kit and turned towards Tommy. The boy shrank back, a look of alarm on his face.

"It will make you better, sweetheart. Don't be afraid." Martha had never needed the horrible looking creature, so prayed it would work. She cringed at the bottom of the bed as the leech was attached to her son's bony arm.

Amy cuddled up to her. "What's he doing, Mam? Why has he put that slug on our Tommy?"

"It isn't a slug, my dear," answered the apothecary. "It is a leech. They suck the blood, and take away the foulness of the humours that invade the body when

179

someone is unwell."

Amy pulled a face. "Does it hurt, our Tommy?"

After the initial squeal of—she hadn't known if it was pain or disgust or fear—he lay, staring up at the ceiling as stiff as a board, as if he daren't move.

"It should not do so," replied the apothecary for him. "Some of my patients express instant relief, others, well..."

Martha was more concerned with how she could pay the man. She had no money at all, for she hadn't been paid by the farmer. "Would you like a cup of tea or something?" she asked. Although not payment of cash, it might make him more amenable. "I had better go down and speak to the constable. He might like one as well."

Tommy found his tongue. Still staring upwards, he called out, "Don't leave me, Mam."

"Amy will stay with you, my darling, won't you?" She prised her daughter from her leg, and looked into her face.

Her daughter shook her head. "No, I want to come with you."

What should she do? "It will only be for a minute or two. The nice apothecary will stay here." She turned to the man. "How long does it take?"

"We have almost finished. Yes, it must be full." He held his bowl under Tommy's arm and the leech dropped into it.

"Ugh," chuntered Amy. "I hope I never need one of them."

"I hope so too. You'll be fine, now, Tommy, but I'll stay with you a while longer. The constable will have to wait. You're more important."

* * * *

Ronnie sat up and stretched. The sofa was not the most comfortable place to sleep. His long, lanky legs, curled up to his chin, had soon become numb, and draping them over the arm of the couch had given him pins and needles. Easier to give up.

His clothes and the few books he owned had all been damaged, even the handkerchief, although he had managed to salvage a small corner of it whilst everybody else had been occupied with other things.

The door in the clock on the wall opened, and the little cuckoo came out and announced five o'clock as his father came downstairs, tucking his shirt into his trousers. No point asking if he could borrow any of his clothes. He would look ridiculous with trousers halfway up his legs.

His mother joined them. She yawned. "Oh, our Ronnie, I'll have to ask around if anyone has any spare clothes, lad. Those will do for today, but just look at the state of them!"

"It doesn't matter, Ma. At least we still have the house. It could have been so much worse."

His father opened the back door. "You're right, lad."

"I'll come with you, Pa, and bring in the cows." He gave his mother a kiss.

"Oh, good lad. Your breakfast will be ready on your return."

On the way to the fields, he murmured to this father, hoping his voice sounded casual, "I wonder how Miss Charlotte fares."

"Um, the policeman said it looked as if Mary Howard must have started the fire and not been able to escape. It's a rum deal, that it is." He took out his pipe and stopped to light it. After taking a deep drag, he offered it to Ronnie who shook his head. He had never had the inclination to smoke. The only time he had tried it, he had ended up having a coughing fit, so had never bothered again.

"You don't know what you're missing, lad. You can't beat a good baccy."

While the birds sang around them and the hills in

the distance reflected the morning sun, they walked on in silence, and then Ed remarked, "Have you heard anything about our Herbert's killer?"

His father had not spoken to him about it before. Taken aback, he replied, "No, I haven't, what with the hullabaloo yesterday, and everything. I wonder if they have any suspects."

Ed turned to face him with raised eyebrows. "Do you have any inkling as to who it could be?"

"Me, Pa? Why do you ask that?"

"Don't look so guilty, son. I wasn't suggesting it could be you."

He let out his breath. "Thank goodness, for a moment I wondered…"

"No, son, although I wouldn't have blamed you." He gave Ronnie's arm a nudge. "I know it couldn't have been you. You're much too agreeable, although you two never did have much in common, did you?"

His red face downcast, Ronnie hurried forward to open the gate to the field where the cows grazed, calling, "I'll see you later, Pa," as his father continued up the track, deep in thought.

Surely he didn't see me? thought Ronnie as he drove the herd homeward. As far as the police knew, his father had been the last person to see his brother alive, but he could not allow him to take the blame. He would have to own up.

Jessica had arrived by the time he drove the cows into the farmyard. He ran over and asked, "Any news on your sister?"

"No, I expect Martha will tell us when she comes. I do pray she'll pull through."

"Me, too."

"Are you as soft on her as she is on you, Master Ronnie?" Without waiting for a reply she added, "I do believe you are. You're blushing. Oo, it's so romantic."

He looked around anxiously. "Please, don't say

anything to my ma. I know she won't approve."

"Why not? What's wrong with our Charlotte? Oh, I know. She doesn't have any money or position. She's just a lowly milkmaid. That's it, isn't it? She isn't good enough." She walked away, chuntering to herself.

Should he call her back and refute her allegations? But how could he deny them? Shoulders slumped, he walked towards the house, but noticed he hadn't locked the gate properly, and one of the cows had escaped. He lolloped after it and retrieved it. "I might have known it would be you, Marigold," he scolded her. "Whenever there's any bother, I can rely on you to have started it." He patted her rump, saying to the others, "Keep her in check, if you please, ladies. She's a troublemaker, for sure."

He received a general mooing for reply and laughed. "If that's a 'yes', I thank you."

His mother hurried out, wiping her hands down her apron. "Your breakfast's keeping warm in the oven. You'll have to help yourself. I need to assist Jessica. She does not have the experience to work alone." She ran towards the byre, but turned before entering. "Have you seen Mrs Holloway yet?"

"No, Ma. Maybe she's gone to the hospital to visit her sister." *Would that I could go,* he wished silently.

"Well, send her in here, if you would, when she does arrive." She disappeared into the cowshed while Ronnie went in search of his breakfast.

He opened the oven door and, with a towel, took out his plate. The heat from the plate travelled through the material into his hand and he almost dropped it as he lowered it to the table. The bacon and sausage slid off, but he picked it up and put it back, knowing the table would be clean enough to eat off. His mother always insisted on a spotless kitchen. Something about bacteria or germs she had heard about that could make you ill, and even kill a person.

Partial to bacon fat, he broke off a chunk of bread, wiped it across the plate to catch the grease before it congealed, and sat back, satiated, examining his hands. The tender left one still seeped puss.

"I'd better put some more ointment on it," he murmured as he opened the cupboard to find the jar. He wiped his knife on his sleeve, dug some out, applied a blob in the middle of his hand, and closed his fist to spread it, before doing the same to the burst blisters on his other hand.

Now, to find a clean bandage. Where would they be kept? No sign in the medicine cupboard. Maybe in the drawer with the tea towels? No, not there, either.

"Oh, well, I'll just have to put the old one back on. It's rather pongy, but it'll do 'til Ma comes back." Unable to tie it with one hand, he gripped it with his fingers.

Could he reach the small remains of Charlotte's handkerchief in his left pocket? Certainly not with his left hand. With his right forefinger and thumb he fiddled about until he found it and pulled it out. The tension of not knowing anything about her condition reared up into his throat, and almost brought up his breakfast as he sniffed the small wad of material. Then he stood up and went to the door, looking out for her older sister. He could not see her along the lane. She should be there. Maybe she had gone straight to the byre, or the barn, or the dairy.

Not the dairy, likewise the barn. He entered the cowshed. Jessica seemed to be having trouble with one of the animals that wouldn't stand still. He went across and whispered in its ear.

"You just need to talk to her nicely," he told Jessica as the animal calmed down. "Treat her like a child."

"Huh…" Jessica retorted, "I know what I'd like to do with her. She's always the hardest one to milk. None of the others act up like she does."

He rubbed his closed fist gently over the cow's neck.

"I told you, Marigold, to be a good girl. Now behave. This young lady doesn't have time to—"

The cow let out a bellow.

"That's what she thinks," called his mother from the other side of the byre. "She doesn't like being told what to do, that one. She has a mind of her own."

The cow kicked out, and Jessica grabbed the pail before she could knock it over. "I give up, Mistress. You can milk her next time." She stood up, shooed the cow out the door and fetched in the next one, arching her back. Her large belly protruded even more in that position.

Ronnie tore his gaze from it when his mother asked after Mrs Holloway again.

"Should I go to her cottage and find out if she's coming today?" he asked. "There's not a lot else I can do around here."

"Yes, please, son. If she isn't coming, you'll have to help out. We'll never manage otherwise, unless you can find somebody else who would be willing. There must be someone in the village who wants to earn a penny or two."

"I'll see what I can find out." He went out and trotted along the lane. Damn, he hadn't asked about a clean bandage. Oh, well, he could do so on his return. And what about Faith? He hadn't seen her all morning, either.

Wilson, the idiot, came towards him. He took off his cap, revealing his bald head shining in the sun.

"Good day, Wilson."

"Good day, sir." Wilson shuffled his feet in the grass verge. "I heard screams."

"Did you? Where from?"

The man pointed back towards the village.

"Someone being murdered, do you think?" Ronnie laughed, intending it to be a joke.

"It sounded like it."

"Well, we had better go and investigate, hadn't we?" He steered him back the way he had come and they hurried on. "When were the screams, Wilson?"

"Last night."

He slowed down. "Oh, there's no need to hurry then. I thought you meant just now."

"I think it was young Master Tommy." Wilson stopped to catch his breath. "That's what Mrs Howard said."

Tommy? Mrs Holloway's son, the boy he had threatened? Could her lateness be blamed on another catastrophe? Her husband had never been found. Perhaps the boy had screamed because they had received news, bad news. He had better find out.

Leaving Wilson behind, he jogged to the Holloway's cottage and knocked on the open back door. When nobody came out after a minute he popped his head inside, calling, "Hello, is anyone in?"

A young fair-haired girl sat at the table, whimpering, her hands over her head.

He reached out to touch her shoulder, but decided he didn't want to alarm her. "Good day," he whispered. "Is your mama about?"

She shook her head.

"Well, is anyone else in?"

Another shake.

He noticed dirty pots beside the sink, solidified food stuck to them, and a half-drunk cup of tea in the middle of the table. It looked as if Mrs Holloway had left in a hurry. "Has your mama gone to see your Aunt Charlotte?"

The girl looked up. He racked his brain to remember her name, but it wouldn't come to mind. Her big blue eyes stared up at him in a disconcerting manner.

A cry from the bedroom above made him start. The girl stood up. "Coming, our Tommy," she called, moving towards the stairs.

"Is he poorly?" he asked.

Ignoring him, she hurried upstairs.

Where was their mother? He went outside. As he was about to go next door to ask if the neighbours knew anything, Wilson came puffing and panting down the entry. "Master Ronnie…"

He waited for the man to continue. "What, Wilson?" He knew he sounded impolite, but had to find out where the children's mother was.

"Police."

Nothing made sense. He nudged the man out of the way and went down the entry onto the street. Beside the constable, two other policemen marched towards him.

"Who are you and what are you doing in this house?" one of them asked, with no greeting or word of salutation.

He took off his cap, releasing his hold on the bandage. It dropped to the ground. As he stooped to pick it up, the policeman put his foot on it. "And what's this bloody item? How come you've left this house with blood on you?"

"It's for my hand. I injured it the other day."

"Doing what, may I ask?"

He couldn't tell them what he had been doing. "I…I fell." He held out his hand for them to see.

"A likely story. I shall have to question you, sir." He turned to the constable. "Do you know this man, Constable Jenkins?"

"Yes, sir, this is Ronald Grant, the farmer's son."

"And can you vouch for him? Did you know about this injury?"

The constable looked at Ronnie, and then back at the obviously senior man, as Ronnie tried to recall if he had made his wound evident when he had been interviewed about his brother's death.

"Well, sir, no I can't."

Ronnie closed his eyes as the senior officer turned to

the third officer. "Take him in for questioning, Constable."

"But, sir, I assure you I…"

"Silence, or do I have to handcuff you?"

"Handcuff? But, sir…"

Mrs Holloway came out of a house farther down the street, and ran up to them. "What's going on, Constable?"

"This man was seen exiting your house with blood on his person, ma'am. We have arrested him."

"But this is Ronnie, the son of my employer. He hasn't done anything. He had nothing to do with what happened."

"We just need to confirm that, ma'am." He turned once more to the constable. "Take him away."

Ronnie grabbed her arm. "Please, Mrs Holloway, please tell them I already had this cut. I've had it for days, haven't I?"

She looked up at the man and pleaded, "Yes, sir, it's true. That's partly why I've been working up at the farm. Please believe me. His mother has enough to contend with, without you arresting her other son for something he hasn't done."

"This is the brother of the murdered man, isn't it?"

She nodded.

"So he received this injury about the same time as the body was found?"

"Yes."

"Doesn't that sound suspicious to you?"

She looked puzzled. "No. His brother had been dead for weeks. How can a new injury have anything to do with his death?"

"That's what we need to ascertain, ma'am."

The third policeman marched Ronnie down the lane, so she saw no point fighting or protesting any longer.

He looked over his shoulder one last time and called, "Please tell my ma. She'll be worrying."

Chapter 15

Helpless that she had been unable to assist, Martha watched Ronnie disappear around the bend. "Please, Officer," she pleaded to Constable Jenkins, "Ronnie wouldn't hurt a fly. You had no need to arrest him like that."

"We have to investigate all possibilities, ma'am. We still have not found his brother's murderer."

"Well, you can't possibly suspect Ronnie, his own brother?"

"Stranger things have happened, ma'am. Most murders are committed by family members, so we find." Constable Jenkins ushered her up the entry. "May we come in and ask some more questions about your husband? And also about Mr Grant—Herbert, that was. I still have not interviewed you about him, and we do not want to conduct our business on the street."

"Yes, of course. I was just trying to find someone to watch the children. I must go to the farm. They won't be fed if I don't earn my crust, seeing as my husband—"

"Yes, ma'am, about your husband…"

The way he kept addressing her jarred on her already fragile nerves. She knew he had to be polite, but did he have to call her 'ma'am' every time he spoke?

They entered the kitchen. Amy flew down the stairs and wrapped her arms around her. "Ma, Tommy wants you."

"Yes, darling, in a moment."

"But he needs you now."

She gave an apologetic smile to the policemen, and gestured to them to sit down, before hurrying upstairs.

"Is he in pain?"

"No." Amy grimaced as they entered the room.

"He's…"

"Don't tell her," came a voice from under the blankets.

Martha pulled them back. "Tell me what?" Then she saw the wet sheet and nightshirt. "Oh, don't worry."

He tried to hide his face. "I'm sorry."

"Never mind, son. Don't beat yourself up about it. These things happen when you're poorly. Come on, let's change your clothes." She pulled his shirt over his head. "Lie on Amy's bed for now."

"Ugh, he'll make my bed smelly," her daughter retorted.

Martha's temper snapped. She flung the sodden sheet she had just pulled off the bed onto the floor and picked up her son, screaming to Amy, "You make his bed up with clean sheets, then, and you can bring all the dirty things downstairs and wash them yourself." She yanked out the bloody nightshirts that still lay under the bed from the night before, flung them at her daughter and stormed into her own bedroom, dropping Tommy onto her bed with more force than she intended. He yelped as he fell on his bad shoulder.

Desolate that she had added to his hurt, she burst into tears as she gathered him into her arms. "I'm so sorry, my darling Tom-tom. Please forgive me."

The second officer's voice came from the bottom of the stairs, "Is everything all right up there, ma'am?"

Trying to pull herself together, she called, "Yes, thank you, sir. I shall be down in a minute."

Tommy stirred with a pathetic look that tugged at her heart strings. "Mam, don't leave me."

As she stroked his hair, she took some deep breaths. "I must, my sweetheart." She covered him with her blanket and kissed his head. "I'll be as quick as I can. You try and catch up on some sleep. Would you like a drink of water first?"

"Yes, please." He snuggled into the covers but then

sat up again. "It still hurts."

"Oh, my darling. I know. You must be brave."

Amy poked her head around the door, a frown on her pretty face. "I've made the bed, Mam, but I don't know how to work the boiler."

Martha stood up and went across to put her arm around her shoulder. "I'm sorry, Amy, I didn't mean it. I was just angry. Leave them there. I'll do them later. But please fetch your brother a glass of water, there's a good girl."

The little girl smiled. "I understand, our Mam. I forgive you."

"Thank you."

She followed her daughter downstairs. The two policemen stopped talking and stood up as a neighbour knocked on the door, asking, "Do you need me right now, Martha, or shall I come back in a bit?"

Martha looked at the policemen. She hoped they wouldn't keep her too long. She really needed to go to work. "Just give us half an hour, if you would be so kind."

The neighbour nodded and retreated.

Martha poured some water from a jug and handed the drink to Amy, who gave the men a peculiar look as she took it upstairs.

"Now then, sirs…" Martha filled another glass and drank it down in one go then filled the kettle, asking, "A cup of tea?"

They both nodded. "That would be splendid, ma'am."

"I'm afraid I don't have any milk. It'll have to be black. I shall ask the farmer's wife to drop some off when she does her rounds."

"Plenty of sugar, if you have some. Let us begin."

Constable Jenkins opened his book and looked at her expectantly. "Have you thought any more about where your husband could be?"

She shook her head.

"And I understand you think the man who rescued your sister from the burning barn could have been your husband, ma'am?" asked the senior policeman.

"Well, I couldn't be sure. It all happened so quickly. Shouldn't you be out there looking for him?" She poured out their teas after putting some cold water in the bottom of the cups while their attention was diverted, so they would drink them quicker.

"We have officers combing the area, ma'am, but it could take days."

Worried about what to tell his mother, she asked, "What's going to happen to Ronnie?"

"He will be questioned, ma'am, and if we are satisfied he had nothing to do with anything, he will be released."

"And if you aren't?"

"If he is found guilty, then..." The man shrugged.

"But he's entirely innocent. I can vouch for that."

"You saw his brother being murdered, did you, ma'am?" asked Constable Jenkins.

"Me?" She stared at him, aghast. "Of course not."

"Precisely."

"So you think he could be the murderer?"

"We shall have to see." They both stood up and picked up their hats. "By the way, ma'am, what do you know about the murder? Even if you did not see it happen, you must know something."

"Me? Why do you say that? I don't know anything at all. Please believe me."

"We will say good day, then, ma'am. If you think of anything at all that could help with our investigations, do not hesitate to contact us." The senior policeman bowed his head. She did likewise, and they went out.

If they found Ronnie guilty of his brother's murder, Charlie would be off the hook. For a second her hopes rose, but then she remembered what had happened to

Tommy. She would never entertain any idea of the vicious blighter returning to the house, no matter whether he had killed Herbert Grant or not. He might as well be hanged. Young Ronnie couldn't possibly be guilty. It would be a travesty of justice if they hanged him for a crime he had not committed.

Amy came downstairs. "Have those men gone, Mam?"

"Yes, dear."

"Will they find our pa and put him in gaol?"

"Hopefully."

"But what will we do without him?" She hid her face in Martha's apron. "I know he hurt our Tommy, but he's still our pa. He didn't mean to do it, did he?"

"Oh, my sweetheart, I don't know what to say." Deep down, her daughter loved her father and, despite his gruff manner and seemingly uncaring attitude, she knew he loved both his children. He had never lifted a finger to either of them before. She bore the brunt of his bad moods, not them.

She prised her gently away and looked her in the eyes. "You have to be brave, my Amy, and look after your little brother for me while I go to work. Mrs Howard will look in on you now and again, to make sure everything is well, and give you something to eat."

"Yes, Mam. I'll try."

"Good girl. I'll just go and check on our Tommy. If you could wash the pots, I would be very grateful."

Amy grimaced but picked up the cups from the table and took them over to the sink.

Martha hurried upstairs and found her son fast asleep, sprawled across the bed. After covering him, she kissed his cheek and tiptoed out, thanking God he hadn't been as badly hurt as she had first thought.

"Will I be able to go to school tomorrow?" Amy asked when she returned downstairs.

Martha looked outside to see if she needed her

shawl. It had felt chilly earlier. "We'll have to see, darling. See how things develop."

"Only, me and Gertie were going to start our secret code today."

"Secret code, what's that?"

"It's so we can write to each other, and nobody else can read it."

"But you can barely write your name as it is."

Her daughter pursed her lips. "I can."

"Anyway, my sweetheart, I really must go. Maybe you could practise your writing. I think there might be some paper in the drawer, and a pencil. You can show me how good you are when I come home." She kissed the top of her daughter's head and hurried out.

Should she tell Mrs Grant what had happened to Ronnie? The farmer's wife would want to know, obviously, but maybe she should wait until the policemen told her. As she hurried down the street, she caught a glimpse of them entering one of the other houses, so it would be a while before they reached the farm.

An eerie stillness met her. Even the geese had disappeared. The burnt-out shell of the barn stood like a spectre, reminding her of her sister. How could they find out her condition, and when she could return home?

Where could Jessica be? Or Mrs Grant? She hurried to the farmhouse, her whole body filled with foreboding.

The farmer appeared from the field. "Good day, Mrs Holloway. May I enquire after your sister?"

Of course, they wouldn't even know if Charlotte was still alive. The condition she had been in when she had left had not looked promising. "Well, she had recovered slightly when I left, sir, but, of course, I can't say about today."

"We weren't sure if you would be coming in this morning."

"Yes, I'm sorry I'm late." Should she tell him about the events of the night before, to explain why?

"Oh, don't worry about that. Any help is appreciated, especially with Faith unwell, and our Ronnie incapacitated." He opened the door and they found his wife and Jessica holding what seemed like a meaningful conversation.

"Oh, thank goodness you're here," exclaimed Martha.

"Why, what's the matter?" Lily sprang up, a look of fear crossing her face.

Although relieved they were fine, she wondered where to begin. Her own problems would seem insignificant compared with theirs, so she explained what had happened to Ronnie.

Covering her mouth with her hand, Lily gasped and leant against her husband. Jessica jumped up and ran to Martha's side.

"What's going to happen to him?" asked the farmer.

Martha shook her head. "Hopefully one of the policemen will come and let you know."

"We need to go and see him." Lily tugged at her husband's sleeve. "Come on."

"But what about the farm? We can't just leave it, the planting, the cows, the butter and cheese…and your milk round."

"We can manage the dairy, sir," Jessica piped up, "can't we, Martha?"

"Well, I haven't the foggiest notion what to do, but you can show me."

"One more hour won't hurt, my dear." The farmer put his arm around his wife's shoulder. "You do your milk rounds, I'll finish off here, and then we'll go and see our Ronnie. All right?"

Lily pulled at her lip and then nodded. "Yes, I suppose so." She turned to Martha. "Did they say where they were taking him?"

"Oh, no, they didn't. Um…where do you think it would be? The policeman in charge should still be in the village, so maybe you could find out while you're there."

"Good idea." Tying her apron, Lily ran out towards the dairy.

"We'd better make a start, our Jessica." Martha grabbed her younger sister's arm and they hurried after her.

"What about our Charlotte?" Jessica asked as they crossed the farmyard. "You didn't say. Will she recover?"

"I sincerely hope so. She needs all our prayers, that's for sure."

They found Lily filling her pails with milk. "Are you sure you two will manage?" she asked, without looking up.

"Of course, Mrs Grant." Jessica pulled a face at Martha, clearly doubting it, but what else could they do, except manage the best way they could?

Martha patted her friend's arm. "We'll be fine, Mrs Grant. Don't you worry."

Lily bent down, lifted the yoke onto her shoulders, and hurried outside. Jessica ran after her. "Don't forget your ladle, Mistress. You wouldn't sell much milk without that."

"Oh, lawks, I'd forget my head if it wasn't screwed on."

Martha rolled up her sleeves. "Right then, where should I start? What's the easiest job I can do without much supervision?"

Jessica sucked in her breath. "Well, I suppose you could fill that cask with milk for the butter. I'll make a start on the cheese."

They worked silently for a while, interspersed with intermittent orders from Jessica. Martha concentrated on her tasks, trying to prevent the occasional grin at the look of pleasure her youngest sister gave on issuing such commands.

Farmer Grant came in, looking harassed. "Would one of you fine ladies come and help in the lambing barn, if you please? The ewes haven't finished lambing, and the orphans I haven't matched with a mother need feeding every couple of hours."

Martha straightened her back and rubbed her hands up and down it. "I'll come. I don't really know what I'm doing here."

"Good. Follow me and I'll show you what I need."

With an apologetic glance at her sister, she followed him.

"I think one of the sows is about to deliver as well," he panted, his face growing redder by the minute. "She appeared agitated when I looked in on her earlier."

"Do you want me to help with her? I used to give a hand at my Aunt Elizabeth's farmstead before I married."

"Oh, that would be marvellous. As you know, I must go with Lily to see what we can find out about our Ronnie." He took out a handkerchief from his pocket and wiped it across his brow. "All my farmhands are out with the ploughs, harrowing or sowing. We have to sow the seeds now, or I shall have nothing to harvest later in the year."

"Of course, Mr Grant. I fully understand."

He mopped his brow again, shaking his head. "One of my carthorses is lame as well, just to add to the mayhem." With a glance across at the farmhouse, he added, "I really can't spare the time to leave things, but…"

Faith appeared at the door. "U…U…Uncle Ed, I can't find Auntie Lily. D…d…do you know where she is?"

A groan escaped his lips. "That's all I need," he muttered under his breath, but loudly enough for Martha to hear.

With her hand on his arm, she told him, "I'll sort out your niece. You finish what you need to do before Lily comes back."

With a grateful smile, he hastened towards the

nearest shed, shaking his head on passing the burnt-out barn.

Martha went across to Faith, still in her pink, fluffy dressing gown. "What did you want your aunt for, my dear? She's doing her milk round."

"O...o...oh, yes. I forgot."

"Everything is in an uproar at the moment. Ronnie..." Martha closed her mouth. No point worrying the simple girl by telling her what had happened. Better change the subject. "Have you had any breakfast?"

The girl nodded. "Y...y...yes, thank you. Where's Ronnie?"

"I think he went to the village earlier." That was the truth. No need to expand on it. She ushered her inside. "Make yourself a cup of tea."

"H...h...how's Charlotte? She's not dead, is she?"

"She's going to be fine," Martha assured her, adding, "honestly," when Faith put her head to one side and frowned. "Now, I must leave you. There's so much to be done."

"I...I...I feel better today. Do you want me to do something?"

"Oh, that would be such a help if you could. But only if you really feel up to it. You could work in the dairy with Jessica. You're used to that, aren't you?"

"Y...y...yes. I'll take my cup of tea upstairs and put some clothes on. I...I...I can't go to work in this, can I?" She laughed as she held out her dressing gown and curtseyed.

The girl had such an engaging, naïve innocence about her, reminding Martha of her own young daughter. She couldn't help but smile.

As she hurried out, though, her thoughts returned to her own situation. Where could Charlie be? Watching her, at that very moment? She glanced around at the hills and woods behind the farm, and a shiver ran down her back. Maybe they would have been better off if he had died in that landslide. At least little Tommy wouldn't be lying injured in his bed. Oh, how she wished she could go home and enfold him in her arms. Could he be crying for her?

A squeal erupted from the pig shed. She hastened inside. Two tiny piglets lay in the straw beside the sow and a third could be seen sticking out of her rear end. Martha gave it a yank and it dropped to the floor.

"You're a big one, aren't you?" she muttered, wiping it with straw, as a fourth emerged, then a fifth. Before long, twelve tiny bodies were suckling at their mother. "Have you finished, now?" she asked the sow as she patted her head, and received a grunt of satisfaction for her reply. "Well done, old girl. Have a rest now. I'll be back in later."

One job done. What next? A sheepdog bounded up to her. She bent down to it. "Where's your master? Has he gone?"

"No, Lily hasn't returned yet," came a voice from the lambing barn. Inside, she found the farmer tending one of the ewes. "She's feverish," he said, examining her udders. "She's produced two healthy lambs." He pointed to the little bundles of white and black fur, trying to approach her to suckle. "But she doesn't seem to be producing any milk. I'm worried she might have mastitis, for her udders are warm and swollen. It's too late to put the lambs with another ewe, they're too old now. They were born yesterday. We'd better feed them by hand with those in that pen."

She looked over to where he pointed, and saw three little bodies lying cuddled up together, one with a pink nose and tiny horns, unlike the others.

"You have various breeds of sheep, Ed," she remarked.

"Well, all mine are Gritstones, the black and white ones. I breed them for their hardiness, and their thick wool crop, so I don't know where that little one came from. It looks like a Whitefaced Woodland. A ram must have infiltrated my ewes from Farmer Briggs's stock. I know he has some."

She laughed. "How naughty. But wouldn't there be more?"

He handed her a bottle of milk. "That's the least of my worries at the moment." He showed her how to feed the lambs.

Lily entered. "I haven't been able to find anything out," she said, almost in tears. "I couldn't find the policemen."

"Well, my dear, there's no point in us going anywhere, if we don't know where he is, is there? And there are so many jobs around here I need to see to. Maybe we should wait a while until we do know."

Lily walked back out, chuntering.

As a mother, Martha sympathised with the farmer's wife. Her own situation was bad enough, but to have one son murdered, not knowing who had killed him, and now the other son arrested for a crime he couldn't possibly have committed, maybe even his brother's murder, must have been too much to bear.

"Shall I go after her?" she asked.

Ed shook his head. "No, finish feeding these, if you would. I'll go."

Later, as Martha went towards the farmhouse, she thought she saw a movement up in the copse, where she had seen Charlie earlier in the week. Her heart beat faster. Could it be him? Where were the policemen when you needed them? She would willingly hand him over to them. His bullying tactics had taken their toll. She hated him more than she could have thought possible. Hurting her little Tom-tom had been the last straw. She had forgiven him for pushing her down the stairs the year before, causing the baby she had been carrying to be stillborn, when he had sworn it had been an accident. Anyway, she had been to blame, for riling him when he had been in his cups. She should have known better.

And what about the other miscarriages she had suffered? Admittedly, they probably hadn't been anything to do with him, but some part of her brain told her they might not have occurred if he hadn't been so violent. He hadn't wanted the babies, anyway. He had said they would only have been more mouths to feed. His wages wouldn't stretch to it. Not when most of his money was spent down at the boozer.

Shielding her eyes with her hand, she peered upwards, but couldn't make out anything. Perhaps she had imagined it but, as she rounded the corner of the burnt-out barn, she jumped when she heard, "Psst."

Her head shot up. Who was it?

It came again. "Psst, Martha."

"No," she moaned. Her heart sank. "Don't let it be him."

His arm snaked out and grabbed hers and pulled her inside the black shell.

Trying to yank it away, she hissed, "Leave me alone. I want nothing to do with you." But he kept a fast hold.

"Just give me something to eat. I'm starving."

"I hope you do starve, Charlie Holloway. Now clear off before I call someone."

"Please, Martha. I'm begging you, just a crust of bread, or a bit of cheese." His dirty face pleaded with her. "You used to love me."

"That was before... anyway, I can't. I can't just go in and steal food from my employer."

I mustn't falter, no matter how hard he beseeches, she thought, as her resolve began to waver. So used to obeying his every command, could she resist?

"How's our Tommy?"

"You have a cheek, Charlie, asking me that. I've had to leave him crying in agony, so I could come here to earn a few shillings to feed him and our Amy." Maybe she exaggerated but, unwilling to let him off the hook, she vowed he should suffer for what he had done.

His neck seemed to disappear as he hunched his shoulders, and a tear fell down his grimy face into his rough beard. "If I could take back what I did, I would willingly do so. I would give my life for my children, you know that."

"I might have thought so at one time, but not now, so there's no need for waterworks. You've burnt your bridges this time, Charlie. I have no sympathy for you." She turned to leave. He did not try to stop her. Breathing in deeply so her resolve would not waver, she walked away without a backward glance.

Outside the farmhouse, she met Lily with a basket of apples. "I may as well bake some pies, seeing as I can't go to see Ronnie." She took out a rather wizened green apple and rubbed it on her apron, then took a bite. "They need using up. They're going soft." She looked up at Martha. "Are you well, my dear? You're rather flushed."

Twiddling her fingers, Martha replied, "Yes, I'm just…" Her voice caught in her throat and she gritted her teeth to try to prevent a sob from escaping.

"Come on in. I've not long mashed a pot of tea."

"No, Mrs Grant, I must do some work. That's what I'm here for."

"Five minutes won't hurt." The farmer's wife gave her arm a gentle tug, and she found herself being helped onto a chair in the kitchen.

"I should be the one to look after you, after all you've been through, but…" Martha broke down and the whole story came out about Charlie turning up, seemingly from the grave, and how he had hurt Tommy.

"Oh, my dear, I had no inkling. Where's your husband now?"

No matter how much she hated him, she could not betray him and tell her he was hiding in her barn, so she just shrugged.

Lily poured out two mugs of tea. "Drink this and

then off you go to your little boy. I wouldn't have let you stay today if I'd known."

"But I have to work. I have no money."

Lily went to a shelf and took down a blue tin. "Here, take this for now. Call it wages for what you've already done." She handed her a pile of coins without counting them. "And I'll make you a parcel of food."

Martha hugged her. "I'm so grateful, Mrs Grant. I don't know what to say."

"That's what friends are for, my dear."

With a direct look in her eye, she pleaded, "Please don't tell anybody, will you?"

"What? About your husband being alive and well, and roaming the countryside, instead of being in jail where he belongs? Weren't there any witnesses last night?"

"Um…well…yes. I suppose the whole village will know by now, anyway. They'll be whispering behind their hands, saying, 'That Holloway woman deserves everything she receives, putting up with a husband like that'."

"No, they won't." Lily took a jar of pickles from the pantry and added it to the food she had already put on the table. "I'll have the jar back when you've finished with it. Anyway, I don't know the ins and outs of your private life, but I'm sure there are worse husbands out there, so don't you go worrying about what other folks think." She poured some milk into a jug and continued, "Nip across and ask Jessica for some cheese and butter while I find something to put these things into. That should tide you over for a few days."

"Oh, thank you so much." Martha hurried out to the dairy, hoping against hope that Charlie did not waylay her again. She would have to run all the way home to arrive before he took anything off her. But how could she pick up the cheese without having to explain the story to her younger sister? Now she had been given permission to leave, she just wanted to return to her son. She didn't want to be held up any longer than necessary.

Fortunately, she found Faith on her own in the dairy. "G...g...good day, Mrs Holloway. Y...y...your sister isn't here," she said.

"Oh, that's fine. I didn't come to see her. I...I'm just fetching some butter and cheese." She didn't want to be greedy and take a full portion from the ones already wrapped. Searching around, she found some greaseproof paper and wrapped a small amount in it.

"Sh...sh...she went off with a man."

"I beg your pardon?"

"J...J...Jessica, a man called her, and she went out to him."

Oh, no. It had to be Charlie. "How long ago?"

"I...I...I don't remember." Faith twiddled with the edge of her apron, then pointed to the vat in front of her. "B...b...before I started stirring this."

That could have been one minute, or fifteen.

"I'd better go and find her. You carry on with what you're doing."

Where to investigate first? Should she tell the farmer's wife? They could search together. But that would mean admitting she knew Charlie had been there. But not if she pleaded ignorance. Faith hadn't said she had recognised him. She may as well have a quick look around first, alone. No sign of anybody in or near the burnt-out barn, only the flattened area where he had been earlier. She wondered, for a fleeting moment, what the farmer would do with it. Not her problem. She needed to concentrate on the task in hand.

She could hear the farmer in the lambing shed. No mistaking his deep voice. They couldn't be in there.

After searching all the barns and outhouses, she tried the stables. The whiff of hay tickled her nostrils as a young groom came over to her, holding a currying brush. "Good day, ma'am." He bowed low.

"Good day. Have you seen my sister?"

"Um, no ma'am. I can't say as I've seen any young lady this past few hours or so, more's the pity—that is, until your delightful self turned up."

She replied, with an exasperated roll of her eyes, "Thank you," and walked away. The last thing she needed was some young whippersnapper flirting with her.

Lily would be wondering where she had gone so she picked up her skirts and ran back to the house. She would have to tell her.

Her young sister flew at her as soon as she went through the door. "Oh, Martha. Thank goodness you're here."

"Thank God *you're* here, more like. I've been searching the whole farm for you since Faith told me you had gone out to see a man."

"Oh, Martha, it was Charlie. He's alive, or... But he...and he... Oh, my!" She buried her head in her hands.

Martha raised her eyebrows at the farmer's wife, who stood, cracking her knuckles, but no explanation seemed forthcoming. She turned her attention back to Jessica. "What happened, darling? Did he hurt you?"

Jessica shook her head. "Not really."

"Well, either he did or he didn't. Where is he, anyway?"

"He's... Oh, Martha, I'm so sorry."

What could have happened? She pushed her sister away and looked her in the eyes. "Jessica, just tell me."

With a deep breath, she whispered, "I've killed him."

"You've what? You've... How? I mean..."

Jessica took Martha's hands in hers and said slowly, "He called me out of the dairy. I couldn't believe it. I thought he was dead. We all did, didn't we?" She looked puzzled when Martha didn't agree, but continued, "He grabbed me, and dragged me up to the copse. He had his hand over my mouth so I couldn't scream. He kept saying horrible things, like how he would kill me if I didn't go quietly. I thought I was going to die."

Lily sat down. Thank goodness she had stopped cracking her knuckles. The sound made Martha shudder. She waited patiently while her sister composed herself again.

Jessica continued, "I've never been so scared, but…but, when we arrived, he let go for a second and…"

Martha nodded, encouraging her to go on.

With a glance at Lily, Jessica blurted out, as if she needed to say it before she lost her courage, "I kneed him in the crutch and, when he bent over, I picked up a big stick and hit him on the head."

"Oh, my goodness." Martha grimaced. "Then what?"

"He fell down. I could see a lot of blood, but I didn't wait around. I ran away as fast as I could. He didn't come after me. I didn't hear him shout or anything. He must be dead, mustn't he?"

Martha looked at the farmer's wife. "Has anyone been up to check on him?"

"No, you arrived just as Jessica started to tell me what had happened."

Martha sat her sister on a chair. "Could you make her a drink, please? I had better go and see…" She had no need to finish the sentence.

She hurried out. What did she want to find? Earlier that morning she had wanted him dead. But Jessica would be hanged for his murder—if she had killed him. She would be able to plead self-defence, though. She had been in fear of her life. No jury would possibly convict her.

At the copse she didn't know whether to be relieved or disappointed when she didn't find a body. A patch of blood betrayed the spot where he had fallen, but he could not be dead, unless dead bodies stood up and walked away.

She hurried back down to the farm to give her sister the good news. Or bad news, in her case. She realised she had been hoping he was dead, that she could continue her life without his constant whinging and whining, or his threats and violence. Not that she could ever admit the thoughts to anyone. She knew it to be a sin, to wish someone dead. She wouldn't be able to look the vicar in the eye the next time she went to church. He would surely know her thoughts. Much better to pretend relief.

Halfway down the field, she halted. A noise—or rather a cry—came from the dry stone wall over to her left. An animal in distress? Or...

Did she want to find out?

Chapter 16

After a brief hesitation, Martha carried on walking. She didn't want to know what had made the sound. But then it came again. Could she just leave him there, in pain? She wouldn't do so to an animal. Maybe, it would be wiser to find a farmhand, or the farmer himself. That way, she would be safer. He—or it, if a wild animal— would be less likely to attack her if she had someone with her.

She could see a farmhand raking hay down near the farm. Maybe he would accompany her. At full pelt, she weaved around the startled sheep that ran in all directions, and hurtled towards him, leaving the gate at the bottom open behind her.

He looked up in surprise. "Good day, ma'am. Is everything well?"

"Actually, I think there's someone hurt up there." She pointed up the field. "I heard a cry," she added.

He dropped his pitchfork and wiped his hands down the side of his trousers. "You had better show me," he replied as he closed the gate behind them, just in time to prevent the sheep escaping.

When they neared the spot, she pointed and fell back so he could go ahead of her. The moaning had stopped.

"Over there, did you say, ma'am?" the farmhand turned and asked.

She nodded. "Yes, I think so."

"Well, I can't see anybody, or hear anything, now. Could it have been farther up?"

She approached closer and looked up and down. "I don't think so. Yes, there's the patch where some of the stones have come loose from the top of the wall. I remember seeing that." She looked over it. Nothing untoward. "Maybe I imagined it." She turned with a frown. "I'm sorry to have bothered you."

In her heart, she knew she hadn't done so, but what other explanation could she give? She took one more look up and down both sides of the wall. Definitely nobody, or nothing, there. If it had been Charlie, where had he gone?

The farmhand doffed his cap and gave her a patronising look. "I'll wish you good day, ma'am. Next time you think you hear an animal in distress, please…" He didn't finish, just stalked off with a shake of his head.

After another glance all around, she followed him as far as the gate. He closed it behind her and picked up his pitchfork, still shaking his head.

"I apologise again for wasting your time," she offered as she walked past him. "I know things are hectic here at the moment. The last thing you need is some female sending you on a wild goose chase."

He doffed his cap again without replying, and carried on with his work.

Head up, she continued to the farmhouse. Lily stood alone, rolling pastry, when she entered.

"I've sent Jessica home," Lily explained. "You'd been gone so long, I was becoming worried."

"Well, I couldn't find Charlie, so he can't be dead."

"Thank God for that. Did you not see any sign of him at all?" Lily stopped. "Where could he be, then?"

"That's what I'd like to know." Martha sat down and wiped her hands across her weary face.

Lily patted her arm, leaving a floury mark on her sleeve. "Oh, my dear, don't give up hope. He might walk in that door, as bold as brass, any moment."

Did she want him to? That was the leading question.

"Anyway, let's have that cuppa." The farmer's wife went across to the kettle, but Martha jumped up and took it from her. As she poured the tea, the smell of baking filled the air, making her stomach rumble. Lily must have heard it, for she picked up a pie from a plate of freshly baked ones, and put it on a plate, saying, "Here, you must be starving. Have one of these, or two, if you would like." She placed another one beside the first.

Martha bit into the warm pie. "Umm, that's delicious. I wish I could make pastry like this. Mine's always too hard." She rolled the firm apple around her mouth, savouring the taste.

"You need cold hands," Lily explained. "That's what I say makes the perfect pastry. Anyway, back to the subject in hand. What are you going to do about Charlie?"

Martha took a sip of tea, then shook her head. "I really don't know, Lily...I mean, Mrs Grant. What do you suggest?"

"You can't go to the law because it might put Jessica in jeopardy. You're stuck between a rock and a hard place, aren't you?"

Martha had never heard that expression before. It summed up her position, though. "Yes, I am. I suppose I shall just have to see what happens." She stood up. "But for now, I really must do some work. Where would you like me to start?"

"I thought you were going home to your son. There's the money over there and the parcel of food."

"But that was before Jessica..." Martha bent down to tie the lace that had come loose on her shoe. "No, I can't leave you in the lurch as well. I'm sure Tommy will be fine for a few more hours. The neighbours will look after him and our Amy."

"Well, Martha, if you are certain. I expect Faith would appreciate some help in the dairy. She isn't the brightest match in the box, but she means well. I ought to have gone to see what she was doing before now, but what with everything..."

"I'm on my way now. We'll make something between us, even if it's only cottage cheese."

Lily laughed. "You're a good soul, Martha. Thank you."

Martha smoothed her dress and went out.

She found Faith sitting in a corner, hugging her knees and went across, intending to help her up. "Why are you sitting there?"

"I…I…I didn't know what to do." The girl stayed on the hard floor, her arms wrapped around her.

"About what?"

"Him." She pointed to the far dimly-lit corner. Martha gasped, taken aback at the sight of Charlie, lying in a heap. Even from that distance, she could see his clothes covered in blood. He didn't appear to be moving.

Hands pressed together, she approached him gingerly, prepared for a sudden attack. She didn't want to be taken unawares if he was shamming. But she need not have worried. He didn't even open his eyes, just lay motionless. She touched his face with the tip of her finger. Warm. Then she reached inside his jacket and felt his chest, but could not be sure if she could feel any movement.

She was startled as Faith whispered into her ear, "I…i…is he dead?"

She swivelled around, almost knocking the girl over. "I'm not sure."

"H…H…Herbie's dead."

"Yes, I know, but that's different."

"Why?"

Before she could think of an explanation, Faith caught her bottom lip in her teeth and screwed up her face. "M…m…my mama's dead, too."

Martha put her arm around her. "Let's go and find your auntie, shall we? I think we need to tell her about…" She pointed to the lifeless body beside them "…don't you?"

The simple girl let Martha lead her outside. In the sunlight, she noticed red spots on the girl's frock.

"Oh, my goodness, he didn't attack you, did he?"

Faith shook her head.

With a sigh of relief, she continued, "So, how do you have blood on you?"

At that point, the farmer came towards them. "What's happening? Why aren't you...?" He appeared to notice his niece's misdemeanour. "Have you been hurt?"

Faith looked up at Martha as if for confirmation that she could tell him what had happened.

Martha spoke instead. "I don't think so, Mr Grant, it's... We were just on our way to see your wife, to tell her..."

"T...t...there's a dead man." Faith indicated inside the dairy.

Martha turned to go back inside to show the farmer what she meant. "Well, we don't know he's dead."

"Do you know who it is?" he asked as he followed her in, gently urging his niece towards the house with, "Go and find your aunt, my dear."

"Yes, it's my husband."

"Your husband? But I thought... No, they never did find him, did they?"

She did not reply, too anxious as to what they would find. Charlie still lay in the same position they had left him.

She stood back as the farmer approached him, asking, "How did he receive these injuries? They look recent."

For a second Martha had hoped he would assume they had been sustained in his fall but, of course, the farmer would recognise fresh blood. He dealt with it every day, slaughtering animals.

"That's how we found him," she admitted, thinking she did not need to implicate Jessica just yet. Maybe she should find Lily and ask her not to say anything. She felt sure her sister would not be likely to broadcast the fact, although her aunt Elizabeth would want to know why she had gone home in the middle of the day, so perhaps she had told her. Maybe it would be easier to admit the truth, after all. There were too many people involved to keep it a secret.

Her fingernails bitten to the quick, she watched him pull apart Charlie's jacket and feel his chest, as she had done earlier. "I couldn't tell if he was breathing. What do you think?" she whispered.

"Charles," shouted Ed in his ear, startling Martha. "Can you hear me?"

She thought she heard a faint reply. Her heart leaped. With her face covered by her hands, she closed her eyes.

"Charles," Ed called again.

She peeped through her fingers and held her breath.

Someone tapped her on her shoulder. With a start, she turned to see Lily. "Phwah, you scared me," she cried.

"I'm sorry, I didn't mean to," Lily whispered.

"Well, Mrs Grant," said the farmer. "I think you've been very fortunate. But we need to take him to hospital straight away."

"He's not dead, then?" asked Lily. "Faith told me he was."

"Not far off. Would you go and find one of the farmhands, my dear, to help lift him into a cart?"

"I'll go," volunteered Martha, unable to bear any more. "I saw one earlier, up in the field."

"But…don't you want to stay with your husband, in case he doesn't make it?"

They would be suspicious if she said no, so she nodded.

Lily released her hand, which she hadn't realised she had been holding, and went towards the door. "I'll find somebody. You stay here."

Charlie opened his eyes and raised one of his fingers.

Martha backed away, fearful that, even in his weak state, he might attack her.

"Martha," he whispered.

Ed moved away so she could come closer. She didn't want to, though. Her whole body shaking, she stood rooted to the spot a few feet away, unable to move.

His eyes closed again and his hand went limp. In fact, his whole body seemed to sink. Ed picked up the arm and let it flop to the ground. He bent closer and put his face to Charlie's mouth. "I'm sorry. I think we're too late," he muttered as he took off his cap and crossed himself in the way Catholics did.

Martha had never been particularly religious. Her faith extended to attending church on Sundays, and believing in heaven and hell, the same as most people she knew. For a brief moment, she wondered which way Charlie's soul would go.

"Should we say a prayer?" she murmured, unsure as to the correct procedure to take in the case of a sudden death.

"Um, yes, that would be appropriate, if that is what you wish." Giving her a curious look, Ed stood with his head bowed, his cap in his hand. When she didn't start, he glanced up at her. "Which one would you like to say?"

"The Lord's Prayer?"

He nodded and began to recite it. "Our Father…"

She joined in, not really taking heed of the words, more afraid of the repercussions of her husband's death. Would her sister be arrested and put in jail? She couldn't bear the thought of that, especially in her condition. Maybe she should take the blame herself and say she hit him? But what about her children? She couldn't do that to them. Now fatherless, she couldn't deprive them of their mother as well.

Once they had finished the prayer she turned once more to the farmer. "Are you sure?"

"That he's dead?" Ed examined the body once more. "Yes, my dear. My condolences to you and your family." He replaced his cap. "I suppose I had better inform the authorities. Have you no idea how this came about?"

She looked up at him. No words would come out.

Lily hurried in, followed by the farmhand Martha had upset earlier.

He gave her an apologetic look. "Maybe you were right, ma'am, when you thought you heard something. I'm sorry for doubting you."

"It matters not now. I…he…" A lump in her throat prevented her from continuing. She felt she should cry, but no tears would fall.

The man looked over at Charlie, as Lily put her hand on her arm, asking, "How is he?"

"Dead."

The farmer's wife's eyes widened. "Oh." She nudged Martha towards the door. "Have you told Ed about Jessica?" she whispered, so the men couldn't hear.

Martha shook her head.

"Then don't say a word. We don't want her implicated. No, we shall have to concoct some other story." Once outside, where they could talk more freely, she continued, "Maybe…maybe we could take his body to the cliff and dump it. No, that wouldn't work. Ed and his foreman would have to be let into the affair, and the fewer people who know about your sister's involvement the better. Anyway, leave it with me. I'll come up with something."

"But what if Jessica's told my aunt?"

"Um, that could be tricky. I don't think your aunt would cover for her, do you?"

"I really don't know. She's very upright and staunch, despite her profanities, but I don't think she would let her favourite niece go to prison. I'll go and see them now. If your husband wants to know why I've left, you can tell him I couldn't bear the angst, so ran off."

"Very well." Lily cupped her chin in her hands. "Oh, my goodness, what a state of affairs—my Herbert, then our Ronnie, and now this. What are we going to do?"

Martha heard the men's footsteps, so she ran across the farmyard and up the lane towards the village to her aunt's smallholding.

Chapter 17

The cottage looked deserted. Peering through the front window, she couldn't make out anybody in the front room. But then, nobody would be there in the middle of the day. Creeping around the back, a cockerel confronted her. "Shoo." She tried to push him away. He opened his beak, put back his head and crowed loudly. "Just go away," she hissed at him in as quiet a voice as she could. "I need to find my sister. I don't want you announcing my arrival."

"Hello, Martha," her aunt's voice came from behind her. "What are you doing here? I thought you were helping out at the blooming farm."

She froze. What should she tell her? Turning slowly to face her, she uttered, "I just came to enquire about our Jessica."

"She's tucked up in her blinking bed, sound asleep."

"Oh, did she…did she say anything?"

"About what?"

"Uh…why she came home?"

Her aunt shifted the basket of eggs to her other hand. "Not really. I couldn't make any damned sense of what she tried to tell me. Perhaps you could enlighten me."

"Me? No. I…um…" *For goodness sake,* she thought, *she'll grow suspicious if you keep stuttering.* "May I go up and see if she's awake?"

"Help yourself. I have my flippin' chores to complete." Her aunt went inside and placed the basket on the table, then picked up an empty one and walked down towards the vegetable garden.

Martha ran up the stairs.

Her sister lay in bed looking up at the ceiling. She sat

up as Martha entered. "What's happening? Have they found him?"

Martha sat on the edge of the bed and took her sister's hand in hers. "Jessica, you have to listen to me. You haven't told Aunt Elizabeth, have you?"

The girl shook her head.

"Good. Now, you don't know anything about Charlie's injuries, understand?"

"But..."

"And you must not tell anyone, is that clear?"

"Oh...They have found him, haven't they? He's dead...isn't he?" She began to cry.

"Well, yes, but we don't want you taking the blame."

"But I did it."

"I know, but you could go to prison and you wouldn't wish that—none of us would. You don't want your baby being born in such an awful place. So, you mustn't say a word to anyone. When you last saw him, he was still alive so, in theory, you didn't kill him. Just plead ignorance."

Jessica touched her belly. "I don't know if I can. What if the police ask me questions? How will I be able to lie?"

"I know it'll be difficult, but you must. You won't actually be lying, just being economical with the truth. Only Mrs Grant and I know about it, and we won't tell anyone, so it's up to you."

Jessica looked her in the eye. "You'd really lie for me, our Martha? You're the most honest person alive, but you'd really do that to save me?"

"Yes, I would."

"But he's your husband."

"*Was* my husband. But...never mind. How are you feeling? Do you think you could come and do some work after your rest? I feel really guilty for causing such mayhem to the Grants."

Jessica pushed back her sheet and lowered her feet

to the floor. "It's the least I could do. After all, it's my mayhem, not yours."

"Well, let's not argue over that. Come on."

Jessica dressed as she waited, and they hurried downstairs and outside, meeting their uncle as they opened the back gate.

"My two favourite nieces. Where are you going in such a hurry? Come to think of it, what are you doing here at this time of day?" His glass eye looked even more incongruous with the sun glinting on it when he winked with his good one.

"We're just off back to the farm, Uncle Will. See you later." Martha could tell from Jessica's demeanour as she shrank from him that she couldn't bear to be around him for long. Martha felt exactly the same. His smarmy manner did not lend itself to familiarity. Not on their part, anyway. His ideas might have been entirely different. She shuddered.

"I can't imagine what Aunt sees in him," she muttered as they hurried up the lane. "He's creepy, isn't he?"

"You can say that again. I keep away from him as much as possible." All of a sudden, she bent over and moaned, "Ohhh!"

"What's the matter?"

"I…I don't know. Ahhhhhh!" she screamed.

Martha looked at her in dismay. "Is it the baby? What should I do?"

"I…it can't be. I'm only seven months gone."

"Let's take you back. You can't stay here for everyone to ogle." She steered her back the way they had come. "Oh, no."

Jessica looked up at the tone in her voice. "What?"

"Wilson. He's coming towards us."

"He's harmless. Ohhh!"

"Not another pain? Oh, my goodness."

Wilson came up to them. "What's the matter, Miss

Jessica? You don't look well."

"I'm sorry, Wilson, she isn't and I must take her home. Good day."

"May I help?"

"No. Thank you very much, anyway."

He pulled at her sleeve. "I don't like seeing my friend in pain."

"I know, but please leave us. I don't want to be rude, but you can see our quandary." She pulled his hand away.

"What's a quand-er-ary?"

"Please, Wilson." Losing her patience with the man, Martha yanked her sister away when she moaned once more.

Her uncle ran towards them. "What's happening? I heard screams. Is this man molesting you?" Before they could reply, he turned to Wilson. "I'll have the authorities onto you, sir."

"No, Uncle. He's only concerned. He doesn't mean any harm. Please just help me take our Jessica back home before this baby is born here and now."

"It can't be born yet. It isn't due for ages." Her sister straightened, seemingly less distressed. "I think I'm fine now."

"I don't care. I'm still taking you home." Martha grabbed one arm while her uncle took the other and they manhandled her towards the cottage.

"Honestly, the pain's gone. It was probably just a stitch from running." Jessica resisted their attempts and tried to pull her arms free.

"My darling sister, we were hardly running. We had barely broken into a trot."

"Well, whatever you call it, I'm fine now. I need to…" A grimace crossed her face and Martha could see her grit her teeth.

"I don't believe you, so you're going back." She received a glare that would have floored a less persistent person but, adamantly, she urged Jessica onwards.

"Listen to your older sister for a change," her uncle added, "instead of being so self-willed. You can't go your own sweet way all the while, much as you would like to."

Jessica raised her eyes. Martha grinned. Her sister needed telling sometimes, and she was in complete agreement with him for once.

With a pat on Wilson's arm in apology of her uncle's suspicions, they left him, still chuntering, and helped her to the house.

Aunt Elizabeth came from the outhouse, her arms full of logs. "What's going on?"

"I think it's the baby," answered Martha. "But it's too early."

Aunt Elizabeth dropped the wood and took over from her husband, swearing profusely when a log landed on her foot. "Let's have her up those blasted stairs and back into bed." Between the two of them, they hauled Jessica up, still protesting, leaving Will downstairs.

"I'll let you cope with her, my dear," he called. "I'm needed out in the field."

"Yes, that's it," replied his wife. "Run off and do your stuff. Leave us to do the flipping hard work." She turned and winked at Martha, whispering, "He would be useless here, anyway. He's much better out of the way. But I just like to make him think I'm mad with him for deserting us. It keeps him on his toes, if you know what I mean."

Martha didn't. She had never had the courage to employ such tactics.

Another whine from the bed had them fussing again. Aunt Elizabeth felt her niece's bump. "I wonder if we ought to call a midwife."

"But I keep telling you, it's not due for weeks." Jessica wiped her hair back from her hot brow, her face turning red.

"But it might have other ideas. It's better to be safe than sorry, that's what I always blinkin' say."

Martha backed towards the door. "I'll go and find one. The old lady who delivered my babies died a few weeks back. Who's taken her place, Jessica?"

"I don't know. I haven't been to see one for a while."

"Someone in the village is bound to know. I'll go and find out. Wait here," she added, trying to make light of the situation.

"We won't be going anywhere, my lass. Just blooming hurry," her aunt retorted, as Jessica arched her back and gave another loud moan.

As she rushed down the stairs, Martha caught her toe in the folds of her dress. With a curse she grabbed the handrail. "That would be the last straw," she mumbled as she jumped the last three steps. "The nail in the coffin, the…" She tried to think of another expression she could use to try to keep her mind from her troubles, but failed.

As she hurtled towards the village she saw Wilson again. *Oh, no, I don't have time for him,* she thought uncharitably, *even if he might know who I should go to.* It would take too long to explain, so she ran past him, avoiding his outstretched hand, calling "I'm sorry, Wilson, I must dash."

Who would be the most likely person to know a midwife? Who would be the biggest gossip? Probably Mrs Howard, but she would still be in mourning for her daughter, Mary, as well as minding her Tommy and Amy, so she didn't want to bother her.

Two ladies stood looking in the milliner's shop window, discussing the benefits of twill against serge. Not well acquainted with them, she did not know if they would be a good prospect.

Maybe the baker would know. She had plenty of buns in the oven. Martha laughed aloud at her own joke as she opened the shop door.

"You sound very cheerful, Mrs Holloway," the baker greeted her. "What can I sell you, today?"

The smile on Martha's face vanished. "Actually, I haven't come to buy anything. It's our Jessica. Do you know if we have a resident midwife nowadays?"

"Your sister? I didn't think she was…"

"Due for weeks," Martha finished for her. "That's what she keeps saying, but she definitely looks like she's in labour to me."

"Oh, dear. If the baby's coming early, he won't stand much of a chance, will he?"

"Not without someone to help him along, no. So…?"

The baker sucked in her lips and stroked her chin. "I can't… Old Mrs What's-her-name died, didn't she? No, I'm afraid I don't know. Someone must, though. Have you tried next door?"

"I'll go there now. Good day."

An elderly customer, hobbling with a stick, had been about to enter as she ran out, and she almost knocked her over. "Sorry, ma'am." She took her arm and helped her into the shop, probably more quickly than she was accustomed to moving, repeating, "I am so sorry. Good day."

She rushed through the open butcher's shop door and blurted out to the queue of customers waiting to be served, "Does anyone know a midwife, or someone who could assist my sister?"

Several of the smarter-dressed ladies looked down their noses at her. She was not bothered. She just wanted help—from anyone. "Please…my sister might be in labour."

One of the other ladies whispered to her companion, "I know who she means. She shouldn't be in that situation, a young lass like that. It's her own fault."

Martha tried to ignore her. Seeing someone she considered to be one of her friends, she tugged at her apron. "Do you know anybody, Susan?"

The young lady shook her head and pulled her apron

out of Martha's hands, as if she didn't want to be contaminated, then hurried away.

"I thought this to be a Christian community." She began to lose her rag. "Never mind the morals, please, just help me. What if she were your daughter?"

"My daughter would not have found herself in that predicament," the first lady uttered, her nose in the air. "She knows right from wrong."

"Anybody can make a mistake. It isn't Jessica's fault our mother died and left her motherless." Her temper finally frayed with the judgemental people. "Oh…piss off, all of you," she bawled.

The collective intake of breath at her profanity filled the shop. Martha didn't care. Sticking out her tongue, and with the whispers of, "It's no wonder her sister is the way she is, with her for an example," and the butcher yelling, "Now less of that, young lady," ringing in her ears, she swept out, her dress swirling around her legs.

Along the street, she stopped and took a deep breath. What had made her do that? She never swore. Well, maybe a few muttered oaths in private, but never in public. She would not be able to hold her head up again.

Susan came out of the butcher's shop. After hesitating for a moment, her so-called friend walked towards her. "I'm sorry, Martha, about your dilemma. I…" She looked around her and then dragged Martha into an alleyway, out of sight. "My aunt who lives at the end of the village has helped with a few births. She might be of use."

"Oh, you mean the one with the big garden, where we used to play as children?"

Susan nodded as she peeped out of the alleyway. "I'm sorry to be so secretive."

"I understand, Susan. You can't be seen condoning my sister's situation by talking freely to me." She sighed. "It isn't my fault she's in this predicament. I did my best." She smoothed down the lace collar on her blue dress.

"But this isn't helping her with her baby," she declared as she patted Susan's arm and stepped out onto the street. "Thank you," she called, before hurrying towards the aunt's house.

In haste, she sidestepped people as carriages and horses, even bicycles, drove past, threatening to run her over, and reached the house as the lady in question walked down her front path towards her, dressed in her outdoor coat and hat.

"Oh, good day, ma'am. I don't know if you remember me? I'm…"

"Martha Holloway, Bridge as was. Of course I remember you. You used to play with our Susan, didn't you? Such a delightful child you were, always polite and obedient. I can't recall ever having to scold you or—"

"Yes, thank you." Martha didn't have time for reminiscences. "But…you're going out?"

"That had indeed been my intention." The lady pulled her kid glove farther up her arm.

"It's just that my sister, Jessica, is more than likely in labour."

"And?"

"Well, Susan said you were adept at delivering babies, and I wondered if you would be able to help."

She received a disbelieving arch of the eyebrows. "I may have assisted at one or two births, but I would not call myself 'adept' by any stretch of the imagination. And it was some while ago. Your sister? She's the young one who got knocked up by an unknown father?"

Martha gulped at the use of such a crude expression. "Um, yes, I suppose you could put it that way." But she needed to stop wasting time and find out if the lady could help. "Are you going anywhere important, ma'am?"

"I was about to call on a friend. But I could, maybe, afterwards, see my way to…" She looked down at her attire. "I would have to come home and change first, though, of course, so it could be quite a while. Do you not know anyone else?"

"I don't, do you?"

"I suspect that most of the villagers shun your sister, anyway. Am I right?"

"Yes, I hate to admit it, but you are. You wouldn't have any qualms about being seen assisting an unmarried expectant girl then?"

"Me? No. I couldn't care less about what other people think. Anyway, I had better be off. My friend will wonder why I am late. I am usually so punctual. He will be worrying." Her parasol opened, she walked sedately down the street, leaving Martha surprised at her statement. She had assumed it to be a lady friend, but one should never assume. Her mother had often told her that. One could find oneself in deep trouble by saying the wrong thing.

Who else could she find to help straightaway? A groan escaped her when she saw Constable Jenkins approaching—the last person she wanted to speak to. She turned and began to hurry in the opposite direction, but he called her. "Mistress Holloway, please wait. I need to speak to you, ma'am."

With a sigh, she waited for him to catch up. "I'm in a hurry, Constable. I need to find a midwife for my sister."

"This won't take a minute, ma'am and, anyway, if you mean your younger sister, I have just come from the farmstead and she has recovered and is sleeping."

"What? You mean she isn't in labour?" She wouldn't mean her other sister, would she? She was languishing in the hospital, miles away, with nobody to visit her.

"Not as far as I know."

"So, I've been wasting my time?" She stamped her foot. "Ohhh." And gained herself a reputation for cursing like a fishwife into the bargain. All for nothing. "Are you sure?"

He ignored her outburst and stood patiently, then

said, "I need to find out more details about your husband's death, ma'am. If you would be so kind as to accompany me."

Her heart sank. For a brief while she had almost forgotten about him. "Where to? Am I being arrested?"

"No, ma'am, we should return to the farm where it happened. We need to establish the facts."

"Yes, sir, of course. But first, I wish to leave a note for the lady who lives over there, to tell her she's no longer required to deliver the baby. Please may I have a page of your book?"

With a shocked expression, he clutched his notebook to his chest. "No, certainly not, ma'am. This is official property. I cannot go around giving out pages to any Tom, Dick or Harry."

Well, I'm not a Tom, Dick or a Harry, she thought, but remained silent. She would just have to hope the lady wouldn't come, anyway.

"Have they removed his body yet?" she asked as they walked along the lane. She sniffed loudly, then delved into her bodice and took out a white handkerchief and blew her nose as loudly as she could, playing the part of the grieving widow. "I don't think I could bear to see him." From the corner of her eye she saw him give her a peculiar look. Was she being too melodramatic?

"I am not sure, ma'am. I have been out and about, mainly looking for you. It seems strange that you should leave your husband so urgently after his demise."

"I was distraught," she sniffed again, dabbing her eyes with the handkerchief, "and what with my sister and everything…" Could she possibly squeeze out a tear? But he wouldn't see it, for he had marched ahead, and she had to take extra steps to keep up.

Two farmhands loaded her husband's body onto the cart as they entered the farmyard. Tears fell down her cheeks, unbidden, as she crumpled to the ground, genuinely distressed, as the realisation hit her. Dead. Even though she would not have to endure his torments any longer, she had loved him at one time. And Tommy—he idolised his pa, or had done, before he had stabbed him.

The policeman helped her up. "Come on, ma'am, you must remain strong. I know it's difficult."

She went over to the cart and asked the driver, "May I have a moment with him before you take him away?"

"Certainly, ma'am, we're in no hurry. Take all the time you need."

Lily came across and put her arm around Martha's waist. "I'm so sorry, my dear," she tried to console her, but the tears would not stop. Tears for their short but happy courtship, their marriage. She had been truly contented for the first year before he had changed. All the frustrations of the last few days came out in her outburst of sorrow, and she felt as if her heart would break as she climbed in beside his lifeless body and gave his cold cheek one last kiss.

Pull yourself together, lass. Think of your two beautiful children. Surely they were the point now. Amy, at least, had been conceived in love, and her little Tommy—she couldn't love a son more than she loved him, no matter that he had been conceived in a moment of rage. She had to be brave for them.

The cart pulled away after she had climbed back down and wiped her eyes.

Lily asked, "What about Jessica? How is she?"

Martha motioned towards the policeman. "*He* said the labour had stopped. It looks like a false alarm."

Lily looked anxious. "What has the constable to do with her? You haven't told him, have you?"

"Oh, no. I won't breathe a word, and I advised her not…" She stopped as the man in question came across. "The constable was looking for me to ask me about my husband," she stated in a louder voice, "and he called at my aunt's first."

"Well, you had better come inside, both of you, and

I'll put the kettle on." The farmer's wife gave her a secretive downturn of her mouth as she led them inside.

Faith had been sitting at the table, her head on her arms. She jumped up. "H...h...has he gone, Mr Holloway?"

"Yes, my dear," her aunt replied.

"I...i...it wasn't me," she protested, eyeing up the policeman.

"What wasn't?"

"I...I...I didn't kill him."

"Nobody is suggesting you did, my dear." Lily took her in her arms. "Why don't you go and check on Faithful? I'm sure he would appreciate a cuddle."

The girl skirted around the constable, wringing her hands under her chin.

"Why, ma'am, would she think...?" he began after she had left. "She has never been a suspect."

"You have to make allowances for her, sir. She's very simple-minded," Lily explained. "Pray, take a seat." As she poured out the tea, she asked, "Are there any suspects yet?" She gave Martha a sideways glance as he looked down at his book.

"Well, not yet. It's somewhat of a mystery. That was why I needed to interview Mrs Holloway, ma'am. In private would be preferable."

"Oh, we don't have any secrets, do we, Mrs...Lily?" Martha grabbed the farmer's wife's hand, anxious not to be left alone, unsure if she could keep her guard up on her own. "There's no need for her to leave."

"Well, it is highly irregular, but given the circumstances..."

Lily sat down next to her.

"I shall need to speak to all the farmhands as well, ma'am."

"Yes, of course. I'll round them up as soon as you've finished with Mrs Holloway, sir."

"Now, I'm puzzled, ma'am. Where had your

husband been hiding since the landslide? Did you have any inkling that he was still alive? Had he made contact with you before yesterday?"

Martha's eyes opened wide. How could she lie? She twiddled a curl between her fingers. "I…um…"

Lily put her arm around her, glaring silently as the policeman looked down to write in his book, and screwed up her face as if to tell her something.

Ah, she realised, *pretend to cry.* She put her head in her hands and tried to sob, but it came out more as a cough.

"Can't you see the poor woman's distraught?" Lily handed her a clean handkerchief with which she covered her face. A hysterical cackle bubbled up inside her, and she fought to turn it into a cry. How on earth could she be laughing at a time like that? Her husband lay dead and she was laughing like a hyena! She had to stop. But she couldn't. The more she tried, the more it came. Drat her propensity for hysterics. It had landed her in trouble more times than a little.

Her abdomen ached, and she clutched it as she dared to look up at the constable. The astonished look on his face made her giggle all the more.

"It's hysteria," she heard Lily explain. "It happens sometimes. I'm sure you've seen it before, sir."

"Well, ma'am, not to this extent."

Martha could barely hear him through the cackling, and could barely see, either, for the tears streaming down her face.

"One way to stop it…" began Lily, and before Martha knew her intention, she felt a slap on her cheek. A hard slap that stung. But it had the desired effect.

"I…I need the lavvy." She pushed back her chair and ran outside. She had not lied. She had almost wet her knickers. On the lavvy, she tried to compose her frayed nerves. *Take deep breaths,* she told herself. *Try to remain calm, no matter what he asks.* In a bid to obey her own command, she breathed in deeply, and blew out in short bursts several times.

Anxious not to keep the policeman waiting too long, in case he became suspicious, she went out. Seeing the horse trough full of water, she dipped her finger in and dabbed it across her hot face. She would have loved to have taken a whole handful, but the green slime on the top put her off. After a quick wipe around her face with her apron, she pushed back her shoulders, and re-entered the farmhouse to find the kitchen empty.

"Oh!" she exclaimed. "Where's he gone?"

Lily came out of the pantry, her arms full of bags of flour and sugar. "He decided to give you a while to compose yourself, and has gone to find some of the farmhands to see what they know." She put the bags on the table. "That was a show you gave there."

"I know. I'm sorry if I embarrassed you. These laughing fits attack me now and again, usually when I'm nervous." She pursed her lips. "Or sometimes they just happen. I can't control them. I see a funny picture in my mind and off I go."

Lily broke two eggs into a bowl and whisked them. "You knew your husband was still alive, didn't you?" she asked, not looking up.

Martha couldn't lie to the farmer's wife. She had been so good to her, it wouldn't be fair. "Yes."

Lily looked up then. "How long had you known?"

"Since the day after the mudslide."

The beating stopped. "And you never told anybody?"

"No. He warned me not to, he..." She had been about to bring up the subject of Herbert's murder but stopped in time. "Anyway, this won't help with the chores. I've wasted enough time already."

"Well, I don't understand how you could keep something like that a secret but, first, you need to sort out your story for Constable Jenkins. I'll back you up as much as I can, but there's only so far I can go."

"I know, Lily, I...I mean, Mrs Grant." She wanted to hug the woman but didn't know if it would be appropriate. "I'm really grateful for all your help. My own mother couldn't have done more."

"Yes, she was a good 'un, your ma. A real friend to me and my family. I'm sure you miss her. I don't mind if you call me by my Christian name. I think we're sufficiently acquainted by now."

A knock on the door heralded the return of the constable.

"Come in, sir." Lily gave Martha an understanding look as she motioned to him to take a seat. "Did you find anybody?"

He remained standing and took out his notebook. "Yes, ma'am, and he had some informative information."

"Oh? What was that?" She raised her eyebrows at Martha.

"I don't know if I should tell you, ma'am. No, I had better not." He put his book back inside his pocket.

"Was it concerning my husband?" asked Martha, her heart in her mouth.

"Yes, and no, ma'am."

Lily put her bowl on the table. "Well, either it was or it wasn't, sir."

He looked from one to the other, clearly unsure as to whether to divulge his newfound secret. "Actually, it concerns your son, ma'am."

"Mine or Martha's?"

"Yours, Mistress Grant."

"Ronnie? Are you letting him go?" Her face beamed.

"Oh, I couldn't say that, ma'am. No, your other son, Herbert Grant, the one who was murdered."

Martha drew in her breath. "But what has his murder to do with my husband?" She had her own suspicions, but what could the policeman have found out?

"I cannot say anything further on the subject,

ma'am. I need to speak to my superiors first." He walked to the door. "I shall still need to speak to you, Mistress Holloway, but I must inform them straightaway. I may return later today, or it might be tomorrow. Good day."

After he had left, Martha let out a sigh. "I wonder what that was all about, and who gave him this new information?"

"Um, I wonder," repeated Lily. "I felt so cheerful for a moment, thinking my Ronnie was coming home. How can they think he had anything to do with that episode at your house? It just doesn't make sense."

"No, it doesn't, Lily. I'm so sorry he became involved. I tried to tell them he had nothing at all to do with it, but they wouldn't listen. Just because he had a bloody bandage."

"But that was for the cut on his hand."

"I know, that's what I said. I do pray they'll release him soon. If only we could find out something. It's so frustrating." Martha took the spoon from Lily who had been scraping the cake mix into the baking tin. "Let me finish this. You run after Constable Jenkins and demand to find out when they're releasing him. Surely he'll know something. He won't have gone too far."

Her hands wiped down her apron, the farmer's wife nodded. "Yes, I will," she sang as she ran out.

Chapter 18

Left alone, Martha's thoughts returned to her own son. If only she'd had time to pop in and see him while she had been in the village. She'd had half a mind to do so, but the constable had put it right out of her mind. Her own poorly son! How could she have forgotten about him? What a bad mother.

But she would make it up to him…somehow.

And what about Charlotte? How did she fare? Buxton was such a long distance away. She could not possibly make the journey over there again. She had to keep the bailiffs from her door. Not that she had anything for them to take from her sparsely-furnished stone cottage. She didn't own anything fancy, just the bare essentials. Not like Susan's aunt. She remembered going into her house and being amazed at the show of pretty ornaments in the cabinet in the corner of her front room. No, they had never had any money left over for such fripperies. Anything spare, Charlie spent in the alehouse. And now…would she even be able to earn enough to feed the children and pay the rent?

The cake in the oven, she wondered what else to do. After washing up the sticky utensils—she licked the remainder of the cake mixture off the spoon, glancing around guiltily as she did so—Lily still had not returned, so she went outside to the lambing shed.

"Ah, just in time to feed the orphans," declared Ed as she entered. "My other shire horse has developed a lame foot now. I must examine it before I decide if the farrier needs calling in. Will you be able to manage?"

"Yes, sir, leave it with me."

The sounds of the ewes and lambs bleating, the smell of the straw and hay, and even the faint whiff of dung, calmed her jagged nerves, as she sat feeding the helpless little animals, giving her time to think once more. What could the constable have found out, and who from? Who would be incriminated?

Later that day, about to go home, she went out into the farmyard and shooed the geese out of her way, wondering why they were kicking up such a gaggle. Looking ahead, she saw a figure approaching. She ran into the house, screaming. "Lily, Lily, your Ronnie's come home."

Lily came hurtling down the stairs. "Where? Where?"

"He's coming down the lane." She grabbed her friend's sleeve and pulled her out the door.

Lily ran and wrapped her arms around him. "Oh, my son, have they released you? Have they really?"

"Obviously, Ma, or I wouldn't be here, would I?" he laughed. "Unless you think I did a runner and escaped over the wall."

"Let me look at you. Did they treat you well? You look thinner. Did they feed you?"

"Yes, Ma. I've only been gone a day. I don't think I would waste away in that short time, even if they didn't."

"Come on in and I'll put the kettle on. You must be starving." She dragged him into the kitchen and took out the biscuit tin.

Although eager to return home, Martha also wanted to know what had happened at the police station. "Did they just free you, or are you still…?" She blew out her cheeks, unsure what the procedure would be.

"Well, yes, I suppose so. They just said I was free to go, so I didn't hang around for them to change their minds, and legged it hotfoot."

Lily picked up his bad hand. "And how is your wound? It still looks rather fetid to me. Let me dress it for you. I bet they didn't even give you any ointment in there, did they?"

"Ma, stop fussing. Please. It's fine." He pulled his hand away and wiped his brow with the back of it.

"Didn't the police say anything else?" asked Martha.

"What about?"

"About her husband, Mr Holloway?" Lily chipped in.

His bottom lip curled upwards, he looked pensive for a moment, then shook his head. "No, what about him? Is he still around? I would have thought he would've been far away by now." He sipped his tea as the two women exchanged glances.

Martha said in a low voice, "No, he's dead."

He almost spat out his mouthful. "Dead? How come?"

"Someone attacked him yesterday. Are you sure you didn't hear anything about it?"

"No. I would remember. It's because of that blasted… I'm sorry Mrs Holloway, I know he was your husband but…it's because of *him* they arrested me."

"Yes, I'm sorry for the misunderstanding, Ronnie." Martha turned to Lily. "I really must go home, now. Oh, I almost forgot…my package. Is it still all right…?" She went across to the dresser where Lily had put the jars of preserves that morning, and picked them up.

"Yes, of course, my dear. The cheese and milk are keeping cool in the pantry. I'll fetch them for you." She returned with the items and put them all into a tapestry bag. "I hope your little boy's feeling better."

"Thank you. I shall see you in the morning—that's if I'm still required?"

"Oh, yes. That's a certainty. Good day."

"Good day to you both." She hurried out. Should she call in on Jessica on her way? No, her son's welfare concerned her more than her sister's. He would think she had deserted him. Whenever her children came in from playing, or from school, she would always be there. He wouldn't understand why she had to work. And she still had to give him the bad news.

The bag clonked against her leg, so she picked it up and carried it in her arms, not needing any further aggravation. She had enough of that already.

Amy ran towards her as she approached, and gripped her round her waist, burying her face in her frock. "Oh, our Mam, why have you been so long?"

"I had to work, my darling, you know that." She eased her daughter away so she could continue to the cottage. "How's our Tommy?"

"He keeps crying for you."

"Is his injury paining him? Oh, my poor little boy." She ran inside the house. Tommy sat in a chair, guzzling a glass of fizzy drink. He didn't look particularly upset.

"Hello, our Mam. You've been gone ages and ages. I thought you wasn't ever going to come back." He jumped up and ran to her. "Mrs Howard made me some special lemonade. It's ever so fizzy."

"That's good, my sweetheart." Should she tell them straightaway? But she couldn't bear to knock the grin off his face. It would wait.

"So, Mrs Howard's been looking after you? That's good. How's your shoulder?"

"It still hurts a lot." He tried to pull down the neck of his nightshirt but it wouldn't go far enough, so he lifted the whole thing over his head.

"Mrs Howard checked it for him earlier," explained Amy.

"Aye," Tommy laughed. "And you should've seen her face when she saw I wasn't wearing any drawers. It was so funny."

"She shouldn't be shocked. She has children of her own."

Martha put the jars of pickles and fruit into the cupboard and was about to take the dairy products into the pantry when he said, "Aye, but she said none of her boys had a winky as big as mine." He lifted his and pointed it around the room.

"Tommy, don't be so rude. You know you shouldn't show it to people." Amy's face showed her disgust.

He repeated the action, making his sister squirm and squeal, and run to the door. "You're not people. You're my sister."

Martha intervened. "You must be feeling better, our Tommy. Turn around. Let me see your back."

She untied the knot of the bandage, revealing a puncture wound of about half an inch wide. It didn't look to be festering. "You're lucky, my boy. It's a good job you're healthy. I'm sure that makes a difference to how quickly injuries heal." She tied it up again and asked, "Have you had any dinner?"

"No, we…" Tommy began.

Amy stopped him. "Mrs Howard made us some lovely sandwiches."

"Oh, yes. They had something called…what was it, Amy?"

"I can't remember. Some sort of fish."

"They were scrumptious. Can we have some, Mam, when our pa comes home?"

A good time to tell them? No time would be a good time.

"Well, I'm afraid I have some bad news, my darlings," she began. "Your—"

Before she could continue, a knock came on the door. She started, imagining for a split second that it was her dead husband. "Open that, Amy, if you would, but you, Tommy…" She helped him put his nightshirt back on before the visitor could see him in all his glory.

Ronnie poked his head around the door, his cap in his hand and his hair a mess.

"Good day, Mrs Holloway, I'm sorry to bother you."

She wondered why Tommy hid behind her. "Good day, Ronnie—again."

A clean bandage covered the young man's hand as

he stood twiddling his cap. He seemed ill at ease as he cast occasional glances at her son, who still skulked behind her. "I…I actually came to ask about your sister, but now I'm here, I would like to apologise to your son for my inappropriate behaviour the other day."

Martha pulled Tommy from behind her. "What's all this? What inappropriate behaviour? You didn't say anything to me, our Tommy."

"It were nothing, Mam, honest."

"I regret to say I threatened him," Ronnie admitted. "And I've had nightmares about it ever since, especially when I was in that police cell, thinking they would find out and put me in prison for that, along with whatever other crime they claimed I'd committed. I have never done anything like that before in my life. You must believe me. As I say, I am truly sorry." He continued twizzling his cap, his eyes downcast.

"Well…um…" Martha could not believe this usually docile young man would intimidate anyone, and for what reason? She turned to her son. "What were you doing, our Tommy, to need to be warned off, eh? You'll feel the back of my hand if you were up to any monkey business."

"Nothing, Mam. I weren't doing nothing. He just…"

"No, Mrs Holloway," beseeched Ronnie, "honestly, he wasn't. I was just in a foul mood, because I'd hurt my hand, and I couldn't find my…um…something I'd lost. Please don't chastise the boy. He really didn't do anything wrong."

She turned to her son. "So, what did he threaten you with, then?"

"He told me I mustn't tell nobody I had seen him at the gully."

Although nothing seemed to make sense, she didn't have the energy to pursue the matter further, especially if the man insisted he was sorry. "Well, if you're sure, shall we forget about it?" She put her arm around her son.

Amy had been watching the interaction with her mouth open. She stepped forward. "Mam, while you're sorting this out, please may I go to Gertie's house?" She looked up at the clock. "She should be home from school by now."

"Um…yes, I suppose so. But don't be too long. I have something important to tell you both."

Ronnie looked up then, seemingly about to speak. She didn't want him spilling the beans, so she shook her head at him, hoping he would understand her meaning. He appeared to do so, for he didn't say anything until her daughter had gone out.

"Thank you, ma'am. What I really came to ask…" He hesitated. "No, it doesn't matter. You have enough to contend with, without me adding to your woes."

"Just spit it out, Ronnie." Martha slumped onto a chair, pulling Tommy onto her knee. "You said something about my sister. Which one did you mean?"

He looked puzzled for a second, then his eyes opened wide. "Your Charlotte, of course."

"I should have known. You're sweet on her, aren't you?"

A red blush spread up his face, and he wavered between shaking his head and nodding.

"You don't have to deny it, Ronnie. I think she feels the same."

His eyes lit up. "She does?" He pulled at his hair, trying to flatten it.

"Yes, I think so." Martha could sense Tommy falling asleep on her lap. She shifted position to make herself more comfortable and wrapped her arms around him. "What did you want to ask?"

"I wondered if it would be appropriate to go and visit her."

"Well, it would be too late to go today. By the time you reached Buxton, it would be time to come home. How would you travel?"

"My father said I could borrow the pony and trap."

"You've already asked him?" At his nod, she continued, "And you've told him your intentions?"

"Yes. He hummed and hawed at first, saying it was highly irregular. But when I told him I…" He sat down and traced his finger along the grain of the table, then said with a rush, "that I intend to ask for her hand in marriage, he almost had an apoplexy."

"I'm not surprised."

He smiled. "So, that's why I've come here, to ask you if…if…"

"But what did your father finally say?"

"He said after all that had gone off, it wouldn't be the end of the world if I married a milkmaid." He looked up apologetically. "I don't mean…"

She put her hand on his arm. "I understand. You are now the heir to your father's farm, and our Charlotte has no dowry, no money of her own."

"And, as she has no father to ask for her hand, I wondered if you would give it."

"Me?" She scratched her chin, biting her lip. "Yes, I suppose I am her nearest relative. Or should it be Aunt Elizabeth? I'm not sure. Anyway, if it's up to me, I give you my wholehearted support. You're a lovely man, Ronald Grant, and I couldn't ask for a better brother-in-law, even if you do go around threatening young boys."

"Oh, Mrs Holloway, I promise I shall never do anything so horrendous ever again."

"I was only teasing, Ronnie," she tried to reassure him. "I know it isn't your usual character. Please don't give it another moment's notice."

He stood up and held out his hand. She gave him hers and he bent low, bestowing a kiss on the back of it.

"My, what a handsome suitor you'll make, young man. I quite envy my sister," she joked, as he put his cap on and loped towards the door.

He blushed once more, grinning, his piercing blue

eyes animated. "So you think it would be fitting for me to call on her tomorrow?"

She felt a moment's pang of jealousy of her sister, but replied, "I'm not sure what the hospital staff will have to say about it, but yes, it's fine by me."

After he had left, she took Tommy upstairs, tucked him up in bed and stroked his fair hair back from his face, then kissed his forehead. "You sleep, my little lamb, and dream the dreams of the innocent, for your life is about to be turned upside down."

She crept out—although she knew he probably wouldn't have awoken even if she had stamped—closed the door and leant on it, sighing. He would, more than likely, not awake until the morning. Should she tell Amy on her own, when she came in, or should she wait until she had them both together?

Without arriving at any conclusion, she went downstairs and searched through the pantry to find something with which to make a meal for she hadn't had time to go to the shop before it had closed to buy any provisions with the money Lily had given her.

* * * *

The following morning, Ronnie rose with the larks before his parents. He examined his hands. Would they cope with reins for such a long journey? They would have to. Nothing would put him off. He could wear gloves for protection.

His mother came down, her hair in a dishevelled mess. "Oh, good morning, son."

He placed a cup of tea on the table in front of her. "I thought I'd fetch the cows in before I go."

"I don't know how many milkmaids we'll have today." Lily yawned. "I might need you to milk them as well, if Miss Jessica doesn't turn up."

"Aw, Ma. I need to leave early."

"You're intent on it, then?"

"Yes, I have never been so intent on anything in my whole life. I feel so…how can I describe it?"

"I do remember being young and in love, son. There's no need to describe it to me." She wiped her hand across her face. "I know your father gave you his blessing, but are you sure about the girl's feelings? She might not be quite so enamoured."

"Oh, she is, Ma. Mrs Holloway told me."

"Well, that's it then. If Martha Holloway says her sister's in love with you, it must be true."

"Aw, Ma, don't be sarcastic. I didn't say she was in love, just that she likes me."

"I know, son, I'm just having you on." She turned his hands over and examined them. "They're healing nicely, thank goodness. Bring in the cows and we'll take things from there."

Once eventually free, he jumped into the trap, grimacing at the pain in his leg from doing so too quickly, picked up the reins and urged the pony forward, wishing she would go quicker.

"Come, on," he encouraged her. "You can do better than this. Faster, faster."

Chapter 19

Amy had been so tired by the time she had come home the previous evening from her friend Gertie's house, she had barely been able to keep her eyes open long enough to eat the meal Martha had concocted from a few manky vegetables and some chicken stock she had forgotten about. Tommy hadn't awoken again, so she had left his in the pantry and trudged up to her bed. *Her* bed. Not theirs, or hers and Charlie's, just hers. How odd to sleep on her own every night. She had dropped to sleep, remembering the many nights of passion they had shared, shedding a tear for the few happy bygone days of yore.

About to wake the children to give them the bad news before she went to the farm, a loud knock on the door made her run downstairs.

Constable Jenkins stood on the doorstep. "Good day, ma'am. I am sorry to bother you so early, but I have important news."

"It must be important to be up and about at such an unearthly hour, sir. Pray, come in." Her heart beat fast. What could he possibly be about to divulge?

"It is with great regret, ma'am, that I have to inform you that your husband has been named as the murderer of Herbert Grant."

"No," yelled a voice from behind her. "My pa can't be a murderer." Tommy came running down the stairs. "Tell him, Mam. It can't be true, can it?"

She tried to think of a possible explanation. "Who's named him, Constable?"

He sat down. "I cannot divulge that information, ma'am."

"They'll lock him up. Mam, don't let them do that." Tommy began to cry.

"Ma'am?" The policeman looked at her, puzzled. "Why is he…?"

"I haven't told the children yet," she explained.

Amy came downstairs, already dressed for school. "Told us what, Mam?"

"Oh, do you intend going to school today, darling? You don't have to, if you don't want."

"Yes, Gertie said we're doing nature today, looking at leaves and plants and things. That's my favourite lesson."

"Oh, but you might not want to when I've told you the bad news."

"I will, don't worry. I love anything to do with nature."

She sat down, lifting Tommy onto her lap. "Now, my darlings, you must both be very brave."

Amy walked across to pour herself a glass of water. "It's about our pa, isn't it? I already know. He's dead."

Martha gasped, as Tommy tried to jump down. "How do you…? Of course, I should have known it would be all around the village. I'm so sorry you had to find out from someone else. I really wanted to be the one to tell you."

"He's dead. What does it matter who told me?"

Martha could not believe the disregard on her daughter's face.

She pulled Tommy towards her as he made to run away, yelling, "He can't be. What are you talking about? He was only here the day before yesterday."

"I'm so sorry, my darling."

He shook his head, looking at her with tears in his eyes. "You mean really and truly dead, like that Herbert Grant?"

"Yes, I'm afraid so, my darling."

"But…but how? Eh?"

"Someone…killed him." She hugged him to her bosom. "I know it's a lot to take in. Would you like to go back to bed? I could bring you something up to eat later."

He shook his head. "No, Mam. I want to hear the policeman."

She turned to the constable. "What happens now, sir?"

"There will be a court case, of course, ma'am."

"But how can they try a dead man?"

"The truth needs to be proven, ma'am." He stood up. "I shall keep you informed. I just wanted to let you know before it was made public knowledge."

"Yes, thank you for that." She followed him to the door, Tommy clinging to her skirts, as she pondered the turn of events. Who could have been the informer? The policeman had learnt something the day before, maybe when he had been speaking to the farm hands. Who could it have been? Her Uncle Will frequently worked on the farm, and she had seen him there the previous day. Could he be capable of snitching on her husband? He was sneaky enough. But why? She would have to find out. She would call around there on her way to work.

Once Tommy had calmed down, and while the children ate their breakfast, she nipped out to see who could look after him, even though he insisted he wanted to go to school with Amy. She knew how much tussling and pushing went on in the playground and didn't want his shoulder knocked.

Mrs Howard agreed, so she took them both to her house, until the time Amy would need to go to school. Tommy didn't want her to leave him, so she had to prise herself free from his clinging arms, while her neighbour bribed him with the promise of some of her famous fudge.

The heavy rain from the night before had left huge puddles in the ruts on the lane, slowing down her footsteps, and she eventually made her way to her Aunt Elizabeth's farmstead. She entered the open door, wiping her shoes on the coconut mat.

Jessica sat at the kitchen table in a pensive mood.

"Hello, are you well enough to come to the dairy?" Martha asked. "I know the Grants could sorely use your help."

"Yes, I suppose so."

Martha told her what the policeman had told her.

Jessica still sat, biting her nails, but did not give any reply, or even any reaction, as if she had not heard.

Martha asked, "Is Uncle Will in?"

"No, thank goodness. He's already gone to work."

"You really don't like him, do you? Why?"

"I've told you before, he's creepy, and his glass eye looks at you with evil intent. Why do you want him? Not looking for a lover, now your husband's dead?"

She gasped. "What? Why would you say a horrible thing like that?"

Jessica let her forehead bang onto the table. "I'm sorry. Don't take any notice of me. I'm just out of sorts. I can't lose the image of your Charlie…"

Martha put her arm around her young sister. "I know, but none of this is my fault." Or maybe some of it could be. Had Charlie murdered Herbert Grant because he knew the smarmy man had been pressing his intentions on her again, and had wanted to wreak revenge? She had never given the man any encouragement. "Nobody else knows about your involvement with Charlie's death, so are you coming, or do you still have the pains?"

"They've stopped. I may as well come. I need so much for the baby. I've hardly started its layette. All I've embroidered is one nightgown, so at this rate I'll never have enough."

"I've started one as well, so if it's finished you'll have at least two."

"Hah," she exclaimed as she pulled her shawl around her back. "Two won't last long."

"Hasn't Aunt Elizabeth made anything?" she asked

as they made their way towards the farm, hurrying as the rain began to pour down once more.

"Yes. To her credit, she's made some vests and a gown. It won't go completely naked."

Smiling, Martha asked the question that everybody wanted to know the answer to. "Why don't you ask the father for help? Who is he, Jessica? You may as well tell me."

Her sister stopped and looked up, opening her mouth as if to speak, then closed it again. "It's…no, I…" She pursed her lips. "Are you sure you want to know? You're not going to like it."

"Go on. You're going to tell me it was Herbert Grant, aren't you? I know you denied it the other day, but—"

"Herbert Grant? No, why would you think that? No, it can't hurt to tell everyone, now he's dead. It…it was Charlie," she whispered.

Martha jumped back. "What? My Charlie? No. I don't believe you. How could it have been? When…?"

"I warned you it would be unfavourable news."

"I don't believe you," Martha repeated. "You're making it up. I don't know why." Out of the corner of her eye, she spotted a familiar figure. "We'll discuss this later. You carry on to the farm. I can see Uncle over by that gate, and I need a word with him." She rushed over to him, still seething at the new turn of events. Could it be true? But why would her sister lie? "Uncle Will," she shouted as he turned to walk away.

He continued walking, and she had to run to catch up with him. She pulled up in front of him and, pushing her wet hair off her face, looked up at his tall figure. Not in a mood to mind her behaviour, she blurted out, "Was it you who informed the police my husband was the killer?"

He looked slightly non-plussed for a second, and then shrugged his shoulders. "That's no way to address your uncle, young lady. Have you forgotten your manners?"

"I'm right, aren't I?"

"Now why would I tell them a thing like that? It wouldn't be in my favour." He tried to push past her, but she would not be put off.

"What do you mean?"

"Less of your cheek. I want to hear no more about the matter."

She let him walk away up the field, clearly not going to receive the reply she wanted, and hurried to the byre. Who could it have been, though, if not him? It had to be.

As she entered, Jessica screeched, "Have you heard the news?" She looked so much happier than earlier, but Martha was still out of sorts with her, and wasn't sure if she wanted to even speak to her.

"What?"

"Ronnie and our Charlotte. Mrs Grant has just told me he's gone to the hospital to see her and, guess what? She says he's going to propose."

She forced a smile onto her face. "Oh, that. I'm pleased he's going ahead with it."

"You knew? Why didn't you say something?" Clearly miffed at not being the first to know, her sister's bottom lip stuck out.

"It slipped my mind. I do have other concerns, dear sister."

Jessica pushed her stool back. "What did you want with Uncle Will? You didn't tell him about me…?"

"No, of course not, but…well, I think it was he who told the police Charlie killed Herbert."

"Huh? Never! Is that true, that your Charlie was the murderer?"

"Yes, I told you." She plonked down and squirted the white milk into the pail vigorously, trying to relieve her frustrations on the unfortunate cow. She had already had her suspicions, so why couldn't she accept the fact that her husband had been the murderer, and that the village could sleep peacefully in their beds? Also an adulterer, now. With her own sister, if what Jessica had said could be believed. She still didn't trust that, though. Her sister loved winding her up.

* * * *

Ronnie had never been to Buxton and had not the faintest idea of the whereabouts of the hospital, but knew someone would tell him. The journey took much longer than he had envisaged, so a very fraught young man eventually pulled up at the entrance.

"You can't leave that nag there," said a man on a wall, smoking a pipe.

"Oh, where should I leave her then?" Not a good start. He thought the people of Buxton were supposed to be a friendly bunch of folk.

"There's a trough over there." The man stood up and pointed out. "I'll bet she's in sore need of a drink."

So wrapped up in his own ambitions, he had neglected to consider the pony's needs, and felt guilty. "Of course, thank you, sir." He led her across to the trough and called out to the man, "Pray, would you be so good as to keep an eye on her while I visit my fiancée?"

"Oh, like that, is it? What's she in there for? Not having a little bundle, is she?"

"I don't know what…" It dawned on him, then, that he meant a baby. "Oh, no, she was burnt in a fire." He took the pony across to him. "Actually, she doesn't know we're betrothed, yet—in fact, we haven't even stepped out together—but I'm hopeful we will be by the end of the day."

The man took out his pipe and knocked it on the heel of his boot. "Well, good luck, then, son. I hope she's well enough to accept your proposal."

"Me too," he called as he ran up the steps into the

main entrance. "Thank you, sir."

He had never been to such a huge place before, and lost his way several times, even though he had been given the directions by the person at the desk. Finding the ward, and after arguing with the nurse who had said visitors were not allowed, he explained his intention, and she allowed him a few minutes.

He looked down at the sleeping, still faintly blackened face of his beloved and grimaced at the bandages on her arms. He gently lifted her hand and feathered little kisses all over it, then found a chair, sat down beside her and waited, taking in her long, slender neck. If only he could kiss that also.

Her eyes opened. She gasped as she tried to sit up.

"No, my darling, don't move," he whispered, caressing her hand with his thumb.

"I beg your pardon? What did you call me?"

He just smiled, as her eyes darted around the ward.

"Are you alone?" she asked.

"Yes."

"No Martha?"

"No, she's…" Should he explain what had happened? No, better to wait until she had recovered completely. "How are you feeling?"

She lay back. "It still hurts to breathe sometimes."

"And the burns?"

"They say they'll soon recover. Why are you here, Master Ronnie?"

"Well…" He fished into his pocket and took out a piece of paper. "I've written you a poem, although, it's more a little ditty. Would you like me to read it to you?"

Her face beamed and she pushed herself up into a sitting position. "A poem? About me?"

He nodded.

"Oo, I've never had a poem written about me before."

He began,

"On a farm in the middle of Derbyshire," He pronounced the end of the name to rhyme with the following line.

"Lives a lass with eyes just like sapphire."

He paused, wondering whether to continue.

"Is that it?" she asked as if disappointed.

With a shake of his head, he continued,

"When a fire broke out, and she almost died,
I could have saved her but just went to hide.
Such a beauty is she, Charlotte by name.
Although she was burned, she wasn't to blame.
I want to make up for my cowardice
By asking her if she'll give me a kiss."

She sat with her mouth open.

"Don't you like it?" He began to screw up the paper, but she stopped him.

"I love it, but…the end?"

"Well, that's the crux of the matter." He glanced around the ward and noticed that several of the other patients had gathered to listen. Could he propose to her in front of them? What if she declined his offer? He would look stupid.

Her eager face grinned from cheek to cheek, as he took her hand.

"Don't be bashful," said one of the other patients who stood behind him.

"Yes," cried another one. "Go on."

Encouraged by their urgings, he took a deep breath, lifted her hand and kissed the back of it again, then declared, "Mistress Charlotte…"

"Yes, good sir?"

"Mistress Charlotte, would you do me the honour of becoming my wife?"

His proposal met with silence for a few seconds. Everybody around them seemed to hold their breath, then she whispered, "Yes, please."

A great shout went up, bringing a nurse hurrying over. "What's going on here? You're scaring my sick patients."

"He's just proposed," screamed Charlotte. "Aren't I the luckiest girl alive?"

"This is highly irregular, sir, coming in here like that, upsetting my…" the nurse began, adopting a stern posture, but then she smiled. "I hope you accepted," she said to Charlotte.

"Can't you tell?" offered the lady standing behind Ronnie. "Can't you tell by their demeanour?"

"My congratulations to the pair of you."

All of a sudden Charlotte's face fell. "But…"

"What's the matter?" asked Ronnie, in a panic that she might have changed her mind. "You aren't going to retract your answer, are you?"

"No, no, it isn't that. I…what about your parents? Especially your father—he might not give us permission. After all—"

He stopped her going any further. Kissing her hand once more, he reassured her, "You don't have to worry about that. He's given us his blessing."

"Really? You've already asked him?"

He nodded. His cheeks ached from grinning. "May I…? Would it be permissible to…?" He looked around at the few people who still remained around the bed. "…to kiss you now?"

Her pretty face still beamed. "What do you think, ladies?" she asked. "Should I allow him to be so bold?"

One of them rubbed her chin. "Oh, I don't know about that. After all, this is a public place, full of sick people, including yourself."

"Oh," replied Ronnie. "I just thought…"

"Of course you may." The same lady grinned, calling out, "We shall all turn the other way, won't we, ladies?" She cackled like a hen.

Ronnie bent forward, anxious not to hurt his new fiancée, and gently touched her lips with his.

"Call that a kiss?" the lady shouted.

"I thought you weren't going to watch," he retorted, as Charlotte grabbed his head and pressed her lips fully against his.

"Is that better?" she asked, once he pulled away.

Not the ideal location for his first embrace, and not the earth-shattering experience he had envisaged in his dreams, but he flushed with pleasure.

The nurse shooed the other people back to their beds and turned to Ronnie. "Miss Bridge needs her rest now, sir. I am afraid I shall have to ask you to leave."

Charlotte protested, but he could see her eyes closing, and didn't want to exhaust her, not when she had just made him the happiest person on earth.

"May I come back later?" he asked, not worried where he would go in the meantime.

"Yes, of course. Give her a couple of hours. There are some good alehouses in the town, if you would like something to drink, and several stalls selling hot food."

He walked towards the door and turned to wave, but his new love had already fallen asleep.

* * * *

When Martha and Jessica finished the milking, they shooed the cows out to the field and went across to the farmhouse.

Jessica clutched Martha's sleeve. "Do you think Mrs Grant will say anything?"

Martha shrugged. "Who knows?"

Lily lifted the tea strainer from the cup, placed it on its stand and spooned sugar into her drink. "Ah, just in time," she exclaimed. "I thought you would smell the pot." She took down two more cups and saucers. "Faith feels much better today, so she's already gone to the dairy to make a start."

"Oh, good, that will help." Martha took a sip of her tea, trying to remain calm, and not let her quarrel with her sister show. "I understand Ronnie's gone to declare his intentions. I'm pleased for the pair of them. Is his father really in favour of their betrothal?"

Lily stirred her drink. "He says so. I was surprised but, like he said, after all that's happened just lately, life's too short."

"Have the police been to tell you about my Charlie?" The farmer's wife looked up with an anxious face. "About his death?"

"No." She looked sideways at her sister for a reaction, but she sat staring into space. "No, nothing about that. I'm surprised they haven't been to inform you by now. They're saying he is—or was—your Herbert's murderer."

"No?" The farmer's wife's eyes lit up, as if the news seemed pleasing to her. "Well, I'll be blowed. What a turn up for the books."

"I don't think it was him, though." Martha put down her empty cup, ready to go back outside.

"You don't? Of course you wouldn't, he was your husband and, even though he had his violent moments, I'm sure he wasn't capable of *murder*." She said the word with extra emphasis, as if it had some hidden meaning.

The farmer came in, stamping his boots on the horsehair mat. "The rain seems to have eased off for a while, thank goodness. I need to plant that last field up today. Is there one of those for me?"

Lily hurried to pick up the teapot. She seemed animated as she poured out his drink, added three sugars and stirred it briskly. "There you are, dear."

Martha pulled her sister to the door. "We'll do what we can in the dairy before Mary's funeral. Good day."

"Of course, that's today," added Lily. "I suppose we had all better go, seeing as her unfortunate demise occurred here in our barn."

Jessica went out first and Martha began to follow. As she reached the door, she heard Lily say to her husband,

"Thank goodness for that," so she slowed down and listened, just out of sight.

"What?" Ed asked.

Jessica turned around and called, "Are you coming, our Martha?"

"You go on." She gestured, not wanting to be heard by the occupants of the house.

Jessica ran back to her. "You're not still out of sorts with me, are you? I knew I shouldn't have told you."

"It's nothing to do with that," she hissed. "Go on. I'll catch you up."

"But do you think she's going to tell Mr Grant it was me who…you know?"

"No, just go."

Jessica sloped off, her mouth turned down, and shoulders slumped, as Martha heard Lily explain to her husband what she had just told her about Charlie. Everything went silent for a moment, and she thought he was about to come back out, so bent down to tie the lace on her boot. He didn't appear, so she crept closer.

"I didn't kill him," the farmer insisted. "I've already told you. I saw our Ronnie running away, and there lay our Herbert, more dead than alive, right on the edge of the cliff top. That's why I said nothing to the police. I didn't want Ronnie involved."

Martha drew in her breath. The farmer was going to let her husband take the blame when he could no longer defend himself, but at least it partly explained the episode between Tommy and Ronnie.

"But remind me why Charlie Holloway was there."

"Oh, he was there, all right. He came out of the bushes, taunting me about all sorts of things, our Herbert amongst them. I'd had enough of his jibes, so I hit him. He fell, landing on top of Herbert, who sort of rolled. Charlie jumped up to catch him but he fell over the edge."

"And you went down after him? You didn't just

leave him there?" Lily's voice took on a higher note.

"Of course we did, but we could tell he was dead. Looked like a broken neck. Charlie accused me of killing him in the first place, but I said he knocked him over the top, so he would take the blame. In the end, we decided to keep silent about it, and pretend we didn't know anything. I told you all this at the time."

So her Charlie had been involved, after all. But why had her Uncle Will acted in such a strange way? Surely he had not been there as well? It must have been a crowded cliff top.

"But why have the police decided he was murdered because, from what you say, he died from an accident?"

About to walk away, Martha heard, "But we can't keep paying William Lucas, can we? How did that thieving beggar find out, anyway?"

"I don't know, but I need to think of some way out of his blackmailing."

Martha's brain lit up with an idea. She ran into the room to join them. "I know a way."

The pair jumped apart guiltily. "Have you been snooping, girl, listening to matters that don't concern you?" asked the farmer.

"But they do." She looked at his wife. "We could frame my uncle for Charlie's murder."

A look of enlightenment came into the older lady's eyes. "Yes, that would solve our other problem, wouldn't it?"

Her husband looked at her through narrowed eyes. "What on earth are you talking about?"

"May I tell him?" asked Lily.

"If we want him on our side, he'll need to know."

They regaled him with Jessica's involvement in Charlie's death.

"I don't know why I'm helping her out, after what she's done," Martha moaned, after Ed had sat down, wiping his brow.

"She's told you, then?" Lily looked sheepish.

"You knew? About her and Charlie?" At Lily's nod she continued, "Why didn't you say anything to me?"

"What was the point? It would have only upset you."

"But when did she tell you?"

"That morning they arrested our Ronnie."

"And you believed her? She might be covering her own back now Charlie isn't here to admit or deny it."

"No, lass, she was telling the truth."

Martha took a deep breath. "Did she say she was willing, or give you any of the details, how often, or…?"

"You'll need to ask her that yourself, lass."

Martha slumped onto a chair. Could she ever trust her sister again?

"She's still your sister, Martha. She needs your support more than ever, now." Lily patted her shoulder. "Family ties should not be broken."

"I suppose so. She will have a lot of grovelling to do before I forgive her, though."

"That's my girl. I knew you wouldn't bear a grudge. You're a wonderful girl, with so much love in your heart…"

"All right, don't overdo it, Lily. I understand what you're trying to do."

"Off you go, then. We'll frame William Lucas good and proper. We all saw him clobber Charlie, now didn't we?" When they nodded in agreement, she added, "Rest assured, he'll not be blackmailing anybody else. If we stick together we'll make it through this, you mark my words."

Martha made for the door.

Charlie had often flirted with her youngest sister, but she had never suspected him of going any further. But she knew how persuasive he could be. He could charm the birds out of the trees—as the expression went—so her impressionable sister would have stood no chance if he had insisted.

And the bar maid?

Martha had moved the dresser the day before, and found the piece of paper that had fallen down—a note, with the words 'tonight at the ridge'. Could that have been from her? It hadn't been Charlie's handwriting, and definitely not Charlotte's, so who else could have written it?

But did she really want to know? Would it make her feel any better, knowing the truth? Straightening her clothes and forcing a smile onto her lips, she went outside where children's voices drifted across to her.

Down the lane, Amy ran towards her with her friend, Gertie.

"What are you doing, coming here? You know I'm working."

Her daughter looked behind her, and Martha saw Tommy panting along, holding his side.

"Our Tommy wanted to see you, Mam, before we went to school. He's been really sad, and Mrs Howard said we could come and say hello. You don't mind, do you?"

Lily came out of the farmhouse.

Martha began, "I'm so sorry, Mrs Grant. They…"

The farmer's wife shushed her. "Don't worry about it, my dear. It's perfectly understandable." She turned to Tommy who had caught up with his sister. "Come on in, me duck. Do you like dandelion and burdock?"

Tommy looked up at Martha. "Do I, Mam?"

She hugged him to her. "I don't think you've ever drunk it. But Mrs Grant's busy and you'll be late for school."

"Martha, it's fine."

"Me and Gertie are going, Mam. What shall we do about Tommy?"

Lily took the boy's hand. "You leave him with me, child. He can stay here today."

The girls ran off up the lane, giggling and singing.

Martha turned to the farmer's wife. "Are you sure?"

"Yes, my dear. You finish your chores while I look after this little one. He's had a rough time in the last few days."

Martha thanked her and hurried towards the dairy after giving Tommy a kiss. Maybe she would come through this, after all.

She entered the dairy to start another day's work.

About The Author

Married to Don, Angela has 5 children: Darran, Jane, Catherine, Louise, and Richard, and 8 grandchildren: Amy, Brandon, Ryan, Danny, Jessica, Charlotte, Ethan, and Violet Alice.

Educated at The Convent of Our Lady of Providence, Alton, Hampshire, Angela was part owner of a health shop for 3 years and worked for the Department of Work and Pensions for 16 years until her retirement, when she joined the Eastwood Writers' Group and began writing in earnest.

Her hobbies include gardening, singing in her church choir, flower arranging, scrabble, and eating out.

Her first novel 'Looking for Jamie' has been hailed as 'one of those books you can't put down'. Without the help and encouragement from the writer's group, she says her book would never have been finished. The sequel, 'A Dilemma for Jamie' was published in February 2013 and the third book in the series, 'School for Jamie', in November 2013. There will be a fourth in the future.

Lightning Source UK Ltd.
Milton Keynes UK
UKOW04f0834190915

258890UK00001B/17/P